MW00720668

The New Noir Anthology of Cold, Hard Fiction

ICED

The New Noir Anthology of Cold, Hard Fiction

edited by Kerry J. Schooley and Peter Sellers

INSOMNIAC PRESS

Copyright © 2001 by Kerry J. Schooley and Peter Sellers.

All rights reserved. No part of this publication may be reproduced, stored in a retrieval system or transmitted, in any form or by any means, without the prior written permission of the publisher or, in the case of photocopying or other reprographic copying, a licence from CANCOPY (Canadian Copyright Licensing Agency), 1 Yonge St., Suite 1900, Toronto, Ontario, Canada, M5E 1E5.

Copy-edited by Maria Lundin
Designed by Mike O'Connor

National Library of Canada Cataloguing in Publication Data

Main entry under title:

   Iced: the new noir anthology of cold, hard fiction

ISBN 1-894663-11-X

1. Detective and mystery stories, Canadian (English) 2. Canadian fiction (English) - 20th century. I. Schooley, Kerry J., 1949- II. Sellers, Peter, 1956-

PS8323.D4124 2001   C813'.087208054   C2001-902151-8
PR9197.35.D48124 2001

The publisher and the author gratefully acknowledge the support of the Canada Council, the Ontario Arts Council and Department of Canadian Heritage through the Book Publishing Industry Development Program.

Printed and bound in Canada

Insomniac Press, 192 Spadina Avenue, Suite 403,
Toronto, Ontario, Canada, M5T 2C2
www.insomniacpress.com

The Canada Council Le Conseil des Arts
FOR THE ARTS DU CANADA
SINCE 1957 DEPUIS 1957

ONTARIO ARTS COUNCIL
CONSEIL DES ARTS DE L'ONTARIO

Table of Contents

Introduction

Iced is an Uzi in a literary hothouse. Deadly compact, it's easily smuggled into the climate-controlled conservatory of sensitive cops and kinder, gentler dicks. Slip the safety on this peaceful, ordered, over-fed nursery. Let loose a burst and shatter the glass house open to cement-cracking weeds, scrub maple, and any other deviant seed carried on a frigid wind.

This is noir from an ice-hard world where the mantra "Peace, order and good government" means "shut up and do as your told or you'll get what's good for you." It's an earthy mix of veteran crime writers and a new generation of gritty, urban authors. Cynical, paranoid stories germinated in the fecund soil of corruption, lust, obsession, violence, and revenge.

Some of these legends are straight hardboil; existential treats spawned from the cheap pulp issues that grew on America's streets and alleys a half-century ago. Others have roots gnarled back into isolated pioneer landscapes, where evil sprouted in fevered winter cabins.

The writers in *Iced* know where evil festers, and it's not just "out there" in the wide world waiting for the pure of heart to stumble over it. If that were so, Oedipus wouldn't have plucked out his own eyes. Lady Macbeth wouldn't have scrubbed herself raw to get the blood off her hands.

Characters in this book are as corrupt as in any ancient tragedy. They laugh at the wrong times and they screw the wrong people, yet they struggle for order, or meaning, or maybe even redemption on a morally bankrupt planet. Not that they've a hope in hell of finding either.

Because hell is preserved for the politically correct and others who believe in innocence. Such delicate flowers need the heat. They settle in, bank their pages around them, peer out accusingly at the cold, hard world. A world that's been *Iced*.

Two Fingers

by Kevin Burton Smith

Noir may be fiction, but the core of it is truth. It was born into a world hungry for writers who reflected the bitter, cynical reality of post-Depression America. Something that spoke to men who could no longer relate to Philo Vance and Hercule Poirot. Men who'd seen the depths to which people could sink. Kevin Burton Smith brings that perspective to noir fiction. His background as a writer of true crime adds a pungent reality to a tale of friendship and trust, making his fiction so sharp and hard you could break something reading it. The founder and editor of Thrilling Detective Web site *www.thrillingdetective.com*, Kevin is currently working to revive the legendary Black Mask magazine as an online presence. A regular columnist for *Blue Murder*, his non-fiction has been published in numerous magazines. "Two Fingers" is his first published short story.

"C'mon, man," he says to me, "You know I'm good for it..."

I look around. It's mostly just Robbie and me, you know, just two guys sitting in a bar, having a few cold ones. We're in this place on St. Laurent, got it mostly to ourselves, a weird sort of place—part sports bar, part dive, part trendy little nightspot, that can't even seem to decide on a name. It's been "the place where the dance school used to be" for about forever. But they serve Corona right, with fresh lime slices, the glasses are clean, and the food's more than decent. And the staff is cool. They leave you alone. I've become something of a regular.

I'd arrived first, and would have been more than content to just sit here and drink the heart right out of this glorious afternoon. It's one of those unexpectedly bright mid-winter days where the sun just stabs you in the eyes, and the big front windows are cranked opened to let in the air and light and the traffic-rumble from the street below, the tires hissing through the runoff from the melting snow. Every now and then, Sylvie would walk over, take a peek down to the street, stretch a bit, and sigh. The place was pretty empty, just a few lunch-hour stragglers, and a regular or two hanging at the bar watching Rollie polish some glasses.

But I was meeting an old friend.

So I'm having a cold one and a smoke, just grooving on the wonderfulness of it all, playing hooky from work, hiding out from my editor, having a grand old time, when Robbie comes bopping in. His long leather coat's thrown open and his hands are jammed in its pockets, jiggling keys or something, and he's puffing away on a cigarette. He's practically vibrating in place. In the benign quiet of the place, he's like a hyperactive tumour.

"Hey, Terry, thanks for coming. Sorry I'm late. Christ, good to see ya! How are you? You're looking good, man."

The cigarette doesn't leave his mouth, just bounces along in time. His voice is too loud, he's speaking too fast. A few heads slowly start to turn. I figure he'd better sit down, before parts start shaking off.

"Hey, yourself. Sit down, take a load off."

"Yeah, yeah, okay." His head swivels to take in the place. "But, uh, let's go sit over there." He jerks his head towards the back of the bar, away from the light and sound, then wiggles the butt jammed in his mouth at the windows. "The light, man, it's bugging my eyes."

Right. His eyes. They're red lightning. He's obviously wired—the eyes, limp hair, and a face like it was spray-painted with vegetable oil. The coke sweats, probably. Wouldn't be the first time he's come down hard, after indulging in some Colombian nose-steroids. But fuck it.

"Sure, no prob. Lead the way."

I get up, grab my coat, gather up my stuff, and follow him. Robbie weaves his way between the empty tables to a dark booth in the back, far away from the windows. The only illumination is an old Molson clock. It's like a quiet little cave. I don't argue.

Sylvie shows up, and takes our order. Robbie asks for a Bud.

"And you want another Corona, right?"

I give her a grin. "You got it, babe."

"With a slice of lime, in a clean glass, right?" She gives me back a small smile. She's not bad, got good legs, for an older dame. If you're into forty-year-old cooze.

I watch her trot off. Robbie gets settled in and we make small talk while we wait for the drinks. I'm not even sure what we talk about, maybe something about Sylvie's ass, or how much the Habs suck again this year.

Then our drinks come, and I tell Sylvie to run a tab. She nods and goes back to talk to this loser she always seems to be hanging around with. The guy seems to be here all the time, drinking beer, reading fucking *Le Devoir* or something. Like, get a life, man. Sylvie's leaning over him, whispering something in his ear. He laughs, and she joins in.

Robbie clears his throat, and I turn back to him. He ignores the glass Sylvie has brought him and tilts the bottle towards me. "Here's to friendship."

Right. I wave the lip of my glass in his general direction. "Chin-chin."

Robbie figures this is a signal to start reminiscing about the good old days, and he's off. I nod, smile, and tune him out. I know the stories already, even most of Robbie's constantly-changing versions of them. I figure this is all just a build-up to his sales pitch anyway.

The name snaps me out of my reverie.

"What? René what?"

"I was saying that we were always there for each other, you and me, but René, he was always so friggin' tight with a buck. Such a cheap hard-ass…"

"What are you talking about? He wasn't that cheap."

"Aw, c'mon, Ter, you know what he was like. Cheap, fuckin' separatist bastard…always looking down his nose at us, thought he was better than us or something, always figuring out some angle on his own. Thought his shit didn't stink. Wasn't tight, not like us, ya know?"

"Christ, let it rest, Robbie. He's dead, so who cares anymore? And what do you mean, he was a separatist? His mother was as Irish as yours."

"You think that means anything? He was always hanging out with those French butt buddies of his at the end…probably planning to screw us over…"

"Hey, you don't know that. And why are you getting so pissed now? It's been, like, what, eight years?"

"More like nine, but yeah, something like that. But sorry, yeah, I guess I'm being a little hard on him. But look, all I'm saying is, he was a cheap bastard…remember that time at the Kojak, him and that Bambi chick with the boots, and we almost died of friggin' frostbite?"

And he is off again, trotting down memory lane. The Kojak was a pisshole strip joint/biker bar we used to hang out in, out in the boonies, back in the day. We'd all been celebrating and feeling no pain. Lap dances, rounds for the house, shooters, René was running up a huge tab. Then, while Robbie and me were in the can doing a line, he split with some stripper he was hot on. Took the car, too. Left us with the tab, stuck in the asshole of nowhere on the other side of the river, Saint-fucking-Hubert on the South Shore. No cabs, no busses, so we had to hitch. It took us forever to get back into town.

"Aw, Robbie, he was drunk. And horny. He may have been a shit sometimes, but he wasn't cheap. René probably would have made it up to us, you know that."

"But he didn't, did he!"

"Um, because he was killed about a week later. Remember?"

The bottle of Bud freezes halfway to his mouth. "Aw, shit, I forgot. That was right about the same time, huh?"

"Yeah. It was."

"Shit, man, I'm sorry...I didn't mean to, well, like, I know you two were always tighter..."

"I thought we were all tight."

And we had been. The three of us went way back. The three amigos. Two Micks and a Pep. Grew up together in Lachine, did a lot of crap together, hanging out at the bars and stuff, things I'm not particularly proud of. But that was a long time ago. I'm all grown up now—I pay taxes and everything. I've got a decent job, an okay place, a nice car, money to eat in a good restaurant now and then, a classy girlfriend who looks good when we go to clubs—you know, the works. But Robbie, well, Robbie never really grew up.

And just like the old days, he's short on cash. Only this time he really needs it.

"Anyway, Ter, forget it, it's the past. So whaddya say? C'mon, man, you know I'm good for it..." It looks like Robbie's over his preamble. Now he's all contrite, and for Robbie, relatively calm. If he had a hat, he'd be holding it in his hands. As it is, he's scraping the label off his bottle of Bud with his jagged thumbnail, like he's got a deadline.

"Good for it? What about the money you already owe me?"

"Aw, c'mon, Terry, you know I'll pay you back. Really. I've got something good coming up, and I'll pay you back next week." Scrape.

"Bullshit. You've been telling me that for four years."

"Look, man, it's important. I really need that money." Scrape.

"You always need the money. And from what I hear, you may not be around next week."

Robbie's eyes suddenly pop all the way open, like someone's just given him a good rap in the middle of his forehead with a ball-peen hammer. Just to get his attention, like.

"Shit! What'd you hear?" I had his full attention now.

"Not much, just that JaJa's looking for you, and he's rather displeased with your job performance of late."

"Oh, shit, what'd you hear? Really, Terry, no fucking around now. None of that 'job performance' crap. You're not at the *Gazette*, now. What'd you hear?"

Yep, I really had his attention now.

I work the crime beat for the last English-language daily in town. I'm not the top guy or anything, and I'm still crawling my way up, but I've had a few breaks, and I've got some great contacts, the result of my less than exemplary youth. I hear a lot of stories, some that will never make it into anyone's morning paper. Robbie's probably one of them.

First of all, let's get this straight, Robbie may be an old pal, but he's no blushing virgin. He's become a nasty piece of work; he's a thug. He's stolen, he's dealt drugs, he's ripped off everything from cars to warehouses, and he's put some serious hurting on more than a few people. I know, because we used to be partners. We had some times, the three of us, at least at the beginning. Slip kids, running scores and bangin' whores. We were young, we were going to live forever, we were having the times of our lives. But somewhere along the line, it stopped being fun, at least for me. Probably the same day René was fished out of the river under the Jacques Cartier bridge, wrapped in a cheap sleeping bag, the bumper from a '75 Toyota still wired to his feet. The message seemed clear enough to me—he'd obviously pissed someone off royally. Robbie had offered plenty of theories at the time—maybe some side deal of René's went bad, maybe he told a tale out of school. Or maybe he'd just dipped his dick in the wrong well, maybe Bambi already had a "special" friend.

But that's all it took for me to decide it was time for a career change. Robbie didn't see it that way, though. Despite all his theories, ultimately he figured René had just run out of luck. Robbie believes a lot in luck.

I guess you've got to believe in something in that line of work. You certainly can't count on your friends. Let's just say that the pool that Robbie swims in is a little shallow at the honesty end. Loyalties change faster than you can keep track, and nobody trusts anyone else. And everybody talks, eventually. You survive by double-crossing someone before they double-cross you. And the cops and everyone else know it. It's all a big game. Like this big-deal Wolverine Squad, for example, supposed to save us all from the bikers and take down the Hell's Angels and the Rock Machine? A task force made up of cops from the MUC, the SQ, the horsemen, and whoever else wandered in? All that money tossed their way, you think there's an army of detectives out there pounding the pavement? Give me a break. Nah, they're all sitting around, playing with their fancy computers and wiretaps, but really just waiting for someone to rat on someone else. That's just the way it is. Someone always talks. Too bad René found out the hard way.

It's one reason I got out. The fear and constant paranoia about being betrayed was eating me up, and the drugs and booze I used to fight it were killing me.

So I went legit, more or less, took a job working in a warehouse out in Pointe-Claire, trying to decide what I was going to do with my life. An English teacher back in high school, a Mrs. Ticehurst, had said I had a knack for writing, so I started taking night courses, which lead to my burgeoning career as a journalist. Like I said, I'm not the top dog, but I'm getting a rep. In a way, I'm still dealing in info, but at least now I'm dishing it out, not afraid of it.

But anyway, meanwhile, Robbie hung in there, started making a small name for himself as a sort of freelance collector and sometime enforcer, doing the deed for dealers and sharks who didn't want to get their hands dirty. We didn't exactly keep in touch, but we didn't *not* keep in touch, either. I didn't necessarily approve of his lifestyle, but we weren't kids anymore, and who was I to judge?

And then the word got out that Robbie had made a big leap up the food chain, and had gotten into bed with Jacques "JaJa" Gallant. Now Gallant, he wasn't afraid of getting his hands dirty. Allegedly, of course. He was the much questioned, occasionally arrested but seldom convicted poster boy for *Allô Police* and *Le Journal de Montréal*. He ran a small crew, used to specialize in truck hijacking, warehouse rip-offs, extortion, a little dope, that kind of thing, pretty much run-of-the-mill type stuff, until JaJa read a book or took a business admin course or something and decided it was time to diversify. Very nineties, really. Suddenly it's like they're one of the most feared crews in town—notorious, utterly psychotic thugs who would do almost anything for a buck. They were big on wet work and "message" hits—car bombs, chainsaws, and barbed-wire garrottes. Too dangerous to even trust, really. Even the Angels and the Machine were a bit uneasy about them and only hired them on a freelance basis.

And that's the reality of "organized" crime in Montréal. Sure, there are gangs and various affiliations, but they're not exactly always carved in stone. In fact, they're often quite loose, based more on ethnic or linguistic lines more than anything. Sure, the bikers are trying to nail down every-thing right now, but they've got a long row to hoe, if they really think they can control this place. And when someone crosses some disputed line or another, someone has to pay. You read about "a settling of accounts" in the paper, you know someone pissed in the wrong pot. Or, as a cop buddy of mine cheerfully confided to me at the funeral of one hapless biker who'd had his "account" settled, "One less asshole for us to catch."

But JaJa didn't seem to notice any lines or boundaries. Money crosses all lines, and he was more than happy to offer his services to the highest bidder, no matter what hole they crawled out of. And even the bikers respected that, mostly because JaJa's crew was too psychotic to fool around with.

Nice boys Robbie had decided to play with. No wonder he is shitting his pants.

"Relax, man. Sit down. Have another Bud. I'll tell you what I heard."

I hold up two fingers to Sylvie, and she nods and heads to the bar. Smart girl.

Robbie's stuck. He could run out now, but he still needs money and he just has to know what I have to say. He sits down. He almost has to. I have him by the short hairs.

Sylvie brings over the beers and walks off. Robbie takes a big sip of his draft and gulps it down. He wipes off his mustache with the sleeve of his work shirt and reaches for the DuMaurier burning in the ashtray in front of him.

"So, uh, what'd you hear, Ter?"

Ah, Mr. Cool.

"Well, the way I hear it, JaJa's become concerned that someone has been talking with the cops lately, and maybe doing a little skimming every now and then, too. Seems he'd like to discuss these matters with you."

"Aw Christ, Terry! I'd never rat out JaJa! I'm not crazy, ya know?"

"Yeah, well, what I hear is that he'd really like to hear it from you personally. He's even offering a little, uh, cash incentive, for info on your whereabouts. It seems someone said someone saw you popping out of a cop car last week, and JaJa knows the cops have been sniffing around, asking about you. Word is they like you for the CD-warehouse job last month."

"What is this 'someone said someone said' shit? That West Island thing? Hey, man, I'm innocent. I don't even do that stuff anymore. Hell, I ain't been out there in a year. I had nothing to do with some friggin' trailer disappearing. And what am I going to do with a shitload of CDs, anyway? I look like Sam-the-fucking-Record-Man to you? I had nothin' to do with it!"

"Do tell? Um, that's not what I heard, but then, what I think doesn't count, does it? The cops like you for it, and JaJa doesn't like the cops liking you. Especially when he hears you've been traipsin' down Bishop at four in the morning, after getting out of an unmarked."

"Oh God, you didn't tell anyone we were meetin', did you?" He's up off his seat, fumbling for his coat, his eyes running all over the room as if JaJa and his hordes are hiding behind the jukebox, or maybe in the ladies' room.

"Relax. Nobody knows you're here. And who's gonna turn you in? The waitress? The bartender? The professor geek over there with his paper? Maybe the old guy sleeping one off in the corner? Relax, you're safe here. Where've you been hiding?"

"Nowhere, really. I just haven't been home. I've been sleepin' in my sister's van. I tol' Maggie I needed it to move some stuff for a pal."

"The blue one we moved the firewood in last fall?"

"Yeah. I parked it right out front. I got my gear in back, and one of them mountain sleeping bags. Soon's I get some dough, I'm outta here, maybe head out West, or to Florida for a while, until JaJa cools off."

"Clever."

"Ha-ha. Don't laugh, I went to my place the other night, to get some underwear and shit, and they were waitin' for me."

"Waiting? Who?"

"Chickie and Duane, the slick fuck with the knives, you know, from Ala-friggin'-bama or wherever. I almost walked in on 'em."

"What happened?"

"Well, I didn't walk in on 'em, eh? I'm not that stupid. I climbed the fire escape and peeked in the window before I did my 'Daddy's home!' number. When I saw 'em, I got the hell out! You can always buy clean jockeys somewhere else, ya know?"

"So I hear..." I glance at my watch. Shit. "Listen, I've got to phone my editor, okay?" I stand up and scramble around in my pocket for change. "Don't go away, okay?"

I give Sylvie the sign for two more as I pass her on the way to the phones. I make my call, then nip into the can, wash my hands, have a piss. By the time I get back, half of Robbie's next Bud is already gone, along with most of its label.

We stay for another hour, drinking, bullshitting, with Robbie chainsmoking, getting increasingly soused, increasingly strung out, and me getting increasingly annoyed by his wheedling and whining, trying to work his con, beating on the past like a drum. He brings up old girlfriends, old cars, old jobs. The time we spent most of the night breaking into the wrong warehouse. The time we took a boat for a joyride and ran out of gas in the middle of Lac St. Louis. The time the three of us drove to Plattsburgh with three black strippers. The good old days...he just doesn't see why I won't give him some more money. Or hide him out. Or switch cars. We've been pals forever, I owe him, he'd give it to me, blah, blah, blah. Finally, he toddles off to the washroom.

The table is littered with tiny pieces of Budweiser labels, an errant lime slice, and more than a few dead soldiers. I look around—most of the regulars have slipped out by now. Sylvie is closing the big windows, and it's starting to get dark outside. The after-work crowd will be shuffling in soon, and you can hear banging from the kitchen. And then Robbie was back, a little more bright-eyed if not exactly bushy-tailed, traces of white powder still rimming one nostril. He sits down as if he's reached an important decision.

"Fuck it, you're just jerking me around. That's it, I gotta go. If you're not gonna help me out, well, then, Terry, fuck you!"

What do you know? He had reached an important decision. I try innocent on him. "Excuse me?"

He's back on his feet now. "You heard me. You have no friggin' intention on givin' me any dough, do ya? You're just jerking me around like that asswipe René was!"

"Excuse me?"

"Don't play fuckin' games. He was always givin' me a hard time, too. Never picked up his share of the tab, never helped a guy out if he could help it. He got what he deserved. Just totally selfish. Only cared about himself. Just like you. So the hell with you. Fuck you! I'm outta here!"

I look at my watch. Then I look at Robbie, and all he's become, and all he once meant to me. He grabs his smokes and lighter. Fumbles, jamming them in his pocket. Struggles into his coat and staggers out.

"Fuck you too," I whisper softly.

I sit there for a moment, smoking and drinking. When I hear the bomb go off out on the street and feel the shards of glass from the big windows blow by me, I hardly even flinch.

Her Voice on the Phone was Magic
by William Bankier

So often noir is about the weak or venal man choosing the wrong woman and the unholy consequences that follow. Think Fred MacMurray picking Barbara Stanwyck; John Garfield going for Lana Turner; Robert Mitchum chasing Jane Greer. If that's what makes the heart of noir beat, then William Bankier is noir's EKG. For forty years, his stories have chronicled the devastating effects of relationships that turn sour, and ones that were rancid from day one. While his work is subtle, incisive and compassionate, it also reflects dark awareness of manipulation, deceit, and betrayal. In the end, he understands that the only exit leads you to something even worse.

Born in Belleville, Ontario, Bill has lived in Montréal and London, and currently lives in Los Angeles. Sixteen of his best stories were collected in the book *Fear Is a Killer* (Mosaic Press, 1995).

Seebold walked five paces this way, five paces that way, trying to imagine what the woman would look like. Thank goodness it was dark. He could picture friends in cars driving by and saying, "Isn't that Martin Seebold hanging around the telephone building?" Earlier that evening he had spoken with an operator while placing a call to his wife, who was visiting their son in Newcastle. The operator's voice did something to him—and here he was. Blame it on the evening, Seebold told himself, excusing his behaviour.

The weather was a plausible defense. Days of such quality happen rarely in an English summer. The sky had remained clear since morning. Now there was a sprinkling of stars and the breeze seemed to be coming in off the warm sea.

The door at the top of the steps opened and a girl appeared. She came down awkwardly on chunky heels, lugging a shoulder bag and a plastic carryall. Incredibly, she wore a hat.

"Fay?" Seebold said. "Fay Blore?"

"You're 94-81-09-00?" They shook hands and teetered off balance, sharing a suspicion that the best part of this affair might have been those flirtatious words exchanged across the romantic anonymity of a telephone connection.

"How about a drink, then?" he said. She was not ugly, only plain. No style to her brown hair, no feminine appeal in the moist, pale eyes, the heavy jaw. She was short, but not petite. "Do you mind the Alex?"

"The Alex is fine."

They walked to the Alexandra Pub and found a quiet corner. She asked for dry sherry and Seebold brought her a large one along with his double whisky. He imagined his wife criticizing him: "The doctor would be thrilled to see you into the strong stuff." But Sylvia was with Gary in Newcastle and would be there for the rest of the week. So Martin Seebold was free to forget he was fifty-six and to behave like an adolescent down here in Wimbledon.

"I've been a telephone operator for ten years," she informed him. Before then, she had sold shoes in a local department store. Went to school in the borough. Born in a house not far from where they were drinking. Parents retired, probably watching television in the old sitting room at that very moment. A brother named Reg was drifting about some-place or other—getting himself into trouble, like as not.

"I'm local, too," Seebold responded. But their origins were not the same. Born up the hill in the Village, the only son of professional parents, Seebold had elevated himself further by marrying Sylvia and settling in her centuries-old family property on the edge of Wimbledon Common. He skated over this information, concentrating on his two years in the RAF at the end of the War. "I was lucky. I was posted to India with the pay corps. Marvellous."

An hour later the pub bell rang and they were chivvied out onto the pavement. "Care for a burger?" Seebold intended to see the situation through to the end.

"Lovely," she said, taking his arm and heading for the McDonald's sign with choppy steps as if they were crossing a ploughed field. There was safety in the crowded restaurant. If he should encounter a friend, Seebold could fob Fay Blore off as an innocent acquaintance.

"Youdon't have to see me home," she told him when they were outside again.

"Don't be silly. It's a lovely night."

Her flat was not far—down a laneway off the Kingston Road. Seebold found himself, surprisingly, in no hurry to say goodbye. It was like making small talk with the dentist after the session is over.

"You live up there?" he said, observing the iron steps and the narrow landing at the top. "It's like something designed to go on a stage."

"Do you want to come in?" She had expected him to be gone like a thief in the night.

"See you to the door anyway." The adventure had turned out fine. He would enjoy describing it to Lionel Henning next time they played gin rummy.

The steps rose beside the glass-roofed kitchen of a fish-and-chips shop. Seebold followed her to the landing, looked down over a railing at peaks of opaque glass, heard the clatter of plates, the roar of boiling oil as a new basket of potatoes went in, saw steam venting from a grating under the eaves. He felt he was in the engine room of a giant ship, a passenger embarked upon a mysterious voyage.

"No, not again..."

Seebold turned and saw Fay at her front door. It was hanging ajar, the room in darkness behind it. "Have you been robbed?"

"I know who did this," she said. She moved inside and switched on a light.

Seebold followed her, saw the room disarranged but not as destructively as some he had read about. No slashing of upholstery, no daubing of walls. "Don't touch anything," he said. "Call the police."

She went to a drawer that hung open, knitting magazines dragged out and scattered on the floor. She found a battered envelope, checked that it was empty. "Forty pounds gone."

"Ring the police now, Fay."

"I haven't a phone." The operator's wry smile acknowledged the irony. "We don't need the police," she said, moving to the door and closing Seebold in. "I know who did this. It was Reg, my brother. He needed money and he knows where I keep it."

"Couldn't he ask?"

"If I'd been here, he would have asked."

Seebold's euphoria evaporated. Here he was keeping late hours with an uninspiring woman who had a criminal psychopath for a brother. "I'll help you clear up."

"I'll put on some coffee."

With the books back on the shelves, they sat at the kitchen table drinking coffee and sipping brandy. She had put on a recording of somebody playing the piano. It sounded to Seebold like underground trains, but Fay's eyes sparkled when she announced, "Pinetop Smith!" so apparently it was something special.

"What puzzles me," he said, "is why throw down the books and toss the other things around? If it's your brother and he knows where you keep your money."

"I know. Maybe he was drunk." She swallowed some brandy and compressed her lips so thin they disappeared.

Rain began falling a few minutes later. The drops hammered on the glass roof of the fish-and-chips shop. "When that stops, I'd better be off," Seebold said.

After half an hour, they were standing in the doorway watching what was clearly going to be an all-night rain. "You'd better sleep here," she said. He couldn't conceal his dismay. "I mean on the settee. Come on, I won't attack you in the night. Have another brandy while I make up some kind of a bed."

Her sheets were fresh. Tucked in, with the remains of his third brandy on the table beside him, Seebold began to enjoy himself. Who could predict what was going to happen to a man on a given day? He grinned to himself as he took another swallow of brandy. He could hardly wait to tell Lionel Henning about his adventure with the spooky telephone operator.

"You all right?" She was in the bedroom doorway wearing a robe made of a fuzzy brown material. Her hand was on the light switch.

"Like a bug in a rug." he raised his glass, she blew him a sisterly kiss and the room went dark.

Seebold had no trouble falling asleep. The drinks and the hypnotic drumming of the rain on the glass roof overcame the discomfort of the settee. He couldn't tell what time it was when he drifted awake. The room was pitch black, no sign of dawn's early light. His watch was on the coffee table but he couldn't see the luminous dial for some reason. He put out his hand and touched warm, naked flesh.

"It's all right," she whispered. "Do you mind being woken up?"

"What is it?"

"I was lonely." A little girl's voice trying to be sexy in the dark. "I thought I'd come and see if you were lonely too."

The approach was so transparent it annoyed Seebold. Or was it something else that made his skin grow cold? He was being put on the spot, asked to perform. He had never enjoyed responding to overtures. Not just physical demands but anything at all; a request from Sylvia for him to attend the theatre would leave him rigid with annoyance. Because it was not his idea.

"I was asleep."

"Sorry."

At last she had to speak again. "I don't please you do I? I could tell when you saw me for the first time, outside the building. It's one of those things, either it works or it doesn't."

"Don't blame yourself too much." Seebold was calming down. Since he would never see this woman again, he could afford to say something reassuring. He had never revealed this before to anyone, not even Sylvia. Now it was as if it had to be said; he was in the dark confessional and the truth would cleanse his soul. "Sex has never been important to me. I'm not gay, don't get the wrong idea, I just don't care all that much about making love."

"I see." She didn't sound convinced.

"What I am is romantic. The part I go for is the companionship."

"That's the best part." She placed her head on the pillow beside his for a moment. But their breathing never fell into rhythm. Soon she said, "Good night," and left the room silently.

In the morning they sat at the kitchen table in pale sunlight, eating muffins and drinking tea. Seebold was reminded of uncomfortable breakfasts with his landlady years ago when he was at the university, before he gave up school and settled for accountancy.

"Looks nice for my day off," she said, indicating the out of doors with an awkward movement of her head.

"Clouding up later I think I heard it said." She was inviting him to spend the day with her but all Seebold wanted was to get away. "Will you walk home from here?"

"Yes. Up the hill to the Village. The while cottage on the corner of the High Street, facing the Common." He enjoyed flaunting Sylvia's house.

Fay had left the front door propped open when she brought in the milk. Now a tall young man came through and stood close to the kitchen table. He had inherited the same sort of head as his sister—shaped by a potter who had a lot to learn—but his body was well-proportioned. "Too late for breakfast?" He extended a hand to the older man who shook it, half rising.

"This is Martin Seebold. He got caught by the rain last night. My brother Reg. You've got a hell of a nerve showing your face around here this morning."

"What's the matter?"

"You know damn well."

"I don't."

"Forty pounds taken out of my drawer last night. When I came home the place was in shambles." She watched Reg's reaction as he turned and surveyed the sitting room. "We put it back together."

Reg ambled into the other room. He opened the drawer where the knitting magazines were kept, closed it, and walked back into the kitchen looking thoughtful. "Why do you think it was me?"

"Who else?"

"Last time I only took twenty. I borrowed it."

"The way you borrow from Barclay's Bank in the middle of the night?"

"I'd never toss your place. You know me better than that."

"Unless you wanted me to think it was somebody else."

"I have an idea who did it." Reg made a helpless gesture. "Why don't you have a telephone like decent people?"

"Do you want coffee?"

"I have to go and see somebody."

"Have some coffee first."

"No, thanks. My sister thinks I robbed her."

Seebold walked up Wimbledon Hill to the Village. He began to feel better when he reached the top, the High Street shops aligned ahead of him with their pricey merchandise and well-designed fronts. There was a physical difference between down the hill and up the hill, he was convinced of it. The air pressure up here allowed his blood to flow more easily, or perhaps ozone from the trees in the Common was a tonic for his lungs. He always felt safer and happier up here. Down in the town there was excitement but also danger among a different kind of people.

He let himself in, carried the morning mail upstairs to his office, and sat at his desk, looking out across the road at the giant chestnut tree and the pond in the middle distance. He still thought of this room as an office although he didn't work here. When he took early retirement last year, Seebold had spoken in terms of doing a little freelance. But nobody had offered him any such work and he had not pursued it. His redundancy settlement had been generous, and Sylvia's resources were considerable. All Seebold had to do was take it easy and grow as old as possible with maximum grace. His famous heart attack two years ago provided justification for a degree of idleness.

Seebold's head was nodding, his mind filled with images of Fay and Reg on rope ladders scaling the side of a ship, when the telephone rang beside him. It was Sylvia calling from Newcastle.

"Where were you?"

"Where was I when?" After a long separation it took only this brief exchange to re-establish their relationship.

"I rang three times last night and twice earlier this morning. It is now 11:15."

"I wasn't here. I was playing gin with Lionel Henning. Then we watched the late film. When it started to rain, I camped out on his settee."

"Oh, yes."

"My neck feels as if it contains a hot poker."

"I suppose I believe you. With your medical history, I can't imagine you chasing the girls while your wife is away."

"Veryfunny."

"Promise me you won't end up dead in the bed of some teenaged tart."

"Even funnier."

She fell silent and Seebold occupied the time watching the ducks and coots on the pond. It interested him that a belligerent coot chased only other coots. Ducks, much of a size, were left alone.

"I rang to say I've decided to stay another few days."

"Having a good time, then?"

"Good time has nothing to do with it. I'm helping Gary and Rose, doing the things a mother does for her son and his wife. It happens to be more difficult at a distance of several hundred miles."

"I know."

"They could be living somewhere in London if you were a normal father."

"I did nothing—"

"If you'd done nothing, Gary wouldn't have taken Rose this far away."

Seebold remembered the moment in Cannizaro Park when Gary came upon the two of them. On a Sunday afternoon, Seebold had led Rose through a tunnel of rhododendrons to show her the view from his secret lookout. In tight jeans and a cotton blouse, she looked like a muscular young boy. Drugged by the droning afternoon and the waves of fragrant greenery breaking around them, he had put his arm around her slender waist and drawn her to him. Her hair smelled of shampoo. He had kissed the part in her hair.

"Fortunately," Sylvia was going on, "Gary has never told me what you were up to."

"There was nothing."

"So you say. But he and Rose live in Newcastle now, in a very ordinary little house. So don't talk to me about having a good time in Newcastle."

Seebold considered putting down the phone, pretending they had been cut off. But she would only get through again, more disturbed than ever. Like taking the cane, trousers down, gritting his teeth, leaning across the headmaster's desk, Seebold had to absorb his wife's telephone call.

"I'm putting an envelope of photographs in the post. Gary and Rose and the baby. When I get back, we'll decide which ones to have framed."

"So, I'll see you when? Saturday?"

She laughed, and for just a second or two, the buoyant sound made him feel secure. "Don't worry, I'll confirm my estimated time of arrival. Give you time to wash the perfume off the pillowcases."

Seebold put down the phone. Then he picked it up and dialed Lionel Henning. His old friend was ready to provide an alibi. "What have you been up to, naughty boy."

"I'll explain when next I see you. An incredible story, full of moral significance. Never become involved with the common people. They'll drop you in it, plunge you straight down into the roaring fires of hell."

Seebold, after a lunch of cheese and granary bread and a shapely Bosc pear, was napping on top of the bedspread when the doorbell chimed downstairs. The noise dragged him out of a half sleep, in which he had been grinding his teeth. A casement window was open. Sunlight across the end of the bed warmed his feet, and the fragrance of mock orange permeated the room.

The bell chimed again.

When he opened the door, Seebold did not recognize Fay Blore for a couple of seconds. She stood there enjoying his discomfiture. Her cheeks were burned from hours spent in the sun. She had put aside the trappings of premature middle age to appear now in velvet slacks, open sandals, a stylish blouse, and a tiny scarf knotted at the neck. Her brown hair was pulled around and clipped at one side—an improvement—but starry pencilled eyelashes could not save her mismatched eyes.

"You were having a nap!"

"It's all right. Come in."

He sat her down in the living room, under the sloping ceiling and dark beams, all of it centuries old. She stared about the room like a tourist in a museum. "I've come to take you out. I owe you for last night."

"You took a chance."

"You said your wife is away."

"A few more days. We were on the telephone a while ago. "

"Did you tell her about me?"

"I told her I was out last night with my old friend Lionel, playing gin rummy."

"Good old Lionel."

He brought the Waterford decanter to the Jacobean table and poured her a glass of Australian sherry. In crystal, it looks as Spanish as they come.

He went upstairs and changed, shaving in five minutes. He pattered down the winding stairs like a schoolboy, smelling of lemon cologne.

Outside, she said, "I'll leave the choice to you—this is your territory. But remember, it's my treat."

Seebold wanted to get out of the neighbourhood. A bus was labouring up the hill in the distance. He guided her to the stop and they boarded the bus for Putney.

"There's a lovely little place near the bridge," he said.

The giant proprietor was bellowing down the telephone in Italian. After five minutes, he presented himself to Seebold and took the order repeating the word "signore" after each item with mock obsequiousness. But the veal was tender and the sauce of lemon and white wine was delicious.

When they left the restaurant, there was still an hour's light in the sky. The tide was in, the grey water high against the embankment protecting Lower Richmond Road. Seebold led Fay along the footpath towards the brick facade of The Star and Garter. They sat at a table by the window, watching cruise boats heading up to Teddington or down to Greenwich. Conversation was easy, and once when she lowered her head against his shoulder laughing at one of his jokes, he kissed the part in her hair.

Later, they caught a bus on the south end of the bridge. It was dark now. Talked out from the pub session, they travelled along the Parkside in silence, holding hands. Seebold had time to think. She must not come inside with him—her presence in the house would last forever—nor could he go home with her a second time. That way lay disaster.

As the bus approached the turn onto Wimbledon High Street, he got up and put a hand on her shoulder. "I'd better say goodnight."

She was so experienced at being rebuffed that she took it with an approving smile. "Keep in touch," she said as the bus stopped and he escaped onto the pavement.

Seebold took his time walking past the cenotaph, past the pond and the chestnut tree. Inside his iron gate, he studied the silhouette of the hydrangea shrubs. They looked as if they could use a drink. Tomorrow. He searched for the front-door lock, and before he could insert his key, the door swung inward. He stood listening. After half a minute, he reached through and switched on the light. He noticed a mark on the door frame where the jimmy had gone in.

The place had not been ransacked so he was able to inventory the missing articles immediately. The carriage clock from the mantel, several pieces of silver from the cabinet. Suddenly, as sure as death and tax evasion, Seebold knew who had robbed his house: Reg Blore. While Seebold was out for a couple of hours, escorted by Reg's sister. For all Seebold knew, Fay was in on it.

The police. He had the telephone up and had dialed the first two nines when he changed his mind. To cause trouble for Fay without giving her a chance to say something was not right. Instead, Seebold dialed a taxi number. The cab came, and he had the driver take him down the hill to the Kingston Road and drop him a hundred yards from the fish-and-chips shop. Taking deep breaths, he walked down the laneway and climbed the iron steps. Below him, the crash and hiss of deep-frying on a massive scale went on, hidden beneath the glass roof.

Seebold knocked at Fay's door and stood waiting in the dark. If she was willing to get hold of Reg and make him return the stolen goods now, this night, he would forget the matter. Otherwise...

Fay was taking a long time coming to the door. He knocked again, sharply. A light went on somewhere inside, not in the sitting room. He knocked a third time. Voices began whispering on the other side of the panel. Seebold began to feel unsure of himself. If Reg was in there and wanted to make an issue of the accusation...

Another light came on and the door swung open. A girl Seebold had never seen stood to one side in jeans and bare feet and a pajama top. Behind her stood another stranger, a bleached-blond young man, bare-chested and tanned, also wearing tight jeans. These people, Seebold told himself, have climbed out of bed to open this door.

"I'm looking for Fay Blore."

"Hello. Come in. My name is Annie Wickersham." Her manner was airline-hostess friendly but her voice was public school. "This is Bjorn Lindgren. We're friends of Fay's brother. She should be along soon."

He came inside and accepted Bjorn's handshake. The boy looked and sounded like middle-class money from Sweden. "I won't stay if Fay isn't going to be around."

Anne's self-assurance was overpowering. "Please sit down, Fay would want you to." She sat after he did and faced him with her hands draped languidly across her knees. "We used a key Reg gave us—with Fay's permission, of course. I expect she's stalling now to give us time."

Bjorn stood confidently, hands in pockets. All the pose needed was sand and sun. "We're just back from Greece," he said.

"Crete, actually," Annie confirmed. "I've been touring for the past six months—India, Nepal. I ended up in Crete, where I ran out of money. The only thing I could do was take work picking cucumbers and tomatoes." She stared at her roughened hands. "Then along came Bjorn and rescued me. Airfare home." The boy's hand hung close enough for her to take it and press it against her cheek.

Footsteps approached on the iron stairs. Seebold got to his feet. So did Annie Wickersham. "The wanderer returns," she said.

Fay tapped with one knuckle, opened the door, and allowed Reg to enter ahead of her. Seebold's presence stopped them in their tracks. "What are you doing here?"

"I have to talk to you. Alone."

"We're just on our way," Annie said. She took Bjorn by the hand and led him into the bedroom. They were dressed and out the door before the tension had time to escalate.

When the front door closed and their footsteps began retreating down the iron stairs, Fay said, "Well?"

"My house was broken into this evening. While you and I were together."

"That's terrible. Did they take much?"

"A few valuables."

Reg said bluntly, "Why come here? Why tell us?"

Seebold thought, let the confrontation begin. "Because I think you did it."

"Me?"

"The coincidence is too much. I've never had robbers in my life. Last night I came here with Fay and her place had been ripped off. She said it was you. Tonight she and I went out—which you much have known—and somebody entered my house." Seebold was getting into a fine swing. "Too much."

"You bastard. I was with friends. I never left—they'll vouch for that."

"I'm sure they will. Let them tell the police."

Reg made a move and Fay intercepted him. "Get out of here, Reg. I'm not having a fight in here."

"This old creep says I robbed his house."

"Go." She managed to open the door while restraining her brother. "Go home. There won't be any police."

When they were alone, Seebold, feeling easier now because he had done his job as a man, said, "I'm sorry, Fay, but you must see my point. It has to have been Reg."

"He has an alibi."

"Of course he has."

She tossed her shoulder bag onto the settee and turned to face him. She wasn't on his side at all. "Have you any idea how many break-ins there are in London? I saw some figures. Five hundred a day. Something like forty here in the borough. Your number came up."

"That's not how it feels to me."

"What have you got to go on besides your hunch?"

"He didn't leave his name on the wall—a hunch is all there is. But I know it was Reg, it had to be him."

"Then call the police."

"I don't want to."

"Well, what *do* you want, Martin? You're starting to drive me up the wall. I don't know why I bother with you."

She looked helpless, on the verge of tears. He kept his distance. "I want back the things he took. Tell him to return my stuff and that will be the end of it."

She watched him for a few seconds, then turned away. "I'm going to take a shower," she said as she left the room. "We'll talk after."

"I'm not going to hang around."

"Stay or don't stay. I'm having a shower."

He was still standing there as the drizzle of water began hitting a plastic curtain. His sense of outrage was mounting. He was being taken advantage of, right, left, and centre. His house had been burgled, almost certainly by Reg, and Fay couldn't care less.

Seebold looked around the room. He would collect payment in kind. Something to hold against the return of his stolen goods. Not that there would be anything in this fire trap worth taking.

Then he saw it on a shelf near the bricked-up fireplace—a brass peppermill. It was obviously an antique, in need of a polish, but a fine piece nonetheless: cylindrical, inches high, with a jointed handle on top fitted with a wooden knob. The mill was in two sections. He tried separating them, but the joint was tight and he didn't want to damage it.

Feeling a mixture of terror and triumph, Seebold slipped the peppermill into his pocket, left Fay Blore's flat, and took a cab home.

As he placed the peppermill on the mantle piece where the stolen carriage clock used to sit, Seebold was feeling a sense of destiny. Fay's presence in his life was very different from tedious debits and credits that balanced at the end of the day. He had been let in on a mild form of anarchy. Truth be told, he was enjoying himself.

Pajamas-clad, slumped in a wingback chair, his slippered feet propped on a needlepoint hassock, Seebold sipped a drink. It would be a bad thing, he realized, to bring in the police and implicate Reg Blore. If they made a case of it, Seebold would end up on the witness stand explaining how he happened to know Reg, and more to the point, his sister Fay. Sylvia would ask questions and his comfortable life here in the cottage on the High Street might be threatened.

The telephone rang. Seebold put out a hand and took up the receiver. Speak of the devil... But it was not Sylvia.

"I was thinking about you while I took my shower. You've had nothing but grief from me."

Her voice on the phone was magic. Seebold closed his eyes and curled up inside himself like a boy being told a bedtime story. "Not to worry."

"I do worry. I'd like us to start again."

"Listen. I've decided you're right about my robbery. It could have been anybody. I'll bring in the police tomorrow just so there'll be a report for the insurance. But I won't mention Reg."

"That's sweet. I'll tell him. He and Annie are there now. I'm at a call box. Bjorn's coming soon with Chinese food."

He imagined the scene in Fay's apartment—plates, glasses, muffled words—the tribe back from hunting, safe for the night. He felt left out. "By the way," he boasted, "I took your brass peppermill. To make up for the stuff I lost."

"Peppermill?"

"It looks good on my mantel. Of course, if my things turn up, I'll discuss giving it back."

"I didn't even notice it was gone." She sounded anxious. "It belongs to Bjorn. He brought it back from Greece."

"Fine taste, those Swedes."

"He wants to sell it to a dealer. He only left it here for safekeeping."

"There's no such thing as a safe place any more."

"Bjorn will be upset."

"You can tell him I'm chairman of that club."

Seebold did not sleep well. Lying cheek-down, he could feel each beat of his heart. How much longer would the old pump carry on? And why was he not more afraid? Was this final section of his life such a bore that he could anticipate the end with no more interest than he felt during the credits of a bad television film?

He heard a thump below. His eyes opened, focused on the green clock dial. Almost four o'clock—he must have been sleeping, after all. More noise downstairs. The front door juddered open and hit the wall. Then silence. He knew who was down there.

Quickly, he rose and found his robe. He pulled his arms through the sleeves as he crept downstairs, past the bend into the darkened living room. His hand found the switch and turned on the overhead light.

Annie Wickersham was at the mantelpiece, the peppermill in both hands. Reg was at the door, close enough for Seebold to touch him, or be touched by him. He felt no fear. It was as if he was Father and had come upon the children engaged in some naughty prank. He moved to the girl, his hand extended.

"Where's Bjorn?" he asked. "Does he always use you to do his dirty work?"

"He's outside in the car." Annie said. Obediently, she handed Seebold the peppermill.

"Annie," Reg groaned, "don't give him that."

She reached for the peppermill. Seebold fended her off. They grappled. She was beefy under the blouse, nothing soft about her. He was enjoying her weight against him, but he was falling off balance. The fire irons went over with a crash, and as he sank to the floor, Seebold saw fit to raise his voice in a ferocious cry.

Reg's eyes were wild. "Come on. Let's go!" He moved back into the doorway.

When Annie followed, Seebold flung the peppermill at her back as hard as he could. It missed her, struck the door frame, and fell to the floor in two pieces. Reg bent and retrieved the pieces in an odd, scooping motion. Then he was gone. Moments later, car doors slammed, an engine revved and retreated into the distance.

Seebold lay still. Strange, he thought, how his heart could hold up through this kind of stress. Had the doctors been wrong? Or had he experienced some sort of remission? The vital organ seemed to be mending itself.

A forgotten episode from his childhood entered Seebold's mind. Seven years old, he stood on the school stage in front of an audience of parents. A female schoolmate faced him, holding two pieces of a heart made of red paper. To a piano accompaniment she sang, "Are you a tinker?"

"That am I," the young Seebold sang in response.

"Can you mend my heart?"

"I'll try," he volunteered.

Focusing on the open doorway, Seebold could see white powder on the carpet where the halves of the peppermill had fallen. He crawled over and stared at the powder. In television dramas about drug trafficking, a police officer would dip his finger into the powder, taste it, and know what sort of dope he was dealing with. But Martin Seebold would not have known what taste to expect. And, anyway, he was afraid to try.

In the morning, a pair of policemen came around. Seebold allowed last night's forced entry to account for his loss from earlier in the day. He listed what had been taken, with estimated values. He didn't refer to Reg or Annie or Bjorn. The officers went away, bored as tourists.

Jaundiced thoughts, like dregs of stale wine, collected in Seebold's mind as he shaved. But he felt better when he left the house and walked down the hill to visit his friend Lionel Henning. They lunched on Henning's patio, then went inside for a game of gin rummy. Seebold lost two quid. He was concentrating less on the cards and more on his recounting of the Fay Blore saga. It was all fine, self-deprecating stuff—her glamorous voice, her appearance as a dowdy dwarf, that hat which must have been her mother's.

There was a film he wanted to see at the Odeon down on Broadway, so he went there alone at three o'clock and sat in the dark, filling his mouth with chocolate-coated caramels while admiring the way Jack Nicholson attacked a door with an axe.

The pubs were open when the film let out, so he wandered back to the Alex for a couple of drinks while he read the paper. Then up the hill for a light supper, an hour watching the box, and early to bed.

Nobody broke in that night. The telephone did not ring. In the morning, the postman dropped a large brown envelope through the slot. Seebold opened it and found, protected by squares of shirt cardboard, several beautiful photographs of his son Gary, his wife, and the cherubic grandson. A handwritten note was folded between the photos.

Back at the kitchen table, Seebold sipped apple juice and read the familiar script. Sylvia would be back on Monday. He was not to come all the way to King's Cross. She would ring when the train arrived, then she would take the District Line to Wimbledon. Seebold could time himself to meet her there and help with bags and a taxi.

His holiday was coming to an end. Too soon, the bad old routine would begin again. It was difficult for him to pin down just what was bad about his existence here with Sylvia. Never mind. He felt grim and justification was not required.

The day was sunny again, no mention of rain in the forecast. Seebold took out the hose and watered the plants in the back garden. Then he went up to the flat roof outside his study. The potted marigolds lining the eaves looked tired. He scooped water from the rain barrel and gave them a drink.

Next he unfolded a deck chair and reclined facing the sun. After an hour, his face felt crisp so he took himself inside. The last thing he wanted was to get himself fried.

He would have to see Fay one more time before Sylvia came back. This idea occurred to Seebold at four in the afternoon as he was working out a crossword puzzle. It made sense for him to let the girl know that, as of Monday, she must not ring up or appear at the cottage for any reason.

He put on the expensive maroon corduroy trousers Sylvia had bought for him a year ago, when she thought he ought to try dressing young. He slipped his feet into black patent-leather loafers and drew over his head a white knitted shirt with a tiny gold crown on the pocket. Seebold decided to consider himself a well-preserved man heading out to keep some mysterious appointment.

With a bottle of claret wrapped in a Harrod's plastic bag, he set out down the hill. He was anxious to arrive at Fay's place, to see her, even to run into the three kids again. He missed it all—the room, Fay's loud music, the whole atmosphere of their young lives. They were so far behind him on the road, it seemed a sensible thing for him to go back and meet them.

He was in the lane, approaching the iron stairs, when it occurred to him she might not be home. If there was no response when he knocked at the door, he would simply wander away, find a pub, have a couple, and come back.

The door was ajar when he reached the iron landing. Fay's door seemed to spend more time open than shut. Voices murmured within. His rap brought Reg to the doorway. "Fay, come here," he said as if Seebold was an exhibit. "Look at this."

She appeared at her brother's side wearing a flowered shift, barefoot, her eyes wide and bright. "Martin! How lovely, we're having a celebration."

He allowed her to lead him into the dusky room. Bjorn was lying on the settee, a clear place beside him where Fay must have been. He was pinching the stub of a thin cigarette. Annie Wickersham lay on the carpet, her head on a pillow. Reg went to her and lay down. He took the cigarette she offered and drew on it deeply.

"What's the occasion?" Seebold asked, his confidence ebbing.

"We're celebrating a deal," Annie said. "An arrangement."

Bjorn spoke up, "Annie flies to Greece. Annie flies back. With her good clothes and accent, Annie flies through customs."

"Then everybody gets high," Reg said and they all laughed for a long time.

Finally Seebold said, "I brought some wine."

Fay left the settee and came to receive the bottle. As she took it, she hooked her wrist around his neck, drew his head down, and applied a wet kiss to his lips.

With a glass of wine in his stomach and a second one in his hand, Seebold's personal pendulum took an upward swing. He sat with his legs extended, shoes making a glittering V. "So, this is how you lot enjoy your-selves," he commented, a tolerant judge.

"One of the ways," Bjorn said.

"How do I love thee?" Annie recited. "Let me count the ways."

"You can't count that high," Reg said.

Seebold felt an urge to get closer to the life they led, to show some sophistication. "By the way," he said, "what was the white powder that ended up on my carpet the other night when the peppermill came apart?"

The response was silence. Bjorn sat up and put his feet on the floor. He looked from Seebold to Reg to Annie. "What the hell happened in there? You never told me."

"He threw the mill," Reg said. "It broke apart."

"How much is lost? That stuff sells by the gram."

"Hardly anything," Annie whispered.

Bjorn climbed to his feet. "And this bugger knows?"

Fay came in from the kitchen. "It's all right," she said.

"It isn't all right! This guy can do us if he feels like it."

"I don't feel like doing anybody," Seebold said. "Except maybe Fay if the rest of you would disappear."

Fay took Bjorn's arm and turned him. She moved him towards the door. "Go to the off-licence, love. I feel like another nice bottle of wine."

Bjorn was trying to turn back. "We've got to do something about this guy."

"We'll talk when you come back. Reg, go with Bjorn. You know the wine I like."

When the young men were gone, Fay came to Seebold. "You'd better go. He can be terrible when he gets mad."

"I don't want to go," Seebold said.

"She's right," Annie said. "Bjorn goes crazy. In Crete, in the green-house, a man got on his nerves. Bjorn cut him with a trowel. He would have killed him."

"All right." Seebold moved away from the door. There was wine in his glass. "May I finish this?"

"Quickly, please."

He took his time drinking the wine while Fay stood in the centre of the room and Annie went to look out the window. Setting down the empty glass, he said, "Okay if I go to the bathroom?"

"Hurry, for God's sake."

He took his time, and when he came out, Annie said, "They'll be here any minute."

The door was open. Fay propelled him through the open door and stood, wanting to close it. "I'll ring you."

"You can't ring me after Monday."

"All right, tomorrow. Go now."

They heard the clang of heavy steps on the iron stairs. Fay said something Seebold missed and Annie made a moaning noise in her throat. Bjorn appeared first, Reg behind him carrying the supplies.

"What's this?" Bjorn faced Seebold.

"Going home."

"To ring the police?"

"No, I just want to go home." Now, when he could have used courage to bluff his way out in front of the women, Seebold was swamped with fear. This young man could thump him nine ways. He took a breath and felt his heart miss a beat, stutter, and catch up.

"You're not going anywhere," Bjorn said. "Not till I make sure about you."

As Seebold made a move to pass the young Swede, Bjorn grappled with him. The weakness in Seebold's arms was ridiculous. For heaven's sake, he could lift a filing cabinet if he had to. He struggled to break free and Bjorn threw a punch he managed to avoid.

Fay called, "Let him go!" but she remained in the doorway. Annie was a face behind the curtains. Seebold managed to get loose and tried again to pass Bjorn on the railing side. Bjorn caught him by the shoulder, swung him around so his back was to the railing, and aimed another punch. This one landed, driving Seebold against the railing which gave way, letting him step back into space.

He heard Fay's scream as he fell. The glass roof of the restaurant kitchen shattered as Seebold burst through into heat and light, seeing white tile, stainless-steel shelves. He realized there is a hell and we descend into it, literally.

And for Seebold, hell was a cauldron of cooking oil heated to a temperature of almost 400 degrees.

The Stand-In

by Mike Barnes

In a story set far from the city, Mike Barnes challenges the perception that noir is an urban phenomenon, that it lurks solely in a world of dark alleys and mean streets. It isn't that simple. The heart of darkness beats anywhere you find people—and in Canada, the Great North is black as often as it's white. Barnes captures subtle menace and the danger of deception with writing that the *Toronto Star*'s Philip Marchand calls "fiercely alive, marked by a sharp, unerring eye for detail, and a wonderful way with metaphors."

"The Stand-In" appeared in Mike Barnes' first collection of stories, *The Aquarium*, which won the 1999 Danuta Gleed Award for Best First English-Langauge Collection by a Canadian. His stories have also appeared in *The Journey Prize Anthology* and *Best Canadian Stories*.

It was 1980. Almost twenty years ago, now. Ganz was living on an Indian reserve, a small fly-in community hundreds of miles north of Sioux Lookout. He was there as the guest of his friend, a weatherman working for Environment Canada. After Ganz quit his job in Oakville, just getting tired of it, he wrote this weatherman, an old school friend, who invited him up for a visit. The weatherman was feeling bored, put-upon in some way that Ganz never quite understood, although they talked for days over glasses of smuggled-in rye. From what Ganz could see, he had an easy, do-nothing job; but, like many people in that position, he felt he should be doing even less. He told Ganz he could stay for the winter, helping him in return for room and board. Ganz had no other plans.

Soon Ganz was taking all of the weatherman's simple readings: temperature, barometric pressure, humidity, precipitation, wind direction, and velocity. The weatherman napped most of the day. Incredibly, he complained about having to answer the phone when his supervisor called twice a week. Ganz wondered if his friend was losing his mind.

The situation worsened when the weatherman got involved with a local girl, a teenager named Crystal. This romance seemed to make the idea of any duties intolerable to him. All he wanted to do was go snowmobiling with her, speeding forty miles to the next village, where her brother had an empty cabin he let them use. Coming back for the supervisor's calls made his face go grey with hate.

Then, one day, he was all smiles. Forget about the supervisor, he told Ganz. From now on he would only call once a week; when he did, Ganz could tell him what he needed to know. Ganz assumed that money had changed hands.

Fuck him, the weatherman blustered, damning the supervisor but glaring at Ganz. The government was going to automate everything soon anyway. Why wait for them to lay him off?

Ganz paid no attention to these rationalizations. He realized that he and the weatherman were no longer friends, something he had begun to suspect. Yet here he was, *becoming* the weatherman, in a sense.

The weatherman took Ganz to the Bay and bought him a parka and thick, high boots and gauntlets. Ganz hadn't packed for the North. He signed a form allowing Ganz to ring up groceries on his Bay tab. Then he roared off on his snowmobile.

It was November 29. Minus-twenty-two degrees Celsius, as Ganz recorded. The mildest day in awhile.

"What you do with that stuff?"

Ganz looked up from the precipitation tray to see Andrew Mequanawap, his nearest neighbour. Andrew was a quick-stepping older man—maybe fifty, by his limber movements, but with a heavily-lined brown face and almost no teeth. He had an oblique way of speaking, his words seeming to point to many things at once.

"My readings, you mean?" Ganz replied.

"All this shit." Andrew's gloved wave took in all of the instruments and gauges littering the small yardlike toys. His head, black-haired, without a strand of grey, was bare to the minus-thirty-four-degree air, plus a wind chill Ganz hadn't calculated yet.

"Nothing, Andrew. Just keeping track."

Andrew liked to banter. But this time his face stayed stern. "You warn me if it's going to snow? Some big storm or something?"

"Sure."

"Bullshit." Now he smiled, a black crease between two brown pegs. "You're a government man."

This he had said before. All the white men—teachers, policemen, the fly-in dentist who yanked teeth—were *government*.

Ganz mentioned the weatherman.

"He's gone. Disappeared." Ganz must have looked dismayed because

Andrew added softly, like a doctor repeating his diagnosis, "You're a government man, Fred."

Then he walked away, his long strides crunching the snow. Ganz wanted to call after him, invite him in for tea, but the one time he had done so, Andrew had acted strangely, slurping the tea beside the kitchen door and leaving without a word.

The next morning, Ganz found a pickerel lying on his doorstep. A frozen, dull gold bar, dusted with snow, that he thawed on his kitchen table and fried with potatoes and onions for supper.

Andrew stopped by most days for a brief exchange. Making his rounds, Ganz thought, uneasy but also comforted. It was his only social life. He felt the strangeness of his position: not a local, not a government employee (officially); yet not just a visitor, either. Probably no one cared—you got by however you could in the North—but his situation weighed on him. It was a limbo. The native people he passed, on his walks or at the Bay, smiled in greeting, but he sensed an impenetrable mildness, a willed tolerance, in their courtesy.

Once, before the teachers flew out for Christmas, Ganz got together with them and the policeman and his wife. Pouring illegal rum behind closed curtains in the teacherage, they bitched about the cold, the Bay prices, the sullen locals. The teachers seemed especially harried; one of them wouldn't return after the break.

Ganz told them about Andrew's *government* line. Someone joked about this being a *cabinet meeting*. They all got very drunk, cursing and laughing until the tears came. At the time, it felt cathartic, though no one had suggested repeating it.

Ganz didn't hear from the weatherman. He didn't dare ask about him. Stints on UI back in Oakville had sharpened his sense of when to lie low, when to keep the facts of his life as unremarked as possible. Apparently, his credit was still good at the Bay, for Ganz's groceries kept clicking through. He had only a little cash, but there was nothing he needed. Environment Canada's cabin was snug, with a TV and VCR, and stacks of movies. Sometimes, looking around at the bland, IKEA-style furniture, Ganz had the thought that he was in a deserted hotel. Like a science fiction movie. The power on, the kitchen well stocked, but all the other guests gone. *World of One.*

He slept fitfully at night, and napped often during the short, crystalline days. He felt like a mole huddled in a tunnel of cold. The snow machines would roar by, close, sounding like freight trains. Then silence again, like a stopped breath. He always set the alarm when he slept, since his readings had to be taken at four-hour intervals, precisely. This irritated him, and he understood better the weatherman's gripes. The constrictions on him were loose, but constant; a fine mesh of duties and deadlines.

The supervisor still called, but less often. Sometimes he was clearly drunk, slurring fulminations about the coming automation that would "fuck us all. Well, fuck *them*!"

At least once a week, Ganz checked his return air ticket in the drawer of the bedside table. Needing to know it was still there, still good. What kept him from shipping out immediately was partly masculine pride—he was twenty-seven—but mostly curiosity. He knew what was waiting for him back in Oakville: a job search. Then a job or welfare. This, at least, felt new.

The day after Andrew left the pickerel, Ganz walked down the shore to thank him.

Andrew was splitting wood, the axe blows cracking like gunshots. His shack always had a thick plume of smoke rising from it and split wood surrounded it in a thick, ragged wall. Firewood was scarce around the village; Andrew hauled it back from across the lake. Two mongrel dogs guarded the wood against the less industrious.

The dogs ran yapping at Ganz as he approached. Just before they reached him, their chains ran out, snapping them off the ground with strangled yelps.

"Thanks for the fish," he called above the frenzied barking.

Andrew peered at him, shielding his eyes with his hand against the glare of sun on snow. His axe blade rested on the chopping block. He wasn't wearing a coat or gloves.

"You know what I thought of when I saw it," Ganz heard himself babbling. "Luca Brasi. You remember that scene in *The Godfather* when the Corleone family gets a fish wrapped in newspaper? 'Luca Brasi sleeps with the fish.' That's the first thing I thought of."

Andrew was looking at him. He barked something in Ojibwa at the dogs, which slunk back to the wood pile.

"You're bushed, Fred," Andrew said.

Bushed. That word had come up often at the Christmas cabinet meeting. It meant teachers airlifted out, hysterical laughter, singing at the northern lights.

"No," Ganz yelled, then realized it was silent now.

"You're bushed," Andrew repeated, turning back to his work.

Walking home, Ganz had a sudden fearful suspicion of how Andrew's pronouncements could seem so malicious, mocking, comforting, goofy and profound—all of these things, at once.

Maybe they were just the truth.

What mainly got him through that winter was helping Andrew with his fish net. Andrew went out on the frozen lake once or twice a week. "When I go," he said when Ganz asked him about his schedule.

One day in January, he pulled up on the snowmobile while Ganz was fiddling in the yard, adjusting the anemometer. "Get on," he yelled over the idling engine.

"Where we going?" said Ganz.

"Fishing."

He got on behind Andrew. Putting his gauntleted hands up by Andrew's sides as they started, embarrassed to hold the other man any tighter. "Hang on," Andrew shouted as they left the island trail and bumped down onto the lake ice. Ganz hugged him, smelling his smoky campfire smell.

They flew across the frozen lake on a trail packed hard as tarmac by other snow machines. A runnerless metal sled, like an ambulance litter with curved sides, rattled along behind them. Strapped down on it was a tarpaulin-wrapped bundle. All around them was a sun-shot plain of white, flowing in gentle waves and mounds, the soft brush line of the distant shore further blurred by Ganz's tearing eyes. The vastness of the winter was exhilarating. It seemed unimaginable that so much ice and snow could dissolve into blue waves by summer.

An empty oil drum marked the spot where Andrew fished. Two thick, peeled sticks, like flagpoles, stuck out of the ice about thirty feet apart. Standing to one side while Andrew undid the straps on the sled, Ganz stared into the dense brush of the nearby shore. Another small island stood off in the distance. Light crashed all around, in eerie silence. Ganz had fished a few times in his life, sitting in a boat with a rod and reel, but he saw this was nothing like that. Anything might swim into a net under the ice.

Andrew had brought kindling and split logs under the tarp. He tossed these into the barrel and got a fire going. More than comfort, Ganz thought: life insurance. Andrew took a long-handled ice chisel from the sled and started digging with short thrusts around the marker stick nearest shore. Ice chips flew up. Ganz looked in the sled for another chisel to help, but there was only a coil of yellow nylon rope and Andrew's axe.

After a few minutes, Andrew paused, panting. Ganz by this time was so used to Andrew's stoical prowess that his laboured breaths, his hands trembling from exertion, surprised him slightly. Andrew allowed him to take the chisel.

Ganz was clumsy at first. The chisel blade struck glancingly or stuck upright. But he soon learned to aim the blade at the jagged edge of the hole, shearing off corners; to use, as Andrew had, short jabs. It was warmer, working. And he was young and strong; it made him feel proud that he dug the hole faster than Andrew. It was gratifying to strike the blow that brought dark water, like oil, bubbling through the slush.

But harder to finish the hole through the water, the chisel head slow and dreamlike.

When he looked up Andrew was watching him.

"Take your hood down. It's too hot." It was minus-nineteen Celsius, a mild day by Ganz's changing standards.

"Get a tan?" Ganz said happily. Andrew shrugged.

Ganz took the chisel to the other marker (his job now) while Andrew tied the yellow rope to the net attached to the first pole. The system, once Ganz understood it, was ingeniously simple. After Ganz dug another, smaller hole, Andrew brought the rope down and tied it to the net on the second pole. He worked with bare hands in the frigid water. Then he untied the net from the pole, as he had done at the other end. Now they could haul the net down to the first hole without losing it; the continuous loop of net and rope was like a clothesline between two pulleys.

"How did you set it up the first time?" he asked.

"Bunch of holes," Andrew muttered, securing his knots. "Pass it along."

Ganz tried to picture it, the work involved.

"It's easy. The ice is thin then."

Down at the main hole, Andrew began hauling up the net. The yellow rope disappeared into the far hole. Ganz took off his gauntlets to help, but Andrew shook his head. "You'll freeze," he said. Embarrassed, Ganz tugged the gloves up again.

The first few yards brought empty net. Andrew, working quickly, dropped the wet mesh in folds beside the hole. Then, thrillingly, the fish came. First, a large spotted pike. Andrew disengaged its gills from the net and tossed it, thrashing, onto the ice. It flared its gills and lay still. Other fish followed: pale whitefish, glittering pickerel, and something murky and large with whiskers.

"What's that?" Ganz asked.

"Sturgeon. White men don't eat them," Andrew said, gripping the greyish back. "Just the eggs."

All of the fish were alive, some barely, and Ganz wondered how long they had been struggling, swimming in place in the dark.

Two pike close together had snarled the net. Andrew's hands flew like a seamstress's as he untangled them.

"I caught a ten-pound pike once," Ganz said. "My girlfriend's mother made chowder out of it."

"Too bony," Andrew said dismissively, flipping the pike onto the pile of other fish. "I keep them for my sentinels."

His dogs. Sometimes Andrew used words that amazed Ganz. He had only been to grade eight, but he had a curious mind and he read the Bay manager's *Time* magazines after he'd finished them. He had described details of Ronald Reagan's inauguration to Ganz. "He'll be good. Good for business," Andrew announced, with an ambiguous sparkle in his eye. When Ganz ventured that he preferred Carter, Andrew retorted, "No good for business."

When the net was cleared of fish, Andrew motioned Ganz to begin pulling the yellow rope while he fed the net back into the hole. Hurrying now, Andrew tied the net back on to the pole, untied the rope, and jogged over to the other hole to do the same. Ganz felt a strange relief when Andrew stuck his hands out over the oil-drum fire and rubbed them hard, his leathery face untensing with the warmth.

They packed the tools back on the sled, piling the frozen fish where the wood had been, and secured it all under the tarp and straps. Riding back behind Andrew, Ganz surrendered himself to a vision of remaining in the North, making his way up here. Surviving, as Andrew did, by his wits and muscle. Fishing. Shooting the occasional gift of a moose. Picking up summer dollars when the government needed a work crew to build new houses or clear brush. He knew it was a fantasy, but unlike the fantasy he was living, it made his life seem purposeful, vivid.

Back at Andrew's, standing safely out of range, he watched as Andrew used his axe to chop the pike up into chunks. The sentinels fell on the pieces he threw, gulping down the first frozen bites, then licking a piece into softness before swallowing it.

"When are you going again?" Ganz called hopefully.

"When I get hungry." Andrew disappeared into his shack.

But Ganz went with him most times after that. Occasionally, Andrew buzzed straight past in his snowmobile, moody or else asserting his autonomy. Or doing neither of those: he was a mystery to Ganz. Another mystery, which hurt Ganz at first, was that Andrew never offered him any fish to take home, even though Ganz was able to help more each time, and they were netting plenty of fish. The pickerel on the doorstep stood out as a lonely blessing. At some point, Ganz figured, he and Andrew had entered a zone where such simple trades, or gifts, were no longer possible. Why, he wasn't sure.

Once, he forgot himself with the older man, and it was like accidentally turning on the lights in a candlelit room.

It was a glittering February day. The sun actually felt warm again, like a hand on the back of his neck. Walking back from the Bay with his groceries, he took the long way round to pass Andrew's shack. Andrew was smoking by a pile of fresh-split, gleaming wood. For once, the sentinels, two puddles of dozing fur, stayed quiet.

"Hi, chief," Ganz called. It was a simple, dumb mistake. He didn't mean anything by it. *Chief* had just come to mind—like guy, fella, buddy.

"Hello, Custer," Andrew said without missing a beat. He actually brandished his axe, like a huge tomahawk.

Mortified, Ganz tramped on as though he had never meant to stop. He passed through the yard of weather instruments, put away his cans, and lay down for one of his long twilight naps, videos twittering in the background.

Two days later, they took in their best haul ever from the net. Two dozen fish, almost all of them whitefish and pickerel.

As the days lengthened toward spring, Ganz felt himself waking up. His eyes dilated with the light, swimming in new details. Sights jolted him: a bare-armed girl suddenly roaring out of cedars on a snowmobile at dusk, black hair streaming out behind her, nipples thrust against her T-shirt. It was one of the craziest, most sheerly beautiful things Ganz had ever seen, and he gaped after her, slack-jawed within his parka hood.

With Andrew's help, he put more names to the faces he greeted on his walks. Maggie, Crystal's aunt. Archie, and two steps behind him, toothless old Linda—his wife, not his mother. Young Benjamin hunting jays with his air rifle.

He even started studying the weatherman's textbooks and manuals, curious about the science he'd been bluffing at.

Stratus means "layered." Fog is a stratus cloud.

He felt like a tourist again. Displaced, curious, alive. Alive. To be home, he thought, is to be blurred, half-asleep; curled in your burrow. Like the kids—glue-sniffers, Andrew said—who scuffed along the boardwalk, or kicked the front step of the Bay in a mindless rhythm. Old people milling around the post-office window at cheque time, or sitting motionless on their doorsteps. Now that he was emerging from it, the memory of his own numbness, matching the general malaise, chilled him.

Andrew had escaped the sadness, but Ganz thought that he would escape it anywhere. "My son lives in Thunder Bay with his mother," he had said once, and something in his placid, unresentful tone told Ganz that Andrew would be exactly the same man wherever he found himself.

He no longer checked his airline ticket, sure now that he would use it soon. He thought that he would stay until break-up. See the ice melt into blue waves, then leave that new lake.

April began with a ten-day thaw. The temperature climbed to a balmy eight degrees in the midday sun, turning the road into muddy slush. Clouds of preposterous flies hovered over snowbanks. Snowmobile engines raced in the sticky snow, throwing up spray. The sound of dripping water was everywhere.

"Break-up soon?" he said to Andrew.

"No, Fred," Andrew replied. "Getting bushed?"

Ganz felt heartened that it was a question again.

They couldn't go out to the net. Pools of sinister grey were dotting the lake, seeping circles in the snow. The slush was too hard on the snowmobile, Andrew said, though he scoffed at Ganz's suggestion that they might go through.

"You dug those holes, Fred," he reminded him.

Ganz thought of the fish, suspended below the roof of ice, fighting and resting, fighting and resting. How long before they gave up, or died of exhaustion?

One day, after taking his morning measurements, he stood by the front window of the Environment Canada cabin, sipping a Sanka. He felt happy, an awareness that had been sneaking up on him lately; the feeling usually coming with a mild anxiety about what he should do next.

Down the road, then, came a strange sight.

Three Indian women, bundled up, coloured scarves on their heads, were shuffling slowly between the half-frozen ruts. The two outside women supported the woman in the middle, holding her under the arms. Ganz heard a low moaning sound, like wind through a crack. As they drew near, he thought he recognized Maggie, Crystal's aunt, as the woman in distress. The moaning sound came from her lowered head.

He pulled back behind the curtain out of respect, or fear.

Something had happened. Was happening.

Ten minutes later, he was drinking another coffee, more acid for his prickling stomach, when the phone rang.

It was the almost-forgotten supervisor. Drunk at eight in the morning, his voice shrill.

"The dishdric hea—" he blurted, then the line went dead. Ganz knew, with an uncanny certainty, that the district head had just walked into the room. And, furthermore, that he would soon be flying up. It was as if he were in a dream tunnel, seeing events just before they happened, their causes dissolving behind him.

He put on his boots and wandered outside, just as Andrew pulled up on his snowmobile. He left the engine running.

Andrew's face was solemn, somehow strange. Like a dark leather mask hanging in shadow.

"Crystal went through the ice," he said.

Ganz knew he meant Crystal and the weatherman.

"Are they...? Did anyone...?"

"They broke through," Andrew said sharply.

"But you said..."

"It's a river over there. Currents."

The fool. The damn fool, Ganz thought, close to tears.

Andrew throttled down. He stared down at his tough brown hands as if searching for a softness that certain extreme situations called for.

"It's time, Fred," he said gently. Ganz knew what he meant. "I'll be back in an hour." He gunned the engine and veered away.

Ganz went back inside, dazed but strangely clear-headed. When he phoned the airport, the man who sold the tickets said, "Eleven-thirty," and hung up. Ganz felt giddy with tension. The gruff message was like the code word in a spy movie, the next link in the network that would smuggle him past Checkpoint Charlie.

He packed his bag quickly. Checking the rooms, he saw no evidence of his five-month stay but his breakfast dishes. He washed them and put them away.

Bouncing behind Andrew on the mangled road that led through bush to the airport, he felt the lake receding behind him. He would never see it blue. Behind him, the sled shimmied in the ice and mud, his pack strapped over the tarp like a midget's body bag. At the airport, Andrew and the ticket agent muttered together in Ojibwa. Standing to one side in the stuffy shack, Ganz felt a deep shame, partly bracing, for causes obscure to him. It wasn't the deception he had participated in, which seemed minor, almost humdrum, one more loop in a vast web of scams. What made his shoulders slump was the dim sense of a larger sin, something pervasive that had snagged him. Carelessness, perhaps; or its twin, ignorance.

He thought he saw embarrassment flicker, for the first and only time, in Andrew's eyes as they shook hands goodbye.

"Hope you get a cold snap," Ganz said. Or a thaw, he thought.

"Why, Fred?" Andrew asked.

"To get the fish."

Andrew gave his thin smile, which now seemed less ironic, more clearly bitter. "They're not going anywhere."

Sitting in the Twin Otter with the other passengers, Ganz watched the pilot and the ticket agent toss the freight up to the copilot, who stacked it behind webbing attached to either wall. He imagined the fish, wriggling more faintly. Down the road, two boys sprang from the bushes and jumped on Andrew's sled. Ganz watched through the plane's little window as they rocked the sled from side to side for a little ways, then tumbled off again. Andrew never looked back or slowed.

In Toronto, where he drifted a few months later, Ganz got a job driving cab for an old man who owned three cars. The old man's son, also the dispatcher, told Ganz that he could safely keep fifteen percent of his fares undeclared; his father would overlook that much.

Ganz wondered briefly when his face had become the kind of face you knew would understand, and need, that kind of information.

Winter Hiatus

by James Powell

Known as a writer of humorous crime fiction, Jim also has a dark side that informs his best work. Stories like "A Murder Coming" (also the title of a collection of his stories published in 1990) and "Jerrold's Meat" are all the more disturbing because of the way they make us smile; and "Winter Hiatus" is just such an existential treat. It understands the sacrifices we have to make to get along; the parts of our souls that we must purge or hide away. And it reminds us that redemption is nothing but a dream.

Born in Toronto, but a long-time resident of rural Pennsylvania, Jim has been publishing his compelling fiction since 1968. He has garnered a record eleven Arthur Ellis Award nominations from the Crime Writers of Canada—including one for this story—and was also nominated for the CWC's Derrick Murdoch Award.

The fields flashed by, all stubble, stooks, and golden sunshine. Then the train entered a shady slope of trees. Suddenly the trees fell away and there was the sun again, glinting on the church steeples of the town.

West felt the slowing of the train. Then he heard a familiar, unhurried voice say, "Happy Valley. Next stop is Happy Valley." Still smiling, he turned from the window just as Mr. Vining, the conductor, leaned across to collect his ticket. The man had a dependable face, and the visored cap with the Greenfields and Eldorado Line badge, sat squarely on his head.

"Welcome back, Mr. West. You've been a stranger."

Before West could answer, the train gave a jolt and everything went dark.

When the light returned, it was dim and electric. West found himself back on the other train, the crowded commuter, which a second before, had slid to a stop deep inside Grand Central Station.

None of the passengers moved or spoke. For the first few moments, the railway car was all ears and heartbeats. The week before, a roving band of street people and dentists—one of those strange alliances of the moment—had jumped the passengers as they surged out onto the platform, hitting them hard and mauling them badly. The passengers might have withstood the street people just by not showing fear. But dentists expect fear. Not finding it brought an extra frenzy to their attack.

So today the passengers listened until they were satisfied nothing was amiss before moving toward the exits. Those who hadn't formed into groups of four did so now. These foursomes went back to an old commuter custom of playing bridge on the train. Few had the nerves for the game any more. But a foursome remained the basic defensive unit.

West's foursome let the drift toward the door bring them together. Out on the platform, West took the point. He'd been there the longest. The others called him the Old Man although he was only thirty-five.

During the bunch-up at the platform gate, West noticed the singleton with the good shoulders and the alligator briefcase watching them again from the edge of the crowd. West's people had christened the man the Hyena. Singletons were always eyeing foursomes, looking for someone showing the strain, someone whose place they might take. West glanced around at his people as they passed through the gate, wondering if the Hyena had seen something he'd missed. Then his mind turned to leading the way as his group elbowed through the peripheral doubletons and singletons, and into the mainstream of foursomes heading for the downtown subway trains.

The passageway was a dark, littered, bloodstained slope as cold and endless as the turbulent streets above their heads. West set his jaw and lengthened his stride, eyes alert for trouble. But, God, his nerves were shot, his body utterly exhausted. And they were only a month into Winter Hiatus, those terrible weeks between the Christmas rush and Easter when the City, without tourists or day trippers to feed on, feeds on itself.

West tensed. Up ahead, where several passageways entered a small rotunda, a large black man with a scarred face and a filthy bandage on one hand was coming down an exit to the street, holding a garbage can over his head. Moaning like a hurt child, the man hurled the garbage can into the fast-moving column of people. It hit a woman in a business suit sprinting at the edge of the crowd. She collapsed in a heap. West let himself be swept on by. There was no way to help her. The City demanded its daily quota of blood. Her blood, tourist blood, West's blood, it didn't care.

Suddenly West remembered where he'd seen the guy with the garbage can before. He'd worked right down the hall in the Public Relations wing of the City Hall Annex when West first started on the taxi desk. What was his name? He hadn't had the scars then. Morgan. Morgan made himself something of a PR legend by concocting a phony jazz form—the Big Apple sound, he called it—and a whole stable of imaginary musicians who played it, and the out-of-the-way clubs they worked. He planted items in the jazz magazines and staged photographs showing the Rhythm Rajahs playing at Fat Clive and Lady Kat's, or Skoobie Hitchcock packing them in at the Licorice Stick Lounge. He even came up with Potemkin Records, the label they recorded for. Pretty soon all kinds of out-of-town jazz types were wandering around late at night in parts of the City where they didn't belong, looking for Mr. Whitey's After-Hours Club to hear the Strideman Standish Trio, and a lot of them didn't come back alive. And ditto those who went hunting for Ozzie's Platter Barn ("Hard-to-find Potemkins Our Specialty").

West's own job with Public Relations wasn't anything that flashy. A million tourists go back home with five million horror stories about the City's cab drivers. West's job was essentially damage control. He fed the media weekly stories of the "Stradivarius Left in Taxi Returned by Honest Cabbie in Time for Carnegie Hall Concert" variety to help offset all the bad word of mouth. Sometimes he tried to kid himself that he was restoring people's faith in their fellow man. But not now. Come Winter Hiatus, you just held on tight and tried to survive any way you could. Like Happy Valley, a little town he'd dreamed up over the years. If things got too tough, West would close his eyes and imagine himself on a visit there. Happy Valley was his secret strength, a place he'd never hinted about to anyone, not even to Fran, his wife.

The hurrying crowd pounded up a short flight of steps, along another corridor, and down more steps to the subway platform, where a train stood with its doors open. The crowd flowed inside. West found a seat beside a pole. His people stood around him. As the train started up, West saw the Hyena watching from the end of the car. What did the man want? West turned away and closed his eyes.

He was coming down the steps from the railway station past borders of red geraniums and white impatiens. It was late afternoon on a warm autumn day, and the slanting sun made church windows of the bright trees. Before he'd gone a block, Merle and Mert, the Blandish twins, had hailed him by name from their big old car to ask if he wanted a lift. Smiling, he shook his head and patted his stomach as if to say, *Thanks, but I need the exercise.* He strode on down the long, broad street knowing that he could turn in at any gate and be greeted with open arms. "It's Mr. West, Mother. Set another place at the table," freckle-handed Cedric Loomis would boom. He had a baritone voice and a job at the Widget factory where the workers sang songs all day on the production line. And after dinner, West and the Loomises would push their chairs back from the table and talk. When West spoke, they would nod and listen as if his words had weight. And their answers would be well considered, for they knew West to be a serious man who was on a mission so important that they would not allude to it without lowering their voices. "Is everything going all right?" they would ask. And West would lie and say everything was fine.

But tonight West turned in at no gate. He continued on his way, enjoying his walk into the deepening twilight. He had decided he would eat in the dining room at Happy Valley Lodge, where the young waitress was in love with him. Afterwards, he'd go to his room there and finish his paperwork. Which reminded him that on his last visit back, he'd once again sensed that someone had stayed there during his absence. He'd sensed a presence, like a perfume in the air. A familiar perfume. And he thought to himself, *What if Fran had dreamed up Happy Valley, too? What if...*

Something thumped down hard on the subway-car roof. West sprang to his feet, wide-eyed and alert. Not long ago, they'd found an entire subway train filled with dead passengers and crew in one of the tunnels. Somehow one of the moleys, the people who inhabited the underground darkness, had dropped down onto a roof and worked his way up to the motorman, stopping the train where his buddies waited along the tracks. Fran had cried while watching the story on the evening news.

West and his people locked arms and stood in a tight square, each facing outward, ready to kick hard with both feet if the threat came in his direction. There was gunfire on the roof, and West got a glimpse of a body plunging by the window. The crew'd had somebody up there laying for the bastard. Further along the tunnel, he thought he made out a sullen line of faces beside the tracks.

A few minutes later, West's foursome was clattering up the stairs from the subway into a street thick with smoke and gridlocked traffic. In the distance, horns were honking. But here at the intersection, the drivers were out of their vehicles and at each other, using fists, tire irons, bottles, anything, in an almost joyful, a clenched-teeth frenzy, like a berserker's rush to death. West avoided the fighting and led his people over the bumpers and through the intersection. Then they teamed up with others going their way in a kind of flying wedge of foursomes. Behind them they heard rifle fire. A sniper working from a rooftop. They hurried on. He was somebody else's problem.

A City helicopter cudgelled the air overhead, maybe bringing in Carmody, West's immediate superior. Helicoptering in and out was a perk of the top brass during Winter Hiatus. But Carmody was really paying for his key to the helipad on the roof. The City's blood appetite was growing.

Carmody's new job was to set things up so a bus load of day trippers could vanish into thin air every other week without anybody making a fuss about it. Now how the hell do you pull off something like that? West shook his head, glad it was Carmody's problem and not his.

Morgan's problem hadn't been his, either. Morgan's trouble was he felt for the jazz fans who he was putting in harm's way. Didn't he like the stuff himself? So the job got to him and he tried to cut out. But you don't eat the City's bread and run. The boys in the yellow slickers nailed him in the Holland Tunnel. West had heard enough stories to know what happened next. You get pushed face first from a moving car—minus your wallet and shoes—and end up sharing rat-on-a-stick over burning garbage with three guys who look as bad as you do and smell even worse, in some basement in a looted and burned-out neighbourhood where the pigeons don't even come any more.

There was automatic-weapon fire down a side street around the police station. The firemen had the place surrounded. As West dashed by, he caught the flash of an antitank gun aimed at the precinct door. The firemen must have faked that armoury four alarmer for stuff like that. Their grudge against the boys in blue was an old one.

West's foursome reached their corner and turned onto the street. But what they saw stopped them cold, panting and cursing quietly. Last week, a discussion on predestination at the theological seminary across from City Hall Annex turned into a riot that might have spilled out into the street if the police and firemen hadn't forced it back inside. But there were no truncheons or water cannons today. After looting the shops on the street to build a bonfire, the rampaging student factions were manhandling passers-by—the one side forcing them to sing "Che Sera Sera," the other "I Did It My Way"—while they lugged out armfuls of the seminary library to feed the flames.

West's people waited for him to decide if they were going to turn back. The local Doberman lady eyed them from the doorway of the boarded-up coffee shop on the corner, looking like she'd just crawled out of a hole. The woman smiled, showing her empty gums. As if on cue, her five dogs supplied the teeth.

West had to go in. This morning was his weekly meeting with Carmody. "I'm good for twenty," he said. The others came up with thirty between them. It wasn't enough.

Another voice said, "I'm in." It was the Hyena, offering a smile and a twenty. West hadn't known the guy worked at City Hall Annex.

The woman stuffed the money into her shirt and ordered, "Okay, boys, give old Gracie a cuddle." West, his people, and the Hyena huddled around her as she doled out the dog leashes. The five snarling animals formed a moving circle and escorted them through the theological fury and over to the Annex's sandbagged entrance. The security people opened the iron grill wide enough to pull them through.

West hurried upstairs to his small, doorless office. All the inside doors had gone to board up the windows, or for beds for sleepovers in the cafeteria if things got too hairy. He'd had the office to himself since Morelli went screaming down the hall tearing his clothes off and had to be sent away.

West sat down at his desk. A moment later, the coffee cart arrived, the attendant's sloppy grin announcing they'd issued another brandy ration because of the trouble outside. West sipped at the three fingers of cheap, hacksaw-edged liquid in the Styrofoam cup. When it was gone, he turned his back to the door and poised his pen as if he was working.

The distance to Happy Valley Lodge was flexible, depending on how long West wanted to walk. The sun had slipped below the treetops, leaving the gibbous specter of the moon to accompany him like a ghostly assistant, an Igor to his Frankenstein. He passed a yard where children with well-modulated voices played graceful Happy Valley games. Here, at least, was a corner of the world you could bring children into. Here even darkness was a friend.

Suddenly West thought he saw someone cross the road a block ahead of him and disappear down a side street. "Fran!" he called, and broke into a run. But when he reached the corner, she was gone. Looking back the way she'd come, he recognized Colonel Ramsay's street.

West walked until he reached the two stone pillars topped with lanterns at the foot of the Ramsay driveway. Hudson was on duty, dressed like a gardener, pretending to be putting down mulch on a flower bed. He returned West's nod with a smile. West knew there would be another man watching from the house. He found Ramsay in the dim around back: a large, rather overweight old man down on his knees, classifying a freshly dug pile of dahlia roots with an indelible pencil by the light of a kerosene lantern.

"My dear chap, what a pleasure to see you," said Ramsay as the new arrival helped him to his feet.

"And I you, sir," said West, marvelling to himself how he always seemed to acquire an English accent around Ramsay.

The old man paused a moment to brush off his knees before saying, "Is it getting bad, old man?"

"Yes, sir. Very bad," said West.

Ramsay's sympathetic look changed quickly to a frown. "Still, isn't it a bit early to be drinking?"

"There was a brandy ration, sir. They might have become suspicious if I hadn't taken it."

Ramsay looked relieved. "Quite so," he said. "I hope you understand how vital they are to us, those reports of yours. Information from the very belly of the beast." He put a hand on West's shoulder. "Just hold out a few months longer. A year. Two at the most," he urged. "Doctor Vasco's going great guns with his creep deflection ray. We'll be in production within—"

"Sir, I thought I saw my wife just now."

Ramsay looked away. "I was afraid you had," he said. He pursed his lips and added, "All right, Fran is working for us, too. Mayor Farr and the town council had to be sure you wouldn't betray us. We've only survived this long because the City doesn't suspect we're here. So Fran was ordered to meet and marry you. The falling in love part was her own idea. But she thinks the City's become too dangerous for you. She came here just now to plead with me to order you home."

Ramsay shook his head. "I wish we could, old man," he said. "But when the creep deflector devices are in place, the City will slide right around us without even knowing we're here. Then you can both come back for good. And we can tell the whole town what you've risked for us all, you and a few others. The Few, that's what they'll call you. They'll sing songs about you at the Widget factory. And one day, when the cities have all crept together and ground themselves to powder, we will emerge, a little island of sanity amid the asphalt madness." Colonel Ramsay gestured toward the horizon. "And then the sound of the jackhammer will ring out across the land as we reclaim the fertile soil beneath parking lot, freeway and..."

Someone knocked on the door jamb. West jumped and swung around in his chair. The Hyena was standing there with a stack of files and a desk calendar under his arm. He smiled and introduced himself. "Mr. Carmody told me to bunk in here. Said you could use a hand."

West went cold inside. Was that it? Was he the one the Hyena expected to replace in the foursome? He forced a smile. "The more the merrier," he said.

"Hey, I like your work," said the Hyena, flapping the arm with the files. "My favourite's that joint promotion with Air India, the Indian Tourist Bureau, and the Sabu film festival at the Museum of Modern Art:

'Himalayans Cheer Cabbie Hero Returning Sacred Eye of Goddess.'" They both laughed.

West took some comfort from the laughter. Maybe he was getting paranoid. "Did Carmody show you my latest, the 'Melba Dinwittie' one?" he asked. "What did you think?"

The Hyena busied himself arranging his things on the empty desk. His faint "Hey, great," stayed with West in the elevator all the way up to his boss's office on the twenty-eighth floor.

Goddammit, "Melba Dinwittie" was good stuff. There she is, delegated by her church to come to the City to buy a second-hand Nutley Trill-Master organ. To her horror, the Nutley man informs her that the congregation's five years of potluck dinners and bake sales still came up a thousand shy of the price of a used Trill-Master. In the cab returning to the hotel she tells her woes to the kindly driver. She's so distraught by things that she leaves her purse with the church organ money in the back seat of the taxi. What shall she do? How can she ever face the congregation again? She passes a sleepless, tearful night. But come dawn, the desk calls to inform her that a few moments before, some cab driver had returned her purse and gone away without leaving a name. Melba Dinwittie flies downstairs. Not only is the church money intact, but someone had added the extra thousand needed to buy the organ!

West stepped from the elevator and strode down the hall to Carmody's office. All right, so maybe "Melba Dinwittie" wasn't in a class with the "Sacred Eye of Goddess." But it was a solid piece of work with a nice little twist at the end.

West found Carmody standing at a window looking out across the City and rattling the change in his trouser pocket. He was a nervous, balding little man. At his desk, Carmody was constantly picking things up and putting them back down. Carmody turned from the window and gave West his hurt puppy-dog look. Why was West forcing him to be the heavy?

"'Melba Dinwittie' won't hack it. Not by a long shot," he said, glancing at the ceiling. "The big boys upstairs couldn't swallow that extra thousand. They think you've lost your touch. Know what? So do I. I can't carry you any longer, kid. I've got my own problems. Like how to make goddam busloads of goddam day trippers vanish without nobody blinking a goddam eye." He rattled his pocket change again, his thoughts on his own troubles, waiting for West to speak.

West worked his lips but nothing came out.

Carmody said, "But I'm not leaving you high and dry. You just need a break from the pressure. I've been checking around. There's an opening over in B Block."

West found his voice. "For what, pushing a coffee cart?" He knew what that meant. On coffee-cart pay he'd have to move back to the city. Fran had as much as told him she'd walk out the door before she'd do that. So there he'd be, alone and holed up in a cubicle at the Y, going sloppy and nipping the brandy and missing days. And when you've missed enough, the City cuts you loose. After that it's three squares from a dumpster, sleeping in a cardboard box, wearing your socks until they dissolve into slime in your shoes, and never daring to look at the desperate thing shuffling along next to you when you pass a store window.

"So big deal," said Carmody, heartily, going over and sitting down at his desk. "So you push some cart. Meanwhile, I'm looking around. I'll find you another slot. When you're rested. When you're up to it."

West took his boss's place at the window. Somewhere down by the docks a thick column of oily black smoke from a chemical fire coiled up into the grey sky. *Well, this is it,* he told himself, *time for a big career decision, time for the singing to stop at the Widget factory.*

West turned from the window. "I'm up to it now," he insisted. "Give me the goddam busloads of goddam day trippers."

Carmody raised a skeptical eyebrow. "I'm listening," he said.

"So let's meet Cyrus Dumple, day tripper," began West, the words falling from his mouth with the ease of a public relations man fighting for his life. "Dumple and his wife and forty other members of the Jolly Oldsters Club of Chickentown, Pennsylvania, have charter-bused it into the City for a day of shopping, a Radio City Musical Hall matinee, and an early dinner at Mamma Leone's. But Dumple decides he doesn't want Italian. So he strikes out on his own to try one of those Rockefeller Center places where you can eat and watch the skaters. Now, Dumple knows full well that the bus that picks them up again in front of the Winter Garden Theater between 7:00 and 7:10 will not wait for the tardy. But he underestimates the distance back, and is a few minutes late as the theatre marquee hoves into view. But what's this heading toward him? It's his bus! But now it has the words 'Happy Valley Express' in the panel above the windshield. As it passes, Dumple sees the Jolly Oldsters out in the aisle dancing as spry as you please to the music of a live combo. He runs out into the street, shouting and wav-ing his hands over his head, chasing after it. He catches up as the bus slows in crosstown traffic. Dumple jumps and slams his hand against a window trying to attract somebody's attention and catches a glimpse of his wife laughing at something Warren Rupp, the retired insurance man, says. Before Dumple can jump again, the traffic is moving and the bus glides for-ward. Dumple runs after it shouting 'Wait for me! Oh, please, wait for me!' but the bus picks up speed, turns the corner, and disappears downtown."

West folded his arms and looked at Carmody.

His boss picked up his letter opener, looked at it, and put it back down on the desk. "I don't get it," he said flatly. "What the hell's 'Happy Valley'?"

West told him. One by one, he gave up each of his creations: Mr. Vining, the railroad conductor; Colonel Ramsay, the dotty old dahlia grower who thought he was a spymaster; Mayor Farr; Dr. Vasco, the crackpot inventor; the Blandish twins; Hudson; Loomis the baritone; the waitress at Happy Valley Lodge who loved him. He named each quiet street, described the principal buildings and landmarks, told him what it looked like on a winter night when the lights from the houses coloured the snow, and how the honeysuckle smelled in the summer darkness.

"Sounds like my kind of place, kid," admitted Carmody, a touch wistfully. "But, like they say, so what?"

"So we've got our work cut out for us, spreading the word about this wonderful Shangri-La of ours. I see lots of magazine articles and picture spreads: 'Small-Town America Alive and Well in Happy Valley;' 'Down-Home Food Best for What Ails You, Says Cancer Specialist Praising Happy Valley Cookbook.'"

Carmody got the idea. "'A Voice in a Million: Modest Cedric Loomis, Unsung Village Nightingale,'" he suggested.

West nodded, adding, "'The Ramsay Dahlia: Doubtless God Could Have Made a More Beautiful Flower, But Doubtless He Never Did.'"

"I like it," grinned Carmody.

"And how about we play up His Honor Otis Farr, Mayor of Happy Valley, cracker-barrel philosopher/Nobel Peace Prize nominee," said West. "We hire some actor for the part. There's one of the Fruit-of-the-Loom boys who might just fill the bill. And we get a CUNY prof to write his stuff, things like 'Those who think history repeats itself will be forced to relive it.'"

Carmody leaped to his feet. "How about 'I've never met a payroll I didn't like'?" He punched the air and shouted, "I love it, kid! We're talking Donahue at least. Maybe even Johnny. By the time we're done we'll have every dumb sucker in the world thinking the ones who disappear are the lucky ones. They'll go to their graves wishing it'd been them on those buses." He grabbed the phone. "I'm taking this one upstairs to the big boys right now."

As Carmody spoke into the receiver, West turned back to the window. Well, it was done. It was all over. He saw his sad face in the glass and smiled at it. *You poor, stupid bastard*, he told himself. *Where'd you get off thinking you were cut out to be one of the Few?*

Head Job

by John Swan

Take a big risk. Expect a big reward. Just don't, John Swan advises, get your hopes too high. Because in the world of noir, you're going to be sorely disappointed. It's a theme that pulses through the hard-edged fiction that Swan has published in Canadian literary journals ranging from *Blood & Aphorisms* to *Zygote*. His work has also appeared in a collection of linked mystery stories called *The Rouge Murders*. From his home in Hamilton, Ontario, Swan works to spread the gospel of noir through the regular Noir Night reading series he organizes and the Web site *www.murderoutthere.com*.

"No flowers. Why, do you think?"

Flowers? she wondered.

"She's a hooker." A second voice, also male, talking like she wasn't there. Which she wasn't. Not fully. "Who sends flowers to a twenty-dollar lay?"

Hooker. Twenty-dollar lay. Shit.

"The words 'hooker' and 'cheap' don't automatically link, Vender, just because that's your experience. She wore silk to the scene."

"The fur coat, that was fake. Or dog." A snort. "Both, come to think. White with black dots. Fake dog."

A smell. Antiseptic.

"Spoken like a man who's never had to get out of the real thing. It's tough, you know. Mats like a son of a bitch."

"Like you can afford the high-priced spread."

"Everybody's done it at least once."

A loud sigh. "Go on. Tell me."

"Give a woman a fur coat, she has to fuck you on it."

"According to who?"

"It's a given. Dozens of little animals sacrificed, spread out on the bed for your pleasure. Get naked, lay back, feel that long fur all over while you're banging away. Women live for that shit. The whole point in having a fur coat. Wearing it is just one long, pre-bang tease."

She heard movement, weight shifting from one foot to the other.

"Bullshit."

"Bullshit nothing."

"Not my Joanie."

"You ever give her the chance? But it's different when the woman is your wife, I'll give you that. You do it once, twice tops. Spill—and you're going to spill because this is the best appreciation-fuck you'll ever get, definitely, you'll think you grew three inches—so you spill, and you can't get the juice out of the fur. Costs, like, a hundred bucks to have the fucking thing cleaned. That's when she says save the coat for special occasions, like she's doing you a favour, economizing. Only you've got kids to raise and a mortgage to pay before you've got special occasions. And that's it. Coat goes into storage. You see it again maybe when somebody dies."

Weight shifting back to the other foot. "That's your life, Jack."

"Fuck, it's everybody's life. Ask around. In-ves-ti-gate. What you'll find, it's why hookers don't wear real fur. Costs too much to get cleaned all the time, besides which, cleaning's hard on the pelts. Breaks them down after too many times. Her heels though, they were expensive. Show those shoes to Joanie. She'll tell you."

Prada, she thought. The shoes were Prada, bought in Montréal. At last, a man who recognized quality.

What made that strange? She was in bed, two men in the room. Familiar situation. A hooker, okay, but not in Montréal or Toronto anymore. She'd come to the Falls shortly after the casino opened. Add some class to the scene, if the tight-asses on the tourist bureau could get their heads out, let her put brochures in their dispensers around town. No twenty-buck lays. A quality service: model beauty, fashionable clothes, and clinically safe. Worked for Vegas, didn't it?

She cracked her lids, peered between lashes. Small room, lots of white. Two men, polyester ties and three-quarter coats. She didn't know them or the room. What had the one guy said? Scene?

"Don't think you'd find this one on the Queen Street track. Not that bad looking though. Before."

Hurt like a son of a bitch as she said it, "Befow wha?" words leaking from her mouth.

The man sitting on the edge of her bed looked surprised. He was thick and dark. Hairy hands holding a hat on his lap. The other, leaning against the wall, was tall and sandy blond, athlete's body going to fat. "That how you're gonna play it, Gloria? You don't remember?" he asked.

They were cops. She didn't need to see badges. Just her luck: the man who knew Prada was a cop.

"Mind if we call you Gloria?" he asked.

Well, that was her name.

"You're in hospital," he went on. "You've been shot. Once in the right side, a graze. A second time through the jaw."

She tried to speak again. Pain through her skull like a razor.

"Why? Well, now, that is the question, eh? Why shoot the call girl in the head? Reason we're here, come to it, is to try to answer that one. Got enemies, Gloria? Quicker you help us with this little puzzle, sooner we're back at Tim's and you can stop worrying."

So far she hadn't had time to worry, but if the cop had told the truth, she supposed she should. Her brow wrinkled. Her shoulders shrugged.

"No one you know who'd want to hurt you?" the one on the bed helping her to answer.

She shook her head, once. Tiny flecks of light filled the room.

"Someone you pissed off? A shy you owe for those fancy clothes? Anyone's dick make you laugh out loud?"

No, no, and no.

"A neighbour or someone take righteous exception to how you pay your bills?" The cop-on-the-bed's manner was slower, more thoughtful.

She shrugged again. Not that she knew.

"Anyone dogging you, wanting to make an honest woman of you?" the wall-leaner added. "Save you from the street, that kind of shit? Oh, I forgot. No flowers."

She turned carefully to face left. A window. Outside, a downspout draining a neighbouring flat roof. Inside, next to her bed, a plastic pouch on a metal tree dripping fluid into the clear tube plugged into her arm. The cop sitting on her bed took out a stick of chewing gum, unwrapped it, put it in his mouth.

"Had to ask, Gloria. Routine. Truth is, we doubt you were the main target. That was probably the john in the room with you. You interrupted. Got in the way. Wrong place, wrong time."

The wall-leaner picked up the new line. "The one in the bed with two bullet holes in his forehead. Remember him at all, Gloria, the guy you'd been fucking just minutes earlier?"

Gloria wasn't sure. Blanks were filling in, but she couldn't remember being shot, couldn't remember any date that hadn't ended with her leaving on her own pins. But if the guy was a regular, not that there are many in a tourist town, but if he was a regular, she might remember him from a previous date, without remembering the time she was shot. She might even remember taking him up to the room. Christ, it made her head hurt just trying to think about it.

She lifted her arm, the one without the tube, open palm, let it drop.

"She doesn't remember."

"Convenient," the wall-leaner said.

"Give her some room, Vender. Take a bullet in the head, see what you've got left. Show her the picture."

The wall-leaner pushed off, brought up an envelope he'd been holding, nine by twelve. "Shot through the cheek. Messy but not life threatening. Bit of dental work," he took a glossy from the envelope, held it for Gloria to see, "couple skin grafts, she's back sucking dick no time. Big deal."

She remembered recently trolling late in the casino bar, then heading to her own bed alone. When was that? How long had she been in hospital?

"Traumatic stress." This was the cop-on-the-bed. "Remember, you got bounced at The Squirrel's Nest, couldn't recall the brawl for a week. Recognize the picture, Gloria, at all?"

Her eyes widened.

"Concussion. Whole different thing," the wall-leaner said over his shoulder.

"I think Gloria's getting some memory back," the cop-on-the-bed, nudging his partner out of the way and putting his pad and pen in Gloria's hand. "Where do you know him from, Gloria?"

Gloria scribbled on the paper, held it up for the cops.

"Movies. That's right. Hugh Polloy, the actor. Everybody's favourite Hollywood bad boy, making a picture up here where the dollar's smaller. You ought to see the shit's been stirred with the news he's been popped. Press has unrolled sleeping bags in the hospital lobby. Television, newspapers from Buffalo and Toronto, whatever's in between. Networks ready to flip the switch and go live the moment there's developments." He fingered quote marks around the word developments. "How about you give a couple old cops an exclusive, eh, Gloria? Tell us what you know about Hugh Polloy, personally?"

Gloria underlined the word on the pad, held it up again for them to see.

"We know he's in the movies," the wall-leaner said. "On location in Old Towne. Was till Friday at least."

The cop-on-the-bed waved his partner back. "What she's saying is she doesn't remember. She only knows him from the movies."

The wall-leaner stared-down the bed-sitter. "I don't buy it. Crew says, the month he's been on the shoot Polloy's banged everything for sale both sides of the river, at least twice." His attention came back to Gloria. "Rumour is he's hung like a horse. So don't try this 'can't remember' bullshit, a guy who's dick reaches halfway to his knees. Even a whore would remember that. Start writing. Everything."

Gloria wasn't sure what to do. She spotted a cord with a button on the end pinned to the sheets near her right hand. That would bring a nurse or somebody.

The cop-on-the-bed leaned forward, put his hand over the button. "Here's the thing, Gloria. There's two ways to go when you buy it, am I

—58—

right? Some take it on the street, find a dark place to park. They're exhibitionists. I understand. The risk of getting caught is part of the thrill. Others find a room, someplace private."

Gloria waited.

"And they lock the door, don't they? Otherwise, what's the point? Correct me if I'm wrong. So, how did our shooter get into the room? That's the real question I think, eh, Vender?"

Shit, Gloria thought.

"A hairpin maybe?" the cop-on-the-bed, developing the question.

"Straightened paper clip, more like," Vender said. "Women don't use hairpins anymore, Jack."

"Suppose not. Ha!" The bed-cop, Jack, running a hand through his own thick, greying hair.

"Anyway, no keyhole," Vender added. "Electronic locks, the whole hotel. Open with a plastic card. Re-coded for each new guest."

"A pass card then?"

"Only for security staff. Hotel's connected to the casino. All their dicks are licensed and bonded."

"Not that we've taken their word for it, am I right?"

"Absolutely," Vender said. "Everybody's clean. Innocent as babes."

Both cops turned to the woman in the bed.

"See how it is, Gloria? Somebody had to let the shooter into that room."

Gloria wrote. Showed it to Jack on the bed.

"Polloy? He got up, opened the door, climbed quietly back into bed to let the killer put a pillow over his face and pump two shots into his skull? Doesn't seem likely, does it? And where were you while this went on? No, here's what I think, Gloria. I think somebody slipped you a few bucks to open that door."

Gloria waited. What was there to write?

"Wasn't you that killed him, Gloria, not you we're after. No gun in the room, you all shot up. Can't blame a working girl for scoring a few extra bucks. But you should have known he'd have to kill the only witness. You're lucky to be alive. Tell us who it was, we'll post a guard here and go get him. He'll never hurt you again." Gloria didn't respond. "Tell us, most you'll get is a suspended sentence. Write it down, your own words, what happened."

Gloria wrote. Handed the pad back to the cop-on-the-bed.

"'Don't know. Don't remember.' Come on, Gloria, which is it? Don't know or don't remember?"

Gloria shrugged.

"Two shots," the wall-leaner, Vender, said. "To the head. Through the pillow."

Jack nodded. "Sounds professional doesn't it? Our Gloria must have some interesting connections."

"There's a first," Vender said. "A hooker with unsavoury connections."

"I think Detective Vender doubts your veracity, Gloria," Jack said. "Know what that means, veracity? Means he thinks you're lying."

"We can put an end to that."

"How's that, Vender?"

"Let the press in. Couple hours with them, she'll be so shit-tired she'll say anything."

Jack frowned as if he was considering. Gloria doubted they'd let the press in, didn't think the doctors would let them. But she held her index finger up like she'd just thought of something, grabbed the notepad back.

"Marcus. Casino bartender," she wrote.

"Last name?" Jack-on-the-bed, asked.

She shook her head, immediately regretting it.

"What did he have against Polloy?"

She took the pad back and wrote again. "Take pictures. Sell them to papers, magazines."

Jack read it aloud.

"No good, Gloria." Vender, from the wall. "Polloy was really shot, with a gun, not shot as in getting your picture took."

Again on the pad. "Marcus planned it. I open door, I get half. Can't remember what happened in hotel room." But she did remember opening the door, turning the bolt so it wouldn't close again soon as they'd got into the room, and Polloy beginning emptying the mini-bar. "Didn't know Marcus had gun," she continued writing. "Everything screwed up. Can't remember."

Jack read again, then looked up and said, "You're a very lucky little hooker, Gloria." Her eyes widened. "Whether it's a screw-up, or if this Marcus was lying to you and intended to hit Polloy all along, either way you're lucky he's lousy at his job. Otherwise, you'd be dead, too."

He passed the pad back to her, but Gloria had nothing more, didn't move to pick it up again. Her eyelids sagged. She shook them open once, pain searing her cranium, let them drop again, the two men taking up the conversation around her.

"So, Jack, you think I could have the lend of your fur coat sometime?"

"What?"

"For my Joanie. You said yourself it's just hanging in storage. We'll clean it before you get it back. Promise."

"Fuck you."

It was weeks before she had to deal with reporters and cameras, there being more to her injuries than in Vender's version. Reconstructive surgery to her lower jaw. Might be more yet, mostly cosmetic, and to stop the clicking when she moved it a certain way. The cops came back, the two she'd woken to and another, a woman who was supposed to be more sympathetic, she guessed. Didn't matter. There was nothing more she could tell them. She agreed to confess to a robbery Marcus must have botched in exchange for a suspended sentence. Marcus would be tried for murder, with Gloria the chief witness. She used her recovery time to work on her own questions. For starters, the question the Jack-cop had implied: Why wasn't she dead too?

She remembered shifting the lid back on the hotel room's commode. *Escorts don't say toilet*, she thought and remembered lighting a cigarette, seeing herself in the hotel bathroom mirror, shifting her shoulders to let her boobs swing. Not sloppy. Not yet. Face fine. Can't beat good bones, she'd thought. They'd gotten her modelling jobs in Montréal when she was a kid, and Toronto. Mostly catalogue work. Not much money, but enough of what she'd needed once she'd learned where to toss the odd freebie. Her mother had done her a favour, seeing potential in her daughter's face, finding a decent surgeon, and getting the cheeks lifted. Might soon do with a touch-up, though. Wait till the breasts sag, find a package deal.

But the time was coming, definitely. Lately Gloria spent two hours in the gym every morning. Her thighs were the best. Hard and tight. Manmilkers. Christ, what a stupid idea, but that's how the clients thought. Not that many actually got between her thighs.

Gloria remembered putting her blouse back on in the bathroom, enjoying the slick of silk on her skin. Then pulling on her skirt, lighting another smoke, dropping the toilet seat and sitting, waiting, thinking. She'd been getting by, if not ahead. Had never lived on the street, never been kicked out by her old man for screwing a favourite uncle. She didn't inhale, outside an occasional line with a customer. Never on the needle. She'd never been a twenty-buck street whore, but then, she didn't have a pension plan either.

Thunk.

Thunk.

In the bedroom, the silenced shots coming back as clearly as they had that day, though she wouldn't have noticed if she hadn't been listening. She'd flicked ash into the sink.

Nothing then from the next room.

She'd stood, flushed the butt, run the sink, checked herself in the mirror, smoothed her skirt, opened the bathroom door. She'd hesitated, turned back, taken the chewing-gum wrapper from the garbage pail under the sink, put it in her pocket.

That was as far as her memory would take her.

Marcus was the one mentioned Polloy. Maybe the actor had been in the casino, looking for action. Marcus got ideas, did a year of college before landing the summer job slinging booze in the quiet room off the main casino floor. Pay was shit, most drinkers leaving quarters if they were up on the slots. That was what drew Gloria's attention.

"Will you have an office with a couch?" Gloria had teased Marcus when she saw he was proud of his college education. "I have an office with a couch."

"You're thinking psychiatry," he'd said, pulling the points on the red velvet vest the casino made their bar staff wear. "That's a medical specialty. Have to be a doctor first. I'm studying psychology."

He was cute. "Psychologists aren't doctors?"

"Doctors of Philosophy maybe, but not MDs."

"Philosophy, psychology, psychiatry, that's a lot of p's," she'd said, leaning over to straighten his clip-on bow tie, "without so much as a single pucker."

Gloria showed Marcus how the other staff scammed the automatic drink dispensers. Summer left and he didn't, hooked on life and its possibilities. She revealed to him the psychology of the escort business. "It's ninety percent between the ears," she said, "more ways than one." Plant the right idea, create some ambiance, and the johns popped soon as their shorts dropped. She hardly ever stripped below the waist, she said. Dress for convenience and to create atmosphere. Silk in the afternoon, always.

Evenings, with the right clientele, should be sequined gowns and real fur. Money, sex, a hint of mystery. Cruise the attractions by limo. An appetizer rolling past Table Rock, river mist raining on the windows. Up the tower to the revolving restaurant for dinner, then back to the historic old hotel, a suite, for dessert. Could be a fifteen-hundred-buck package. At least that's what she'd thought when the casino opened, shortly after her mother died. That was why she'd moved to the Falls.

Turned out the casino was polyester and denim: pensioners without hobbies; factory workers and housewives, their kids locked in the cars out in the parking lot; boys from Buffalo suburbs, making like street pimps showing their hos the town. Second biggest attraction, after the casino, was still the Hill. Candyfloss and sugar-cone ice-cream parlours, wedged between freak and monster museums. Dioramas of waxed gore: Dracula and Frankenstein drooling blood, Dillinger shot down outside a movie theatre, a near-naked woman hung from a big hook pushed through her gut.

"There's more class on the Rue in Montréal," Gloria told Marcus, grinding her cigarette butt into a proscribed bar ashtray.

Marcus told Gloria about another level of clientele: people who tired of limited-bet tables in the casino and wandered into the bar wondering aloud if there might be something more exciting. High-stakes games, floating in some of the city's many motel rooms, perhaps, or they didn't know. "Surprise us, kid. Anything. We're booked-in till Tuesday."

Gloria cut Marcus a slice for clients he sent her way. She remembered, now, the two of them discussing the Polloy photo scam that she'd told the cops about, and Marcus quickly suggesting a bigger score. Selling pictures to *The Inquirer* or *Screw* would be only one payday, he said.

"Get my face in the shots, my name in the credits," Gloria told him, "I'll have johns lined up to Lake Erie. All I do to keep them coming back is say they're bigger and better than Hugh Polloy. You get your share, same as always."

But who knew if they could even sell the pictures? Marcus countered. Polloy was well-known as a Hollywood stick man. There had to be plenty of photos floating around already.

"There is a way to make it a sure thing," he went on after they'd kicked the first idea to death. "Think of the Hill. We set up our own museum. A shrine," Marcus said. "Posters and clips from Polloy movies, blow-up headlines of his biggest scandals. Pics of half-naked celebrities he's bedded. We get testimonials from all the girls he's banging here in town. You heard he's hung like a horse?"

"How is it I haven't had a piece of him already?" Gloria asked.

"He's working his way up stream. I'll get you your shot. But here's the main attraction, the whole raison d'être for having the museum here in the Falls. We set up a diorama exactly matching the hotel room you rent. We buy as many of the original furnishings as we can and make you the main attraction, right there, telling the paying tourists what happened, hinting at all the dirty little details, confirming their worst suspicions."

"Sex, celebrity, death, it's what the paying public wants. Like the graveyard bus tours to dead celebrities' homes in LA, or the New York excursions to famous crime scenes. Only this is better than all the wax horrors on the Hill put together, because you'll be right there to describe how you entertained Polloy for hours, then had to go into the bathroom for a rest. When you came out, he's shot dead."

"Wait, wait, wait."

"Everyone will speculate who did it. A jealous husband? A professional hit man with mob links? A rejected lover? Who could have killed him?"

"What's this 'killed him'? This 'shot dead'?"

"We do it together. We snuff Polloy."

Even now, she recognized the genius of it. Pull it off, she'd have more johns than could shake their sticks at her, not to mention a profitable front business. No way she'd ever be a twenty-buck whore. She decided Marcus was good to have around, long as he kept getting ideas.

"I'm beginning to suspect I've been a corrupting influence," she told him late that night. But now, weeks later in the hospital room, she still didn't understand where it had gone so wrong.

A few newspaper reporters did follow up when Gloria was released from hospital. Right off, she focused on getting her life back, regaining the income to pay for the row house she rented other side of the highway, that sort of thing. Marcus' replacement in the casino bar, a middle-aged woman looking tired already at the start of her shift, said she'd never heard of him. Shortly after, Gloria was banned from the casino. It was a strain. Hookers don't get disability.

"Kid tells a pretty strange story," Jack said one afternoon, standing in Gloria's kitchen.

They'd already had her down at the station, to prep her testimony for Marcus' trial. "What's your point?" she asked.

Jack looked through the patio doors to the ten square feet fenced off as the unit's private yard space. "Case like this brings a lot of attention to the city. Fella once said all publicity is good, but the Crown Attorney isn't in the ad game. He's careful, wants to make sure it's his best foot he's got pushed forward. Had us follow you, see if Marcus' story played out."

He was dressed in a baseball jacket and blue jeans, black and white hairs boiling over the rim of a grey T-shirt underneath. Cops' day-off clothes. Gloria had on her silk blouse, blue jeans, white sneakers. She was letting her bangs grow out to comb forward, frame her face to at least shadow the scarred cheeks.

"Has it panned out?"

He shook his head, sat himself at her tiny kitchen table. "It hasn't. You haven't rented any space on the Hill. You're barely working. You've lost your pimp. You haven't anything like enough money to start a new business that I can see."

Gloria leaned back against the kitchen counter. "I'm supposed to have started a new business?"

Jack smiled. "Not the type the prosecution would like to publicize in a courtroom full of reporters. Don't worry. Stick to your story, robbery gone bad. Keep it simple, our deal will hold. Marcus' yarn is so complicated it makes the defence look desperate just bringing it up. That coffee fresh?"

Jack took chewing gum from his mouth, stuck it on the underside of Gloria's table. Gloria felt her stomach knot, faced by a decision that had already been made. She lifted the pot, poured, sat in the chair opposite Jack. He sniffed the potent, rancid steam rising from his mug.

"You don't remember?" She shook her head. "Too bad. Weird idea, but ideas are all that drive this world anymore. Pick one you like or one will reach out and grab you." He took his first sip. "Who'd ever figure people would sit inside a casino, mesmerized by flashing lights and sirens, a natural wonder like Niagara Falls sitting right outside the door? You know, I don't think winning even plays a part in it. People win, they gamble it away again." Another sip. "Crazy as it is, the kid's idea could probably work."

Gloria kept quiet, letting Jack finish his coffee. "Well," he said finally, leaning back, "get over the hump, give me a shout. Never know. I might be able to send some business your way." Gloria knew what cop business meant: freebies for snitches and colleagues who might help his career, in exchange for not being hassled every time she found a paying client. "Might even know where to find ten grand to help seed your start-up."

It made Gloria wonder how she and Marcus had thought to finance their dreams in the first place. Marcus wasn't much on details. It would have been up to her.

She laid a hand on Jack's sleeve. "What would Vender say?"

"Vender?" Jack answered. "Oh, Vender would put you to work on the track."

They sat a while longer, Gloria leaving her hand on Jack's sleeve, noticing how brown his eyes were, the wrinkles at the corners that pointed like darts to the rich, deep irises.

"Still got that dog-fur coat around," he asked, "anywhere?"

It was all she could do not to rush straight over. Christ knows she needed the cash, several times, but she couldn't be sure about Jack, that he wasn't still watching, that the whole scene hadn't been a set-up to test Marcus' story. So she waited the weeks that grew into months until Marcus' case finally came up, and she performed her civic duty: reciting an experience of pain and forgetting and betrayal before an eager court.

Even after Marcus' conviction she waited another week before asking the floor maid to call and let her into the hotel room between guests. Slipped the girl ten bucks and went straight into the bathroom, lifted the lid on the toilet tank. Sliced with the thin blade of an exacto knife at the chewing gum she'd used to reseal the top of the foam liner back to the inside of the tank. The plastic sandwich bag she'd slid between was still there.

Gloria counted Polloy's money for the first time, having been too nervous when she'd performed the theft months earlier. She stopped at twenty, all U.S. hundreds, and remembered having left one, and some smaller bills, in Polloy's wallet. Better for their original plan to keep the press guessing about motive.

Now the hard part: getting back out through the main room without looking, wanting and not wanting to remember. It had been tough enough on the way in, with the money as a focus. The bed, a table, two chairs, door to a closet, she'd been in rooms like this hundreds of times. Hell, she'd probably been in this exact room more than a dozen. Not enough in any of them to distract her from retreat; or from the faces and images that began flickering in her mind's eye, bringing the last memory, all of it, screaming back: Polloy in bed, pillow over his head, couple of feathers sticking out through the ticking. Gloria stepping up for a closer look before gathering her shoes and coat to leave. Something red. Movement, another person in the room, pain suddenly burning her lower right side. She spins, falls.

The carpet smell of tobacco and soap. This wasn't part of the plan. This wasn't...shoes approach, stop at her face. She should play dead, but her mouth and eyes are wide.

Don't breathe.

Don't even blink.

A nick in the leather links two tooled holes on the shooter's left shoe. It steps over her, then the other.

Rustling.

Stop.

"Sorry about this, Gloria. If I'd told you this part, you wouldn't have gone through with it," Marcus explains, the memory pulling her back like an undertow. "Some guys, you know, it'll be the ultimate thrill. Basic psychology, really. Defiance against the human condition, a lonely squirt of life against the vast eternity of death, all that. Death in this case represented by a gun-shot wound."

More rustling.

Don't move, don't move.

What does he want?

"You'll thank me Gloria, when you get better. You'll be doing thousand-dollar blow jobs."

An explosion she never remembers as the bullet entered her head.

Coup de Grâce

by Barbara Fradkin

Since she published her first story in 1994, Barbara Fradkin has been a unique voice crying in the darkness. True to Oscar Wilde's dictum, she lets no good deed go unpunished. In the noir world she shares with Wilde, the bad aren't the only ones damned. Just as often, the good must pay a price for their attempts to do the right thing. Fradkin's stories, which have appeared in numerous magazines and anthologies, are all coloured by her experiences from twenty years as a child psychologist. She knows all about the darkness of the human soul.

Born in Montréal and living in Ottawa, Barbara's first novel *Do or Die* was published in 2000. A second, *Once Upon a Time*, is due out in 2002.

I closed the workshop door on the body and hurried up the basement stairs. I knew the cellphone number by heart, but still misdialled twice before my fingers could obey. Relief rushed in when the Pope himself picked up the line.

Detective Christian Levesque didn't really like the name Pope. But his fate had been sealed when he'd had too much to drink one night after a long case and revealed to his fellow officers that, as the youngest of twelve kids growing up in Trois Pistoles, his mother had wanted him to become a priest. The officers had laughed so hard they coined the name Pope and it had stuck. Rumour was, it suited him in more ways than one.

"It's Sam," I said. "There's been another death."

"Who?"

"A high-tech big shot called Richard Potts. I've been working with the family."

"Where are you?" Not a guy to waste words.

"At the Potts home."

"Who's in the house with you?"

"Mother and daughter," I replied. "I put them in the living room when I got here. The body's in the basement."

"Are you sure he's dead?" The Pope sounded breathless, and I realized he was already on the move. I quelled a rush of gratitude.

"I know dead, Levesque. Looks like an accident this time, if it makes you feel better." The last time one of my messy cases had ended up in murder, he'd begun to joke that I was the best advertisement against social work he'd ever seen.

"It does. I'm on my way. And Kaminsky, this time don't touch anything."

I could have protested. I wasn't with the Children's Aid anymore, forced at times to dodge the blunt sledgehammer of the law while I shepherded my fragile charges to safer ground. I'd moved onto the gentler, greener pastures of therapy. But I was too rattled to conceive a snappy comeback. Instead, I hung up and sneaked a peek into the Potts' fashion-perfect living room. Jennie was curled up on the sofa with her arms wrapped around her knees and her long curtain of black hair flopped forward over her face. Her mother, Laura, stood by the window, gazing out at the bleak winter day. Not a tear between them, I noticed. Richard Potts would not be sorely missed.

I don't know how many times in the past six weeks I'd wished the man dead. Maybe a thousand? I'd always considered my murderous fantasies to be a healthy sign, a sign that after nearly twenty soul-battering years on the front lines of family dysfunction, I still cared enough to want to fix things. And Richard Potts' death would certainly fix things, at least for his daughter Jennie, who was thirteen going on sixty. Not because she'd been on the streets since she was ten, like many of my clients, but because youthful play had entirely passed her by.

It took me awhile to realize this, for Jennie was not the usual type of client to pass through our youth-counselling agency.

"She's failing school," her father said when he made the initial phone call. "And she refuses to talk to us. Just sulks in her room."

"Any risky behaviours?" I asked, running through my standard repertoire of questions. "Drugs, late nights, unsavoury boyfriends?"

There was a noticeable silence on the phone. "She's only thirteen," he said eventually, and his voice had chilled ten degrees.

I bit back the retort that thirteen was older than he thought. Parents are remarkably stupid when it comes to teenagers, but that's what pays my rent. "How about next Wednesday at ten? I'll come out to the house."

"Next Wednesday's not convenient."

"Okay." I consulted my agenda. "How about Thursday at two?"

"I'm out of town all next week. And I prefer evenings."

Annoyance flashed through me. I was not used to being treated like a dishwasher repairman, squeezed into his busy schedule. Most people clamoured to see me, and if they weren't desperate for help when they called the agency, they were by the time they got through our waiting list. Mr. Potts and I finally settled on the mutually tolerable time of 4 p.m., and I prepared to hang up with relief.

"What did you say your name was?" he asked.

"Sam Kaminsky."

"And what are your qualifications?"

Ten years in plumbing school, I thought, but behaved myself. "I'm a provincially certified Masters of Social Work, fourteen years with Children's Aid, and three with Youth Counselling."

His dismissive grunt was very faint, perhaps even my imagination. "I was expecting a man."

I got that often, mostly from macho men who think their wayward sons just need an alpha male to whip them into shape. But I pretended to be obtuse. No point wrecking the therapeutic alliance too early. "I know. The Sam is short for Samantha."

The truth is, I'd never been much of a Samantha. By the time I was fifteen, I was a shade under six feet, but still flat as a board. Like myself, my hair never did what it was told, so I kept it in line with a strict two-inch limit. In the big-hair eighties, this was disastrous, and by the time the freaked-porcupine look was actually in style, I'd given up all hope of men, chucked out the skirts and scarlet lipstick, and become just plain Sam.

"Fine, Ms. Kaminsky, I guess you'll have to do. My wife and I will expect you at four the Tuesday after next."

"Jennifer, too."

There was another long pause. "I don't think that's wise."

I could have asked why, but sensed that with this prick, it was all about who was in charge. "That's how I operate," I replied. "If you want my help, Jennifer has to be included from the beginning."

"She won't speak to you."

"That's fine, see you all then," I said breezily, but when I hung up, I unleashed a string of profanities at the silent phone. I hated the pompous little prick already.

And now the pompous little prick was dead. Just to double-check, I slipped back down into the workshop, where Richard's body was still contorted in the grotesque spasm that had gripped him in death. In his hand was the scorched electric heater he'd been trying to repair, and the stench of burnt plastic almost overpowered that of seared flesh. The fuse had blown, plunging the basement into darkness, but enough winter sun slanted through the high window to illuminate the room.

I crept on careful tiptoe as I studied the scene. Nothing suspicious jumped out at me. Richard's tool kit lay open on his workbench, and a precise row of screwdrivers and pliers was lined up on its pristine surface. The heater was plugged into the wall, but still intact, as if he'd only just begun work on it. It was Jennifer's heater, I knew, because she'd been complaining of the chill in her bedroom for weeks. Considering the amount of time the poor girl was forced to spend at her desk, he'd taken his own sweet time repairing it. Perhaps my increasingly blunt hints had got to him, but I doubted it. In the six weeks I'd been working with this family, I'd made absolutely zero progress with Mr. Potts. All I'd managed to do was highlight to Jennifer and her mother what a cold and controlling prick he really was. Which wouldn't have been so bad if either of them had been in a position to leave him. But there is nothing therapeutic about showing someone the bars of their cage when there is no way out.

I heard a scraping sound behind me and whirled around to see Laura Potts halfway down the stairs, swaying despite her white-knuckled grip on the railing. Her pinched face was a scary shade of ash. I moved briskly to herd her back up the stairs.

"I've called my friend on the force," I said. "We should leave things alone down here."

She stood stock-still, her red nails digging into my arm. Laura, even dishevelled and distraught, was better put together than I'd be for the Viennese Ball. "I won't say a thing," she whispered. "They can't make me say a thing."

I eyed her warily. "Just answer his questions. He's a fair man."

Still she wouldn't budge. "Jennie won't need to talk to him, will she? She's so exhausted she won't know what she's saying."

"He will want to talk to her."

"But can't you, I mean, say she's in shock or something?"

"I can probably get him to wait until tomorrow. But Laura, it was an accident. That's obvious just looking at things."

Her grip eased. "Is it? Oh good. I mean—I know it's an accident, but you never know what the police might think. Or the insurance company."

I placed a firm hand under her elbow to steer her upstairs. "Insurance companies don't investigate crimes, Laura."

"But what if they think there was negligence? It's a great deal of money. Richard took out the policy when I was diagnosed with MS, and he knew I'd never be able to work. My pills alone would bankrupt Jen and me in a month. What if the insurance company tries to wriggle out of it?"

"He electrocuted himself trying to fix a heater—that's an accident pure and simple. The police will probably find a frayed wire inside."

As if on cue, a siren whined through the night and groaned to a stop outside the door. I barely had time to hustle Laura back upstairs before the Pope strode through the front door, stamping the snow from his boots. The Pope's not a small man, either vertically or horizontally, and when he's in charge, he seems to grow half a foot. His big head bobbed like a turtle's and his shoulders filled the entire hallway as he lumbered noisily around the house. He had a young sidekick with him, and after satisfying himself that the rest of us were unharmed and the house secure, he led the sidekick downstairs.

When Laura and I re-entered the living room, Jennie finally raised her head, like a corpse coming to life.

"I'm glad he's dead," she intoned.

"Right," I interjected, anxious to head her off at the pass. This was not the moment for soul-baring, not with the Pope within earshot and a perfectly healthy and obsessively careful fitness nut sprawled lifeless on the basement floor. "Jennie, when the police speak to you, I want you to stick strictly to the facts. What you saw and heard, what your father said and did within your presence. In fact," I paused to take a notepad out of my briefcase, "it might help to write down what you remember, so you don't get confused."

Her mother sat down on the couch and folded her arms tightly. "He just wanted to bring out the best in you, honey."

"You always took his side. Never mine."

Laura coloured. In truth, Jennie was dead right, and her mother knew it. Laura had elevated appeasement to a fine art even Chamberlain would have envied, and there was no way she would have taken a stand against the Hitler in her own home.

"I'm sorry, honey," she began.

"Oh forget it!" Jennie snatched up the notepad and stomped toward the door just as the Pope walked through it.

"I've sent for the coroner and the forensic team," he said in his trademark mournful tone. I'd never known the man to laugh. So many dead bodies and wailing relatives piled so high around him, I don't think anybody could reach him. "Just routine, Mrs. Potts, but to save time, Constable McGillvary here will take your daughter's statement while I take yours. Ms. Kaminsky, could you make us all a pot of tea?"

If looks could kill... But they can't, and the Pope acknowledged that by lifting one eyebrow almost imperceptibly as he met my gaze. He wanted me to be a good girl and not fan the flames of this already tense moment. And maybe he wanted me out of the room, too. He'd learned the hard way that I tend to interrupt when I see one of my clients under siege.

I returned fire by drawing my eyebrows together into a scowl, but then dutifully left the room in search of tea. In the kitchen I paced as I waited for the water to boil. Beneath his plodding, coplike approach, the Pope was good, and Laura Potts was no match for his tenacity. God knows what she might let slip, and Jennie was even worse. Like most thirteen year olds, she didn't think of consequences or nuances. On top of that, she didn't plan to live past fourteen, so she might recklessly confess to all kinds of things. I knew from my own experience that if you poked in just the right place, her feelings would pour out in a raw, molten rush.

At my first meeting, I'd found the right place without any trouble. As her father had predicted (indeed, probably orchestrated), she'd refused to join her parents in the initial contact. So I'd received the inventory of complaints in meticulous detail from Richard Potts, occasionally seconded by his wife. Afterwards, I went up to Jennie's room and found her lying on her bed in the dark, staring at the ceiling. Not a muscle moved as I entered. Without turning on the light, I moved the desk chair to face her, sat down, and introduced myself.

"Do you know why I'm here?"

Still not a muscle twitch.

"Your father says he's worried about you."

"Yeah, well, since my father has all the answers, why ask me?"

"Because your answers might be different."

"I have a learning disability, so my answers don't count."

"Where'd you get that idea?"

She turned her head for the first time to look at me. In the faint light I saw the ghost of a stunningly beautiful girl, blonde and blue-eyed like her mother, but with waxen skin and hollow eyes. "Didn't he tell you all about it? That's usually the first thing he tells people—that I forget things and can't organize my ideas."

"Do you think that's true?"

She turned away again. "I think I'm just stupid."

"What makes you think that?"

She gestured to her desk, a Spartan white expanse with a long, lean halogen lamp. "Two hours studying when I get home and three hours after supper. Longer if I don't make it through all the work. Sometimes I'm up here till midnight. But it doesn't stick."

I noticed there were none of the electronic toys that most of my kids had. No computer, no CD or tape player, no television. Not even a phone. Normally I'm not a big fan of electronic overkill, but this room felt positively bleak.

She shrugged it off. "Dad says otherwise I'm too distractible."

"Dad knows everything?"

She rolled her eyes. "It won't work, you know. You being all friendly and chatting to me. You can't help me or fix things, so you should save your breath."

"What would fix things?"

"Nothing. Well, maybe euthanasia."

"You mean killing yourself? Do you think about that sometimes?"

"Doesn't everyone?"

"Ever try it?"

She gave me a sidelong frown. "I'm not crazy, you know."

"From where I sit, you're neither stupid nor crazy. Just desperately unhappy."

She was silent a long while, and I thought she'd shut down, but then, from behind her blond hair, she opened the floodgates. "Why should I be unhappy? I've got everything I need. A beautiful home, a good neighbourhood, a rich dad who's bought me piano lessons and art lessons and even riding lessons. See how hard he tried to find something I'm good at, so he doesn't have to be ashamed of me?"

"You think he's ashamed of you?"

"His friends' kids are all in the gifted program, or the best in their ballet class, or get the lead in the school musical. What can he ever say about Jennifer? Jennifer passed math this term?"

I'd talked to thousands of kids over the years, smart and dumb, and few saw their lives with the brutal clarity Jennifer did. Stupid, she was not.

"Stupid and being bad at school are not the same thing," I said. "Take it from me, who sat at the back of the class praying the teacher would forget I was there because I couldn't read aloud to save my life. It took me till grade ten to realize my ideas were as smart as the next kid's. Ideas are what counts, Jen. Not whether you can read aloud or memorize your times tables."

Jennie rolled over and looked at me with a tiny smile. "Dad's going to fire you in no time, you know. I've been through a dozen counsellors and psychologists and tutors, and he's changed my school five times. Nothing fixes me."

I remembered the agony of walking into the schoolyard as the new kid on the block. "Five schools. No wonder you're angry."

Her eyes unexpectedly glazed with tears. "It's not like I want to be this way."

"If only wishes came true, eh?"

She said nothing. Fought the dam that threatened to break.

I kept my voice as soft as I could, so as not to violate her pain. "I'm here to help, Jen. You, not just your mom and dad. What can I do to help you?"

Wan smile. "Kill my Dad, maybe?"

I remembered those words now as I balanced the tea tray in one hand and pressed my ear to the study door, straining to hear what Jen was saying inside. Thank God the Pope had assigned her to the rookie. Perhaps under his inept questioning she'd just shut up like a clam, something she was good at. Did it during just about every family interview I tried to conduct. Sat staring at the floor through her curtain of blonde hair. Well, black hair by the end—her little rebellion against the tyrant. At the time, I'd regarded the black hair as a good sign. Jennie was coming out of her shell and beginning to believe in her right to be who she was. Of course, it didn't go over well with Daddy, who, as Jen had predicted, fired me the day after the hair turned black.

It was Laura who resumed contact, phoning me two weeks after the firing to ask me to meet Jen and her alone. "I'm not sure I agree with your tactics," she said on the phone. "But you are the only person she'll talk to, and I'm at my wits' end. She's not eating."

Another little rebellion, I thought, but when we met at the back of the local Tim Hortons, I realized it was more like a full-blown hunger strike. Jen looked terrible. Skeletal, skin like chalk, black circles under her eyes.

"No hospital," she said when I suggested it. She seemed hardly able to pull a full sentence together from the threads of her unravelling mind.

"Of course no hospital," her mother soothed. "It's not as bad as that."

"Hospital might not be a bad idea." I ventured in the understatement of the year. I sipped my diet Coke, suddenly conscious of the insidious message it sent. Jen and her mother had ordered nothing.

Laura shook her head. "Sh–she's just like me, can't eat when her stomach's in knots from worry. Once–once she gets through all her school assignments, she'll be fine."

It was the first time I'd heard Laura stutter, another small piece of her being lost to her disease. I looked at the pair of them: Jen in her oversized sweatshirt, and Laura in her fur-trimmed wool jacket. Denial might be a survival strategy that worked for Laura, but it was going to kill Jen.

"Laura, can I have a brief word?"

I practically dragged the woman into the ladies' room, and after checking under the stalls to ensure we were alone, I towered over her urgently. This was no time for clinical subtleties.

"Jennie's close to starving to death. Her brain's shutting down, her heart is probably struggling. Neither of you can fight this all by yourselves."

Laura paled but folded her arms across her chest. "Are you a doctor?"

"I've seen—"

"You've seen! But you don't know Jen. She shuts d–down when school work gets too demanding. If we let up on her, she'll never learn to face life."

It was Richard talking, through this prim and brittle mouthpiece. What would it take to make this woman's own voice come through?

"I call it as I see it," I said brutally. "Now, I'm giving you a day to talk this over as a family. Here's the clinic at the Children's Hospital to call. Either you take her there, or I'm calling Children's Aid."

Laura's big blue eyes widened and she started to sputter, then changed her mind. For an instant, fear tinged her defiance. "I'll take her to our family doctor."

Who was Richard's old college buddy, if I recalled correctly? I shook my head. "That clinic, or the CAS."

Laura stomped off in a huff, grabbed Jen by the hand and hauled her out of the restaurant without even a backward glance. But the glance she gave her daughter was curiously accusatory. How dare the girl cause her such aggravation!

I spent part of the next day lining up an appointment for Jen at the eating disorders clinic, so everything would be in place when Laura called. No call. Surprise. When my cell phone finally rang, it was midnight and I was already in bed, dreaming of rough and hungry men stealing into my room at night. One of them bore an alarming resemblance to the Pope, but I was as yet unwilling to concede an attraction. Attractions and I didn't have a big success rate, and the Pope, a confirmed bachelor wedded to his job, was my worst pick yet.

Faintly sheepish, I returned to reality and answered the phone. It was Jen, barely decipherable through her exhaustion and tears.

"Why are you doing this to my mom?"

"Jen, what's happening?"

"You've freaked her out. She says you're going to call the CAS."

"Only if she doesn't take you to the clinic."

"I don't need the clinic. I don't need any of this help. I ate all my supper."

"And did you throw it back up?"

Silence, then a noise almost like a snarl. "They had a big fight. Fighting's not good for my mom, and now she's back in bed."

"Then let me help. Let me take you to the clinic."

"No! Stay out of it. It's my problem. Daddy always says figure out what the problem is, think of some solutions, pick the best one, and do it. So I'll do it." There was a new determination in her voice, and she slammed the phone down before I could ask her what.

But I had a sinking feeling in my gut.

That determination was still evident now as Jennie faced the Pope's sidekick in the study. Even through the closed door, her voice sounded stronger and her thoughts more together than I'd ever heard. Adrenaline can be quite the energizer.

"I told you," she was saying, like a teenager talking to a very dense parent. "My mother and I left at about one o'clock, and we didn't get back till three. As soon as we got in we smelled the burning. So my mother checked the basement."

"Did she call 9-1-1 or the police?"

Silence. I pressed my ear closer.

"Why not?" the rookie asked.

"Because Sam arrived and she took over."

"That's Ms. Kaminsky? How soon after you came home did she arrive?"

"Only a few minutes. Maybe two or three. We had a meeting set up with her."

I was straining to hear her explanation of the reason for my visit when the French doors opened down the hall and the Pope came out. I jumped back, rattling the teacups. He looked startled, and a funny, bashful look crossed his face before he chased it away with a frown.

"What are you doing?"

"Wondering if I should interrupt," I said quickly. Counselling teaches you to lie fast. "I brought tea, and I was wondering how she was holding up."

"Well, the mother's holding up fine, considering she found the body. Cold piece of work."

God forbid Laura should be without her defences, I thought, but I pasted concern on my face. "What did she say?"

"That she and her daughter had gone out grocery shopping earlier in the day but they'd had to come back for an appointment with you."

Grocery shopping, I thought with disbelief. Had that been Laura's last ditch effort to pretend this was nothing but teenage caprice, that buying all her daughter's favourite foods would stem the ruthless tide of the disorder that gripped her? After Jennie's ominous late-night call, I'd called Laura first thing in the morning, told her I wasn't taking no for an answer, and I was coming out at three o'clock to take them both to the clinic appointment I'd made. Maybe Laura's denial had served her right to the end.

Or maybe that's what she wanted everyone to believe.

"So they were together all day?" I ventured casually.

The Pope gave me a weird look. "That's what she said. Why?"

I knew Laura was lying because Jen hadn't been home when I'd called with my ultimatum that morning, and Laura had been searching all over. The Pope didn't need to know that, however.

So I shrugged my disinterest and let the silence lengthen. The Pope shifted awkwardly and gave me what was probably meant to be a smile. Quick and sideways, like he was jerking it back before I could really notice it. The Pope was trying to flirt, I realized with a flush that spread all the way to my toes.

"Anyway," he continued, his eyes glued to his notes. "Looks like a clear case of misadventure. I've got an Ident team looking over the scene, and we'll have to wait for the PM, but I think you should take the family that tea. I'll be in soon."

The tea was stronger than Turkish coffee by then, of course, but I took it into the living room, where Laura was pacing back and forth, her limp barely noticeable. MS is a capricious disease, and I knew that once the adrenaline wore off, she would collapse. Probably for days. Even now, I could see she was unravelling.

"God, how did I let it come to this? Richard electrocuted, me wasting away, our daughter committing slow suicide—all of us on a path to destruction like some Greek tragedy. I studied the classics, y–you know, before I married Richard and thought I was happy—well, I didn't have to work, did I? And classics isn't a very useful field. Nothing I did was very useful. That's me—window dressing, fancy trim, airy nothingess. And then, ultimately, with my garbled speech and my failing limbs, not even good for that. Flawed, damaged goods, like the daughter we produced—"

I jumped in. "Laura, sit and have some tea. You need your strength for Jen."

"Strength? Oh yes, that. Too little too late."

"The police are ruling it an accident," I said firmly. I had to keep this woman together. "We'll get Jen the treatment she needs. She will be all right."

Laura blinked and nodded to herself several times. At that moment Jen came into the room and the two of them exchanged quick, conspiratorial nods. So, as I'd suspected, they had agreed on their story. But with any luck the Pope would feel no need to poke through the events of the afternoon thoroughly enough to disprove it.

That hope was dashed a few minutes later when he stuck his big ugly head in the doorway and jerked it sideways to signal me out into the hall. His face was grim. No sideways smile, no wishful gaze.

"Ident found a shoe tread in the far corner over by the wall socket. There are traces of sand. Looks like someone might have hidden behind a cabinet there and plugged the heater into the wall."

I grew cold inside. "You mean, waited for him? And plugged the heater in when…"

He nodded. "Not too many guys are stupid enough to work on an electrical appliance while it's plugged in."

"But even so, it's just a shoe print? How do you know it's from today?"

"It seemed a bit damp, like what you'd leave if you came in from the slush."

I glanced toward the front hall, where Laura had everyone's boots neatly lined up. Jennie's were dwarfed next to the Pope's, and a small puddle had formed beneath both. My throat constricted. "Maybe the father stood there himself. Maybe he plugged in the heater to test it."

"We're looking into it. Constable McGillvary's gonna check the footwear in all the closets. Meanwhile, can you tell me anything about what was going on between these people that might make them want to kill him?"

The Pope loomed over me, his sharp eyes boring into mine. In the silence I could hear the rookie clumping around upstairs. The air felt unexpectedly close and I began to edge away. "What I know is confidential."

"I can get a subpoena, but why not save me the hassle? Families that call you usually aren't getting along too good. In fact, in some cases, murder has improved things a lot." He grinned, probably to remind me we were soldiers in the same war, but this was no time for levity.

"Hey, I'm good at my job, Levesque, and I was making headway."

"Never said you weren't. What I meant was, was this a can of worms, here, that you opened up?"

Can of worms? More like a powder keg, with me the spark that lit the fuse.

"There were tensions," I replied carefully. "A wife with MS, a daughter with low self-esteem and a learning disability, a husband with a touch of megalomania… But in the grand scheme of my caseload, this one was peanuts."

"No reasons for murder, then?"

"I can't imagine any." I glanced into the living room, where Laura was now splayed on the sofa, her face a perfect match for the white brocade. "Look, I'd better get her something stronger than tea."

I ducked outside to my Jeep, relieved by the chance to get away. My Jeep does double duty as a junk room. I rummaged around in the mess in the back and finally emerged with a half-drunk bottle of Scotch I kept there for the occasional end to a hard day. When I returned inside, the constable was just coming back from his search. He shook his head.

"No matches," he reported, and I thought the Pope looked relieved. I felt a hundred pounds lift off me, too.

"I'm pretty much done here, then," he said. "I've got a few things to check tomorrow, but I'll speak to the family now."

He filled the pale designer living room with his bulk and perched himself on the sofa to talk to Laura. I couldn't hear the words, but I watched her go stiff with fear and then limp with relief. She sagged back on the sofa, eyelids fluttering, and the Pope gave me a pleading look. I pulled the Scotch from my pocket, and the Pope raised a curious eyebrow at me before I offered it to Laura.

I smiled a full-fledged, flirt-back smile. "Emergency car supplies."

For a while we both got busy, him phoning in his report to his boss and me getting Laura's sister rounded up to take care of them. Once everything was done, the Pope paused on his way out the door. His brow furrowed and he inspected his shoes.

"Can I drop you somewhere?"

"Well, I've got my own car." Nice move, Kaminsky.

"I could follow you, we could maybe grab a bite."

"A bite. Yeah. That would be nice."

He followed me to the nearest Tim Hortons and we wolfed down chili and hot coffee. Luckily, it's hard to talk with your mouth full, so conversation wasn't a priority. Finally, he sucked his fingers noisily and finished off with a soft belch. My kind of guy.

"I'm glad I couldn't find anything to link those two to the death," he said.

"Oh?" I said. A cop with a conscience, a cop who cared.

"Yeah. I mean, the death did look suspicious. What guy works on a heater plugged into the wall? And there are those prints by the wall and similar prints in the snow by the back door that leads to the basement."

"Oh really?"

"But they could have been there awhile. We haven't had snow in a week."

"So are you ruling it accidental?"

"Well, I'm not closing the file yet, not till I check out the guy's finances and stuff, but I'm leaning that way. Then his wife and daughter can try to put this behind them and get some help for their problems. You're going to stay involved, right?"

A cop who cared. I'd felt it the other times I'd met him, when the messy lives that I worked with had exploded into crime. Ugly and inept, we were two peas in a pod. Now, watching me, he grinned, and I felt my whole body begin to hum.

"We should go," I said. "They're closing the place around us."

Outside, he stood by my Jeep and looked at the jumbled mess in the back. His breath puffed in the chilly air, but he looked like he didn't want to leave.

"You got anything else stashed in there besides that Scotch?"

"You like vodka?" I opened the door for him. Inside, I started the car and turned on the heater. We passed the bottle back and forth, and the Jeep slowly grew toasty. I shed my jacket, he his parka. Then he leaned over, took the bottle from my hand and planted a clumsy arm around my shoulder. I tilted my face, and somehow we connected. Inexpertly. Groping beneath sweatshirts and devouring any bare skin that came in reach. Blind instinct, that's what we were, unleashed from years of fruitless yearning. We scrambled over the seats into the back and sprawled out on my tangle of sports gear. Unzipped and bleary-eyed with need, he reached to move something out of the way. His hand closed on something and he pulled it free. Stared at it.

My boot.

He turned it over, looked at the tread, and looked at me. I met his gaze. I'd forgotten the boots, thought I'd hidden them well enough earlier, when I'd gone out for the Scotch and changed into my spare pair. I could see the bleak anguish in his eyes. He wanted me. Maybe...maybe even thought we had a chance at something, but he was too good a cop to turn his back on his job. Or on the truth. No matter how twisted that truth became.

No matter that some people squandered the precious lives that were placed in their care, that some people didn't deserve the families they'd been given. I'd even offered Richard Potts one last chance, gone to the house early to tell him the desperate lengths to which his daughter might go, and what I planned to do if we were lucky enough to find her alive. He'd dismissed me with a flick of his hand and a cataloguing of the legal ruin I'd face should I presume to meddle further in their lives.

The Pope wouldn't see the thousand shades of good and evil in the world I inhabited. To him, good was simple.

It had to be.

Damn Richard Potts.

Avenging Miriam

by Peter Sellers

Jon L. Breen, writing in *Ellery Queen Mystery Magazine*, called Peter
Sellers, "one of the key figures in the Canadian mystery renaissance
of the 80s and 90s." Peter was the founder and editor of the
acclaimed *Cold Blood* series of Canadian short crime fiction
anthologies, which comprised six volumes published from 1987
through 1998. In addition to editing, Peter has published crime and
dark fantasy stories in *Mike Shayne Mystery Magazine, Alfred
Hitchcock Mystery Magazine, Ellery Queen Mystery Magazine, Hardboiled*
and numerous anthologies. A collection of his stories, *Whistling Past
the Graveyard*, was published by Mosaic Press in 1999. He is a three-
time finalist for the Crime Writers of Canada's Arthur Ellis Award
for Best Short Story.

"'I just want to put it behind me and get on with my life.' That's what one
of them said." He handed the paper to Kieran, who read the first few paragraphs of the article and saw the quote for himself.

"I must confess, I find the cold-bloodedness of that even more incomprehensible now than I did when I first read it," Sebastian went on.
"Imagine. Saying something like that, as if she had just failed a big math
test, or dented her father's car. Instead of kicking another fourteen-year-
old girl to death."

To Kieran, it did seem a rather cynical attitude, but then he wasn't yet
familiar with all the facts in the case. He'd been in Europe on an extended holiday when it happened. The two or three paragraphs were all he'd
read about the case before sitting down with Sebastian. Even had he not
been away, he didn't follow the paper much even in the best of times.

"What's this got to do with me?" Kieran asked, handing the clipping
back.

"As you well know," Sebastian began, "thanks to the Canadian justice
system, none of these killers will serve more than a token amount of time
for their crime. Three years at most. In some cases, that means they'll be
out in time to apply for their first driver's license, or to attend their high
school graduation. Somehow it doesn't seem fair. So I want to hire you."

"To kill that girl?" he pointed at the paper Sebastian now held.

"To kill them all."

That meant nine. The group of children who had beaten their friend and schoolmate to death one evening after dinner, while other kids were having piano lessons, writing in their diaries, or hanging at the mall.

Kieran didn't have to consider this proposal for long. "I'm sorry to disappoint you, but I'm not your man. I don't kill children for money," he said. "In fact, I've never killed a child in my life."

Sebastian shook his head. "They're not children. Don't be fooled by the acne and the braces and the innocent looks that they can turn on like VCRs. Children don't savagely terrorize and brutally murder their peers. Chronologically they may be thirteen or fourteen or fifteen, but they're not children, I assure you. They're monsters."

"That's as may be, but I'm not going to execute them for you." Kieran took a sip of coffee. "What's your interest in this anyway? You the victim's father? Uncle? What?"

"None of those. I'm not related to Miriam at all."

"Miriam," Kieran repeated.

"I'm not a relative. I'm just a deeply concerned citizen who can see when a gross injustice is being committed, who has the wherewithal to do something about it."

"Well, you're more noble than I am. And I'm still not your man."

As if he hadn't heard, Sebastian took a folded sheet of paper from an inside jacket pocket and held it out. "Here is a list of all their names and addresses. You'll need this, obviously."

Kieran hesitated. He didn't want the job, and he didn't want to see the names. He didn't take the paper at first, but Sebastian did not withdraw it, and eventually Kieran reached out. Once it was in his hand, however, he did not open it. "You shouldn't have this," he said. "If these kids are all young offenders, then nobody's supposed to know who they are."

"Legally, that's true enough. In fact, just for passing you that list, I could go to jail for much longer than any of them will for their crime. But we're both men of the world here. You know as well as I do that every time there's a case like this, even though the media can't mention names, people know. People in the community know. It's not that hard to learn the names."

Curiosity got the better of Kieran. He finished his coffee, unfolded the sheet, and read the names. The victim's was at the top. Then came the names of her killers. They were typed one after another in simple Helvetica. Each name and address was on a single line, then a double space, and then the next name and address. It appeared so innocuous. There was nothing in the way the words looked to give any hint of what the people they stood for had done. Adam and Rebecca and Tiffany—one common or artificial name after another.

Kieran scanned the list quickly, once. Victim and killers. Then he read it again slowly, and then a third time, more slowly still. As he did so, he felt a deep sadness creeping through him. It must have shown on his face.

"It's an awful thing, and terribly, terribly sad, but some crimes are too great to be ignored. When you have the power to make a difference and you don't, aren't you an accessory to the crime? I always thought so. Do you have children, Kieran?"

Kieran did not make a habit of discussing any aspect of his personal life with his clients, but something about this situation felt different. "Yes," he said. "I have two daughters." That was all he was prepared to divulge. The fact that he had seen neither girl in years was nobody's business but his own.

"Well, unpalatable as this might be, before you make a final decision, try to imagine one of your daughters in that situation."

Kieran tried. He tried to imagine what it must have been like for the murdered girl. The incomprehension when the gang of teenagers turned on her. They were all people she thought of as her friends, whom she so wanted to be like and to impress. Why were they doing this? The question must have loomed so large in her mind that she didn't feel the blows at first, as if their mere occurrence numbed her to the pain they caused.

Then terror must have set in. Surrounded, driven to the ground, blows from fists and open hands turning to dehumanizing kicks. The hundred-and-fifty-dollar cross-trainers and the Docs and the trendy hiking shoes slamming into her body as she squirmed, trying to find escape. But there were nine of them, so it was easy to surround her. No matter where she put her hands to ward off the blows, most of her body was left unprotected. For every kick deflected, eight others found their mark. She cried and begged, but mercy was not forthcoming. At some point, one of them, perhaps her leg growing tired, picked up a stick and used that to beat the victim on the head and neck.

Did they talk to her, Kieran wondered, as they were killing her? Did they explain to her why? Did they call her names and abuse her with their mouths as well as their limbs? Did they hurl accusations and condemn her family? Did they laugh?

And then for a moment, they stopped. All nine of them stepped back and let her rise painfully to her feet. They were letting her go. She was bleeding and stunned and every step was painful but they let her stagger away from them. How did she feel then, as hope soared inside her? Did she thank them? Did she thank God or whatever force made them stop? Or did she just make her way as fast as she could, urging her unsteady limbs on, wondering incongruously what she would tell her parents and how she would explain to her teachers why her homework was not done?

In the end, none of that mattered. She hadn't gone fifty yards before they set on her again. That, to Kieran, was the cruellest part: letting hope build and then grinding it out. They beat her and kicked her and finally left her lying on the bank of the small creek where she died.

Kieran shook his head. It was so completely senseless. He couldn't conceive of either of his daughters in such a circumstance. He folded the list of names and placed the tip of the paper against his pursed lips, shut his eyes, and considered for some time.

"All right," he said at length. "I'm your man."

Sebastian smiled with relief. "I know this is a huge undertaking. Thank you for doing the right thing."

"Right isn't part of it," Kieran said. "It's business."

"And I don't imagine there's a volume discount."

Kieran shook his head. "In fact, there's a volume premium. Nine random people, yeah, you'd probably get a break. But nine kids, all linked to the same event, the cops are going to know what's up from the word Go. So that makes the job infinitely tougher. Which in turn means that it won't cost you just nine times X. It's nine times X plus a whole whack of danger pay. You fine with that?"

"This has to be done. And it has to be done right. As my grandfather always used to say, 'The craftsman is worthy of his hire.'"

"Oh, yeah," Kieran said. "I'm worthy all right."

Kieran spent a few days planning his trip to the West Coast. He decided to drive, not wanting airline reservations booked in his name. A seven-day trip would help him get his thoughts together, to make sure his plan was solid.

Sebastian started to explain why he wanted to hire someone in Toronto to handle a job in Vancouver, but Kieran was miles ahead of him. Distance made sense in any job like this. So did time. After they agreed on a price, Sebastian delivered the cash the next day. Large bundles of used, non-sequential bills. Kieran looked at the money, riffled the ends of two or three random bundles, and put it all back in the athletic bag.

"Aren't you going to count it?" Sebastian asked.

"I'm sure it'll be right," Kieran said with a gentle smile, leaving the consequences of error unspoken. He put the package of photographs of all nine targets in the bag with the money and zipped it closed.

Financial matters settled, Kieran explained that it would take time. Sebastian would have to be patient. It might be that three or four or five of the killers would die quickly and the rest would be on guard so Kieran would have to sit back and wait for them to relax again, drop their guards, begin to forget that there might be something out there in the dark waiting for them.

"The wheels of justice grind slow," Sebastian said. "But they grind fine. I'm confident that the job will be done to my satisfaction. Time is not of the essence."

"I've got this gig," Kieran said to his friend Richard. They were sitting in a Second Cup on Yonge Street, watching women go by, talking sporadically.

"Good one?" Richard was from South Africa, and a dozen years in Canada had done little to soften his accent. A former soldier in the South African army, Richard had been involved in some unpleasantness in a couple of the black townships. Later, as a mercenary, he'd fought in the Congo with Mad Mike Hoare, but had been smart enough to say no when Hoare called him up about his projected coup in the Seychelles. Now, he did what Kieran did. They had mutual professional respect and often sat and talked about contracts, clients, and the unreasonable deadlines they were frequently expected to meet. They also turned to one another when they had logistical problems.

"Big one, anyway."

"Somebody famous?"

"Nope. No names you'd recognize. But there are nine of 'em."

Richard whistled. "You could retire on a baby like that."

"No, I have to take 'em out individually. That's the problem. Once I whack the first one, the cops'll know I'm after the bunch."

"How's that?"

So Kieran told him the whole story—who he'd been hired to kill and why he was going to do it.

"That's a tough one," Richard said. "You sure you can't get 'em all in one place and blow it to hell?" Then he made a face and dismissed his own idea. "Naw, too much margin for error."

"I thought about hitting them all in one night. Working it all out. Choreographing the whole thing. Capping them all and leaving town the same night, but there's too many people, too many variables."

"You know, the cops might not be as much of a problem as you think. They can't publish the names of any of these kids, so if they start getting hit they can't put that fact in the paper. And are they going to start throwing armed guards on these kids twenty-four hours a day? You want to draw attention to them, that's a grand way to do it. This young offenders bullshit may work in your favour. Protect you by trying to protect your targets."

It had been unusually dry in Vancouver for the previous few weeks, and there were restrictions on watering lawns and washing cars. Kieran was tired when he got to the city, but instead of checking into his hotel, he drove to the airport and left his car in long-term parking. People tend to notice out-of-province plates. Then he took a bus downtown, checked in, and had a nap.

He killed the first three of them the next night. This had not been his plan. He'd anticipated spending a few days scouting the situation and working out the most efficient and least risky way of picking them off one by one. But as he cruised past the home of one of the female killers, the door opened and she stepped outside. Kieran followed her discreetly. It wasn't that difficult. The car he'd rented was in no way distinctive, and the quarry, like so many teenagers, was oblivious to everything around her that was not of obvious and direct concern to her.

She made two stops on her trip, meeting two young men whom Kieran recognized as additional members of the group of nine. It was better than he'd hoped. They were together, in clear violation of their probation. Better yet, they headed straight for the centre of Stanley Park to toke up. Kieran followed them and they were all dead before the joint went around once. He dragged their bodies far into the bushes. They might be discovered first thing in the morning by some jogger who ducked off the path for a leak. Or they might lie undisturbed for days. Kieran quietly hoped for the latter, but he planned on the former.

As he was driving back over the Berrard Street Bridge, he thought about what had just happened. He hadn't said a word to the kids. He'd just dropped them as cleanly and as quickly as possible. In the instant between life and death, he doubted if they had made any connection between what was happening to them and what they had done to that girl by the side of a rubbish-choked creek. He'd heard that at the point of dying, your life flashes before your eyes. If that were true, did the lives of those three young killers freeze-frame on their viciousness and cause the truth to ignite a spontaneous chorus of, "Oh, so this is why we're being killed. I guess there is justice after all"? Kieran somehow doubted it. He decided then that all the rest of the condemned, like prisoners mounting the gallows or standing before a firing squad, would at least know why.

Kieran had requested a smoking room in the hotel. Once inside, he put the chain on the door and took out the three photos of the dead and burned them one by one. They were high school yearbook photos; their bland artlessness and frozen smiles gave no hint of the rage inside. He wondered what the old scientists—who felt you could tell a criminal just by looking at his face—would have made of these images. He held each photo in turn over an ashtray and watched as the flames melted the photographic paper, twisting the faces grotesquely, making them look truly monstrous. He held on and watched until the flames licked his fingers. When all three were done, he emptied the ashtray in the toilet and flushed.

The next morning, there was nothing in either the *Vancouver Sun* or the *Province* about three bodies being found in Stanley Park. Nor was there anything about three missing teens. That might have been because their being out all night was a common occurrence, or perhaps their concerned parents had phoned the police and had been told that people couldn't be considered missing until they'd been gone a full twenty-four hours.

Whatever the reason, Kieran had a modest reprieve. A chance to get further ahead than he'd initially envisaged. He went over the list while sitting at an outdoor café on Robson Street and decided on another one of the boys on the list. He was finding it difficult to work up as much enthusiasm for executing the girls. The decision to put it off wasn't entirely conscious, but it wasn't involuntary either. He'd taken the money, and he'd do it eventually, he knew he just had to work up to it.

He picked Christopher next. The boy's family had moved him away from the neighbourhood where most of the others on the list still lived. They had settled in the suburb of Burnaby. Perhaps they thought they could move away from the past and the stares and the whispering. But Burnaby was not very far to go. And the reality, as Kieran well knew, was that you can't outrun the past. Let down your guard for an instant, and it will come find you and stop your heart.

He drove to Burnaby, found the new address, and scouted the area thoroughly. Then he went to a mall not far from Christopher's house and waited in the food court. He ate Indian food, drank coffee, and watched the kids who gathered there. Any one of them capable of anything, he thought.

He scrutinized the faces discreetly and suddenly realized, in shock, that Christopher was there. Laughing and joking with a new gang of friends. Kieran took another long look to make sure. He hadn't quite expected it to be so ridiculously simple. He got up and emptied his tray in the garbage, placing it on top of the bin. Then he went out into the mall to wait. He bought a paper and sat by a wishing pond, reading the sports section and watching Christopher.

An hour later the boy left in company with a small knot of friends. Kieran wondered if they would head straight home or stop by a desolate creek and slaughter one of their number. Or if that task was being left solely up to him.

They climbed into a 4 x 4 and set off. Kieran followed as the driver let passengers off at various different points, singly or in pairs. He dropped Christopher off at a corner, and the boy waited to cross the street until Kieran had driven past. Kieran knew where he must be going: he would follow a path through a ravine, across a small footbridge, then up the hill to the far end of the street where his family's new house stood.

Kieran circled the block as quickly as the speed limit allowed and parked near the exit of the ravine. He started walking in. His pistol was in his jacket pocket. He reached the footbridge ahead of Christopher and had just stepped onto the path on the far side when he recognized the figure coming towards him. Christopher must have seen Kieran at precisely the same moment, for he took two or three more faltering steps and then stopped. Kieran kept walking forward. Christopher, perhaps with some primal instinct kicking in, took a step back, then two, but he was still gazing into the gloom, trying to figure out if he should stand his ground or flee.

Kieran didn't want Christopher to run. He said, "Hi, Chris," in a soft, friendly voice.

The familiarity froze Chris momentarily. Who was this, speaking his name, but whom he did not recognize? The same soft, friendly voice said, "Miriam says hello." And then Christopher knew the only smart thing to do was turn and run.

It was probably a root, or perhaps an unevenness of ground, but his toe caught on something and he fell, abruptly and hard. Kieran watched him make one abortive attempt to get up, then the boy began crawling, scrambling along the dirt path, weeping and sniffling with fear. Kieran caught up with him easily. He stood looking down at the boy who lay half-curled on the ground, his hands about his head, making incomprehensible noises of pleading.

Christopher was lean and his legs were long, and under other circumstances, he might well have been able to easily outpace a middle-aged man.

But he was wearing his jeans pulled low around his hips, the tops of his boxer shorts displaying colourful cartoon characters. As he ran, his pants began to slip down his legs. He stumbled and reached down, trying to wrestle his pants higher while still fleeing as fast as he could. His pants seemed reluctant to move, but the boy was unwilling to stop and do the job properly. He kept on his erratic forward pace, his head turning back frequently to stare in wide-eyed panic at the man who followed him. And then he tripped and fell.

It would have been easy to have shot him through the head and leave immediately. But then he thought about the first three and how none of them would ever know why they died with such shocking suddenness. This one was going to know. He was going to know, just as his family was going to know, as soon as his three dead friends were found. Either the police would tell his family, or they'd be smart enough to figure it out for themselves. They'd know that their son had not died in a random act of violence. Not the way Miriam died, but because Miriam died. That made Kieran wonder then what Christopher's mother thought of the boy when she looked at him across the breakfast table in the months since Miriam's death, knowing what she knew about him.

Kieran crouched down next to the prone youth. "Sit up," he said. "We're going to have a little chat."

Tentatively, the boy shifted one of his arms from over his eyes and peered at Kieran, uncertain at first, and then with growing hope. He rose to his knees, sniffled, and wiped his eyes with his sleeve. His lip quivered.

"Don't kill me," he said. "Please."

Kieran indicated a tree with the barrel of his gun. "Sit," he said.

The boy leaned his back against the tree and stared at the gun in Kieran's hand. "Please," he said again.

"Hmm," Kieran looked thoughtful. "Is that what she said as you were killing her? How many times, I wonder? After the first couple of times it must have become easier and easier to ignore."

The boy started to cry again. Kieran waited for a while and the weeping subsided. "Why did you do it?"

The boy shook his head. "I don't know. I don't know why."

"Because other people were doing it? Or did you start it? Was it planned out in advance? Or was it something that just happened?"

"I don't know. I was just there."

Kieran wondered what the truth really was. Had there been a phone tree? "Hi, it's Tracy. Whatcha doin' tonight? You wanna get together? We're gonna, like, go grab a latte, check out this new club, and then, like, beat Miriam to death. Yeah, I think it sounds cool. Call Mike and tell him, and ask him to phone Lindsay. Oh, and you know that new zit cream? Does it, like, work any good?" He hoped it hadn't been like that, but with kids these days, you never knew.

"Wearing your pants like that makes it tough to run, doesn't it? You know why you wear your pants like that? I bet you don't have a clue. It's a gang thing from LA. The gangs started wearing their pants baggy in the crotch like that so they could hide weapons. If you'd had a weapon hidden in there you might not be in the predicament you're currently facing."

The boy had been sobbing steadily and it got harder now. Kieran began to feel somewhat uneasy. He didn't want to stay too long and risk getting caught. "Listen," he said to the kid, "I'm going to teach you another valuable lesson. First of all, you know why this is happening, right?"

The kid looked panicky and blank and shook his head, wiping his nose on his sleeve again. "Miriam," Kieran said softly and the kid started to wail more loudly.

Kieran decided there was little point in dragging things out. "Here's the lesson. Most teenage kids think they're invincible, that they're going to live forever. If they understood and embraced their own mortality, they'd be better off, I think. They'd be more empathetic. Make more constructive use of their time. So I'm helping you realize your mortality right now. This is a valuable life lesson here. One of the secrets of the universe. You're lucky. Not many young people get to die with such clarity of mind."

Then Kieran put the pistol away. Christopher stared in disbelief, as if he could smell mercy. Until, in deference to the surrounding neighbourhood, Kieran reached into another pocket and took out the guitar string.

Kieran stayed in Vancouver a few more days. By now, all four bodies had been found. Nothing was mentioned in any of the papers about the connection between the four of them. But the cops would have linked them instantly, and the rest of the targets would drop out of sight temporarily. So there'd be no more work for him there in the immediate future. There was, however, one stop he could make on the way home.

Just like Christopher's parents, Rachel's mother thought she could run away from trouble. She had taken her daughter to stay with relatives in Calgary. Further than Burnaby but somehow still not quite far enough.

Sebastian had supplied him with the information. The new address, the names of the people with whom Rachel and her mother were staying, the phone number. He'd even provided Kieran with a new photograph of the girl, who had cut and dyed her hair in another vain attempt to hide from destiny. The photo was a candid shot, taken on the street, and it showed the girl in company with an older woman. Kieran studied the girl briefly and then focused his attention on the mother. She was perhaps forty and attractive, with lines that gave her face character and depth. He studied the face for a considerable time.

Kieran figured the cops in Calgary would be on alert, but not like on the coast. He went to the airport and got his car. The rate they charged for parking was usurious, but he reckoned Sebastian could afford it.

The last time Kieran had been in Calgary, there'd been a boom going on. Apparently, in the years since, there'd been some bad times, but if you didn't know that, you'd swear the boom never stopped. There were cranes everywhere. New buildings going up. The oil patch was thriving.

Kieran drove to Rachel's cousin's place. It was a typical subdivision house, rather ugly, squatting behind a bloated two-car garage. There was a minivan in the driveway and a sprinkler on the lawn, but no sign of life. He came back that evening and watched for a very brief time. Lights burned in three or four windows, and he saw silhouetted figures moving behind sheer curtains, but no one came out.

He drove on, past the local schools until he found the high school he suspected Rachel would be attending. Then he went downtown for dinner.

Since he was in Alberta, he had a steak and tried to think of a plan to kill Rachel, but his thoughts kept drifting. He was distracted by snatches of conversation from other tables. He found himself watching female patrons and waitresses as they breezed past his table. As he watched them, the image of Rachel's mother's face kept crowding its way into his head. He didn't bother trying to suppress it, for he knew why she was there. It wasn't just that the mother was attractive and possessed of an energy that the camera captured easily. It was seeing them together, mother and daughter so much like one another, in a photo where they looked happy and very ordinary. But even as he had looked at the picture for the first time, it had caused him to wonder what she thought about her daughter now. How she managed the reality and rationalized the enormity of the crime. He had a desire to talk with her about it. He knew it was time to go home.

After dinner, he went to his hotel and did not leave a wake-up call. The next morning he started driving east. He needed a break. He was about halfway through. The heat would be on in Calgary to some degree. He'd let things cool off all over the place, maybe wait out the winter in Toronto and then finish the job in the spring. He was sure Sebastian wouldn't mind. All the way home, across a thousand miles of prairie and through the vast northern woods, thoughts of Rachel's mother kept him company.

"We're certainly off to a flying start," Sebastian said. "Five down, four to go."

Kieran hadn't been paying too much attention, and it took a second or two before the words sank in. Three in the park. One in the ravine. Four, no matter how you added it up. "Five?" he asked.

Sebastian nodded. "I guess you haven't read this yet." He handed Kieran a newspaper clipping. It was from the *Calgary Herald*, dated the day after Kieran left town. Rachel's body had been found in her room. She had taken an overdose of sleeping pills.

"Her mother's pills?" Kieran asked.

Sebastian shook his head. "They were her own. She'd been having a lot of trouble sleeping, apparently. Really bad nightmares."

No mention was made of nightmares in the article, nor of what might have caused them. Nothing in the brief piece indicated that this was anything other than another tragic teenage suicide.

Sebastian supplied a little more information. "She was also having trouble at her new school. She didn't fit in, and I understand she was picked on a lot. What goes around, comes around, I suppose."

Kieran handed him back the cutting. "I don't suppose there's a rebate for this one?" Sebastian said.

"You can ask," Kieran said.

Sebastian chuckled. "Well, hearing about the deaths of her friends must have helped nudge her along. So I guess you can take partial credit anyway."

Kieran didn't reply.

Kieran spent the winter in Toronto while the fuss died down out west. He monitored the Vancouver media, and when the four killings of the previous autumn had not been mentioned for three months, he decided it was time to go back and finish the job. This time he took the train, booking a stopover in Calgary.

It was not difficult to find Rachel's mother. She no longer lived in the house he had observed in the fall. Instead, she had recently purchased a modest condominium in a residential area near the downtown core. Obviously, she had no desire to go back to the West Coast. Not immediately anyway.

As he watched and followed her for several days, the pattern of Rachel's mother's habits became obvious. Her routine was remarkably consistent and included having lunch most days in the one of the same three restaurants, with the same individual co-workers, or the same small knot of people.

He was struck by the drab ordinariness of it and marvelled, as he always did, at the antlike tenacity that kept people going in such numbingly tedious circumstances.

He also soon discovered that after work she rarely went out with anyone. She either stayed in or walked by herself to a small pub a few blocks from her home. Once in the pub, she also followed a regular routine.

She would sit at a small table for two against the back wall. There was a wall sconce beside the table in which two low-wattage, flame-shaped bulbs burned dimly. By this light, she would read a book while very slowly nursing a glass of red wine. Never more than one glass, and she never stayed much longer than an hour.

Kieran was glad that she didn't sit at the bar. Women sitting alone on bar stools always struck him as tragic, somehow.

Kieran watched Rachel's mother discreetly for some time. She read slowly and occasionally flipped back a page, presumably to pick up a line or a thought she had missed.

Kieran did not talk to her that day. He just watched her surreptitiously for the first few nights. He sat in a different spot each evening. One night watching a hockey game on the TV behind the bar. One night doing the crossword in the *Globe and Mail*. One night reading a book of his own.

Two or three times, Rachel's mother did not show up. But on each of the other nights she was there. At some point, she finished one book and began another.

Finally, after almost two weeks, Kieran approached her. She had just walked in and sat down, and the waitress had not yet come over to take her order. "Excuse me," he said. "I was wondering if I could buy you a drink."

She looked up at him intently without responding right away.

"I'm not trying to pick you up or anything," he said. "I just admire anyone who reads Dickens." He indicated the copy of *Oliver Twist* that lay on the table and then held up the copy of *Bleak House* he had bought several days before and had been pretending to read for the last few evenings.

He ordered each of them a glass of red wine and sat opposite her at the small table. Conversation was guarded and stiff at first.

"Do you live near here?"

"No. I'm just in town for a while on business. My hotel's near here."

"Which one?"

"Journey's End."

She nodded. "Where are you from?"

"Toronto, now," he said. "But I'm from Vancouver originally."

Her face brightened. "Really? That's where I'm from."

"No kidding. What a coincidence! So, how long have you been here?"

They chatted amiably for some time. What she told him was mostly true, based on what he knew of her life already, and she willingly accepted the carefully constructed story he passed off as reality.

"So, I don't want you to get the wrong impression," he said, "but I've been in here a few nights and I couldn't help but notice you."

She looked at him as if expecting the advance to come now.

"You must like it here," was all he said.

She smiled. "It gets me out of the house."

"Lots of things do that. You could take up yoga or join a book club. You like to read."

"I don't feel very social a lot of the time."

"It's none of my business, but you look kind of sad. Anything you'd care to discuss with a stranger you're never going to see again?"

"How can you be sure of that?"

"I'm forty-two years old and I've never been to Calgary before in my life. It's a fluke I'm here now. I had to cover for somebody who got sick. The odds of our meeting again are extremely long. So anything you want to talk about?"

She shook her head. "Not really. Do you have any kids?"

"Two," Kieran said. "Daughters. They live with their mother. How about you?"

"I had a daughter, too."

"Had?"

Rachel's mother shook her head. "She died last spring."

"I'm terribly sorry. I didn't mean to stir up bad memories."

"It's all right. Everything stirs up bad memories. You didn't know."

They sat in awkward silence for some time, Kieran studying the woman's face while she watched the memories that unspooled in her head.

"So what work do you do?" he asked her softly.

She looked in his eyes and smiled. "You don't have to change the subject," she said. "I don't mind talking about it."

"I figured, because you just said—"

"I lied. I want to talk about it, but I try to keep myself under control. That's why I come to this place. Because nobody here talks to me about anything. I think my friends are tired of hearing about it—not that I have that many friends here—so I try to hide. But it doesn't always work. Rachel killed herself."

Kieran let out his breath slowly. "I can't imagine what that must be like," he said. "Losing a child that way."

"You know, it's been almost a year and I still can't imagine it either."

"Was there something specific that happened to cause it? Had there been any signs?"

Rachel's mother looked down at the table again. Her hands played with the stem of her wine glass and then began riffling the pages of her book. "No," she said. "There'd been some trouble back in Vancouver. She got involved with some bad kids. I tried to tell her, but how many fourteen year olds listen to their mothers? I took her here thinking we could leave the trouble behind."

"I guess trouble has a way of following you around," Kieran said.

"Sad, but true," Rachel's mother said with an unhappy smile.

"So things didn't change when you got here?"

"For a bit. A few weeks. A month. But just until she got settled in a little and found the kids here who were just like the kids at home. And then it was like nothing was any different."

"How did she behave?"

"I don't know. She'd do things out of spite. She used to hitchhike to school. This started just before she turned thirteen. I'd tell her not to do it, but then she'd leave the house in the morning, and I'd leave for work a few minutes later, and I'd see her a block or so away, standing by the side of the road with her thumb out. She'd stare right at me, like a challenge. There must have been things I could have done better but, for the life of me, I don't know what they were."

She sipped her wine, and Kieran remained silent. She had more to say yet, and it wasn't his opinion that she was after.

"When I used to see kids on the street, I used to think that they all left home because they were being beaten or abused. I realize now how naive I was. Some of those kids were just like Rachel. There was nothing awful going on at home. Nothing unusual, anyway. They just left. They skipped school. They ran away. She used to tell me that she was spending the night at this friend's house or that one. Those other kids must have told their parents the same thing, I suppose. But they never spent the night at anyone's house. They used to sleep in apartment building stairwells. Why? What was the reason?"

"It must have been difficult for you."

She shrugged. "It had its moments. You know what the hardest thing is? I have so many questions for her that nobody will ever be able to answer. Even if they could, I don't imagine I'd accept them because I don't imagine I could understand."

"It sounds like she was pretty lost."

"Yes. That's what hurts. I never saw the amount of pain she must have been in." Rachel's mother raised her face and held her chin forward bravely. "She was a good girl. Really she was."

Kieran imagined one of the pictures of the murdered girl, her head in the creek, face down, hair matted. Her body indelibly marked by the ferocity of her attackers. He felt the urge to tell Rachel's mother that despite what she might think, good girls didn't do that to children, but he restrained himself. He was starting to feel tired and unclear how to proceed.

"I'm sure she was a good girl," Kieran said. "I guess it's just that everybody's got conflicts. Everybody's confused at least some of the time."

Rachel's mother was silent for a long time. "I'm sorry," Kieran said finally. "This is a bit of a downer. I really didn't mean to stir so much up."

She made a dismissive gesture with her hand. "Most days, it doesn't take much stirring."

"Would you like to go get something to eat?" he asked.

Rachel's mother looked at him a long time before answering.

Kieran took the train to Vancouver the next afternoon. Much of the way, he thought about his time with Rachel's mother. It hadn't been entirely satisfying. He'd never felt the moment was quite right to ask many of the questions he had. And he hadn't been able to divine the answers he was looking for through less direct means. But he still had a job to do. So he forced the disappointment from his mind and tried to focus on what lay ahead.

He dispatched the first three of the four remaining killers quickly and efficiently, over two nights. The third one was dead before the first two bodies had been found; before panic among the families of the killers could erupt; and before the police would go on active alert. The waiting had proven wise. The targets were careless and obviously considered themselves out of the reach of any act of vengeance.

They all cried. One of them announced that it wasn't his fault, that the other kids forced him to do it. One claimed he hadn't done anything at all, just watched. Kieran explained how, if that were true, it was worse than taking part. And the third one pleaded for Kieran to have mercy because he was so young. Only fifteen. "Well," Kieran said, "look on the bright side. You got one more year than Miriam did." Boom.

There was only one left. Kieran's opportunity came two days after he arrived in town. She was walking home from a movie when Kieran pulled the car up beside her, got out, and opened the door. "Get in," he said.

He wasn't at all sure that she wouldn't just scream and run, but she didn't. She stood and looked at him. He waited by the open door, saying nothing and making no move. He could almost feel her mind working. Then she started toward the car. He wondered, as she climbed in and he shut the door behind her, if she used to hitchhike like Rachel did, if she was used to getting into strange vehicles.

When he was settled behind the wheel, he said, "For a minute there, I wasn't sure what you were going to do."

She shrugged. "I thought about taking off. But even if that had seemed the best thing to do, it wouldn't have made any difference, right?"

"No, I'd have come after you."

"I've always known that eventually you would," she said.

"So you know who I am and you know why I'm here?"

"Yeah. I've just been wondering when you'd get here," she said.

"I spent some time with Rachel's mother." He was unsure why he felt a need to explain. As if the delay had inconvenienced the girl in some way.

The girl looked surprised. "Why? How do you know Rachel's mom?" she asked. "Anyway, Rachel killed herself."

He nodded, answering her first question, ignoring the second. "I wanted to try and find out why she did it and how her mother felt about it." He pulled away from the curb.

"I'll tell you why she did it. Because there was this bogeyman out there, who would be coming around one night to splatter her brains on the ground, just like he did to all her friends. One after another."

"That may have been part of it." He felt very calm. "Do you suppose it might have been partly because she felt badly about what she'd done to Miriam?"

She opened her purse and pulled out a pack of cigarettes. The rental car was non-smoking but it seemed to Kieran that it would be petty to stop her. She lit up and blew out a great plume. "I was getting scared waiting for you."

"Oh?"

"I was afraid you wouldn't show up."

"There was no need to fear that," he said.

They drove in silence for several minutes before she asked, "Why do you think this has been happening?" There was a plaintive note in her voice. "Why has someone killed all my friends? What did I do to deserve that?"

"Maybe it wasn't what you did so much as who you did it to and how you did it to them."

"What the hell does that mean?"

"What did Miriam do to deserve to die?"

She crossed her arms and turned away from him to face out the side window. "You wouldn't understand."

"You're probably right. But you could try me."

"Does everybody die for a good reason? Do you ever really know why you're doing it?"

"Sometimes," he said.

"Yeah, right. I don't want to talk about this anymore."

He ignored her. "It should have been quick," he said. "Abrupt, sudden, and painless. Not dragged out. I bet she didn't even know why it was happening."

"So you've never done that? You've never prolonged the agony?"

He thought carefully about how to answer. "No. I've never done it," he said at length. "Unless it was to make sure that the person understood very clearly why they were about to die. Did Miriam have that understanding, do you suppose?"

The girl shrugged. "She probably knew she was going to die because nobody liked her. Would that be enough reason for you?"

He didn't answer. He had driven to an isolated industrial area of warehouses and small manufacturing facilities, and he stopped the car.

She looked around at the surroundings, then at him. "I must be stupid," she said. "I was relieved to see you." Kieran figured the details had fallen into place. "You knew about Rachel. You know about everything that's been going on. You're not here to protect me at all."

"I'm afraid not," he said. He had taken the pistol out of his pocket and brought it to bear. It was not as steady as it had been every time before.

"You're here to whack me." She looked at the glowing cigarette in her hand and laughed bitterly. "My last smoke and I didn't even take the time to appreciate it." She ground the butt out on the dashboard with sharp, angry motions. "Do I get any last words?"

He cocked the hammer on the pistol.

"You're kidding yourself, you know, if you think you don't do what we did. You've tortured us for months. We couldn't sleep. Afraid to go out of the house. Waiting for you to show up. How many of us got the value of your wisdom before you blew our fucking brains out?"

"Are you finished?" he asked. It was taking all his energy to focus on the pistol, to keep it steady and aimed true.

"That's up to you, isn't it?" Nothing happened. It was warm and close in the confined space. "So," she said finally, turning square in the seat to face him, "what are you going to do now, Dad?"

Winter Man

by Eliza Moorhouse

Eliza Moorhouse lives in Vernon, B.C., but her mind occasionally finds its way to the twisted back streets of Hong Kong. She knows them intimately, and from that fertile breeding grown sprang Grant Calvados, the amoral, opium-taking dealer in stolen antiquities. Calvados is the son of an unusual mother and an unknown father, and one of the most extraordinary characters in Canadian crime fiction. "Oriental antiquities became his darkly beloved passion" Eliza says, "easily surpassing his regard for humanity." He lives in a world where betrayal is the best you can expect.

Eliza has won several awards for her writing. This story was on the Arthur Ellis Award shortlist in 1995.

The Hong Kong sun wandered across the carpet and paused at the carved cherrywood bed, mercifully avoiding the old woman's face. Hoarse and puffy-eyed, she was a formidable sight in the morning. Thrusting the first cigarette of the day between swollen lips, she called for the servant, Ana, to bring her breakfast tray.

Finishing the tea and toast with English marmalade to the last crumb, the old dragon had one more cigarette, then screamed for Ana to help her dress.

"The grey dress today, madam?" Ana asked in amazement.

The grey dress and matching cape were the old woman's street clothes, yet they had remained in new condition for she seldom bothered to dress and wandered the streets in old slippers and shapeless black.

"Do as you're told! I'm going out. Important business." The old dragon thrust the breakfast tray aside. "Take that away and ring for the chauffeur at half past eight."

"Master would not like it, madam. I promised that you would stay in the house until family leaves for Canada."

"I am not a prisoner! Do as you're told." She angrily dusted her face with pearl powder and forced one more Double Happiness cigarette from its thin package. There was no fear that Ana would run for help; no one was about. The master of the house, her son, had gone at 6 a.m. as usual, in his Porsche, threading his way through the streets of Hong Kong to his office in a high building in the Central District. And Ruby, her daughter-in-law, left promptly at 7 a.m. for her antique-and-curio show in the Penton Hotel, Kowloonside. The old chauffeur, Jim-Jan, was no threat, for he usually slept until his bell rang. Lazy fool.

Ana produced the old woman's grey dress and cape, wiggling her stubby feet into loose carpet slippers. When Ana had gone, Tu opened a lacquer box and withdrew a bracelet. As the old woman held it up to the light, doorways into yesteryear opened softly. Between the shadows she saw her husband, Lung, dressed in his cadre's best blue wool suiting; felt again the mismatch of irony and tenderness. The bracelet had been his mother's, and he had wanted her to have it on this special day—the seventh day of the first moon, when all of China celebrated birthdays. The Manchu bracelet of gold filigree embraced two dragons, whose heads met in the centre to form eyes of emeralds. Her daughter-in-law, Ruby, asked about the bracelet periodically; indeed, she sometimes came upstairs to the old woman's room and opened the lacquer box without permission.

"When we get to Canada you will have a splendid room with a view of Stanley Park. And there will be no hanging about on the stairs or the streets in Vancouver, old one. Things will be different there. You must learn to live quietly behind doors, listen to music, watch television. Learn to read."

But Tu did not want to go to this city named Vancouver or to this country, Canada. She wanted to die here, in Hong Kong. First, though, she wanted to live a while longer; enjoy sunny afternoons of mah-jongg in the park with friends, tea and laughter with old cronies in the evenings on the stairs, watch the cars and people go by, wander about in her old peasant clothes. She wanted no changes in her life.

And so she needed money so that she could run away. There was a large house in the New Territories where she could go. Her friends had talked about it: board and room was offered in exchange for working the land, and she felt she would like that again; live as she had in her younger days. She could tend the ducks, they'd told her. Well, good, because she would not be carted around like an old sack of ginseng, leaking and spilling life-treasures into the earth.

The bracelet secure on her left arm, Tu left the house on Hennessy Road and climbed into the back of the limousine. They had only driven for about twenty minutes when she yelled, "Stop! Stop here!" Jim-Jan expertly parked alongside the crumbling vendor stands of Carpenter Road. If he had private thoughts about letting the old dragon free at the edge of the Walled City, he gave no indication. Behind the vendor carts, in the shadow of the Hak Nam, one lone shop had opened for the day.

It was perfect. Her nosy daughter-in-law would never discover what she had done. It was far away from the glitz of Ruby's world! Over the noise of jets from nearby Kai Tak Airport, she yelled, "In about fifteen minutes."

The shop's door tinkled as she entered. For long minutes, no one came and her eyes wandered: a rosewood counter with a glass cabinet underneath containing inferior goods; a musty smell; a curtain leading to somewhere, spotted with grease. It began to move. "How can I help you, madam?"

Her gaze met the shrewd green eyes of the shopkeeper. Wizened and unclean, she sensed hostility beneath his extravagant politeness. Through the curtains came the simple, melodic flow of a zither. She felt displaced and fought a sense of alienation, but time was running out, and she must grasp what frugal opportunities were available. Taking a deep breath, she removed the bracelet from her arm and handed it over the counter. "How much?"

The shopkeeper, holding the bracelet up to the light, allowed it to slip away and then return. "Lovely old emeralds. Manchu?"

She nodded.

"And old-quality gold. Hmm." It was worth a great deal, much more than he had. What to do? "Leave it with me. I'll have it appraised for you, then we'll know its true value."

Complications. She frowned. Did one have jewellery praised? "No, I'll take it home with me and come back for this praising."

"I am most trustworthy."

She studied his close-together eyes, the wind-and-thunder angles of his face. "No. I'll take the bracelet home and return in two days. My chauffeur is waiting."

The shopkeeper returned the bracelet slowly, allowing the gold filigree to wander through his fingertips. Then he went to the front window, and rubbing a small portion clear, watched the old woman and her chauffeur drive off in a splendid limousine. He felt a terrible sense of loss. Something uniquely wonderful had come and gone. Money! He needed about a thousand American, or at the very least, five hundred. But who, where?

When outside shadows moved in, the Afghan withdrew a heavy, worn volume from behind the counter and allowed the pages to fall where they may: "It is advantageous to develop supporters at this time." He carefully restored the tome and sat pensively. Who did he know? Who, in all of Hong Kong's substrata could support him now? By the light of a candle, he consulted old lists of names, pages worn and brown with time. Then slowly, like a man coming out of the dark, he reached for the shop key and went out to telephone.

Calvados pushed aside the fresh Shanghai lake crab and went to answer the phone. Seldom interrupted at supper time, he viewed the call with alarm. "Well? My supper sits waiting."

"Calvados? Grant Calvados? It's me, the Afghan."

Visions of the Turkish prison formed, overlain with the face of the

Afghan, eyes and mouth out of sync...oh Lord, how had the man found him? "Where did you get my phone number? It's unlisted."

"Had it for years. Remember? You gave it to me, something about those black pearls."

"Oh yes, quite right." Damn, a botched job. The Afghan had proven unreliable, as usual. "So, what is it this time?"

In a condescending tone, the Afghan told him about the bracelet. "Manchu and worth a fortune! She'll be satisfied with a small sum, maybe two thou American, but I don't have enough to even tempt the old witch."

Calvados hesitated. Dealings with the Afghan always backfired, yet he wanted badly to take a look at that bracelet. "All right, we'll meet. Mad Monkey Bar, ten this evening."

"My leg. I can't go out on the street. Sore leg."

He was lying, of course. No doubt in trouble again. Calvados imagined the shopkeeper's spicy face, lines ingrained with dirt, the eyes of a hundred echoes. He was a fool to get involved, and poised between the risks of acceptance and curiosity, at last agreed to drop into the Afghan's shop on the edge of the City of Darkness.

"With money!"

"Of course with money, fool!"

When Tu arrived once more at the Afghan's shoop, her appearance had altered. Gone was the finery of her previous visit; now she wore shapeless black and appeared to have wandered in from the street. The shopkeeper was obliged to produce a chair so that the old witch could sit and rest. Only then did she proffer the Manchu bracelet, the heads of the dragons meeting in the centre to form eyes of emeralds.

Suddenly there was an undefined presence—a change in the texture of the shadows—and Tu stared at the man who had entered through the curtains, soft as snow in the dead of night. Soft, dark beard, old pock marks, a continental air, lean and sharp like a cruel quicksilver wind. Like her daughter-in-law, he reminded her of winter.

"Ah, friend," said the Afghan. "What do you think?"

Calvados accepted the bracelet. It reflected a prism of light, formed a pattern of loose gold coins against the wall. With a twist of one unruly eyebrow, he claimed the antiquity as his own. The Afghan must have no part of this unspeakably beautiful creation, which for some reason, was being exchanged for a paltry sum. Starting at five hundred American and working up to twelve hundred (damn but the old woman was shrewd), Calvados at last closed the deal. They watched the ancient Chinese woman limp out of the shop and down the street. Calvados considered how easy it would be to strong-arm her when the Afghan interrupted his thoughts.

"We'll sell it at once, and I'll claim only a half." The shopkeeper ignited a stubby candle which defined his face ghoulishly.

"A half? What? You said nothing about this when we met last night, and you've put up nothing!"

"A half. Finder's fee."

"Finder's fee be damned! I got you out of a predicament."

"Either half or the cops will be most interested in your phone number, from which they can get your address easy enough. Come, Calvados. Be reasonable. I'm being most generous in giving you half."

When Calvados crashed the money box into the shopkeeper's skull, it broke open and coins flooded the counter and floor. Even so, he could tell at a glance that the Afghan was dead. Then the evening developed as thrice before, with the elimination of fingerprints and every trace of his presence. Bending over to snuff the candle, his eyes found a worn photograph tacked to the wall, a sunny moment dissected from its sombre background: a young boy and an elderly woman in the traditional garb of Afghani peasants. And he remembered the old Chinese woman. She could identify him. He tried to recall if the Afghan had used his name, but he could not. Damnation, what to do? He gazed beyond the window onto the darkening streets.

Dressed casually in cotton slacks, sandals, and an embroidered barong tagalog, Calvados jumped from the tram part way down Des Voeux Road and climbed a hundred or so stairs up a narrow pedestrian lane that led to Cat Street. For long hours, down the domino of days, he searched the streets for the old woman. He did not think she was a user of the pipe, yet obviously a wanderer and possibly a player of mah-jongg. And while she might never divulge his description as the man in the Afghan's shop, the newspapers were asking for information. He could not chance a return to prison; life held so many delights. He liked to walk among his treasures obliquely, posing choices: should the spare elegance of the Ming be here, or there; should the yin and yang of the jade chess set be under the light; should the gold of the Manchu filigree bracelet lie uncoiled or be fastened to expose the dragon's heads?

On the fifth day of his hunt, at the hour of the dog, he found the old woman in a small park on Magazine Gap Road. He was looking down from the top of the peak out onto the harbour when his eyes swept the picnic tables and penetrated a group of elderly Chinese women playing mah-jongg. But by the time he came down from the peak, they had gone. Cursing his luck, he spent several days casing the park, to no avail.

And then one morning, while inspecting the contents of a jade-traders shop on Carnarvon Road in Kowloon, she brushed past like a ghostly wind from yesterday.

"Jo sun, my friend."

Startled, he dropped the *Hong Kong Times*. Bending to retrieve the newspaper gave him time for composure. "Do we know each other?" he asked innocently.

"Hai. Winter man who praised my Manchu bracelet."

He felt his life slip away, abandoned like a bad play. "How nice to see you again. Shall we go somewhere and have tea? My car is just around the corner."

"We shall walk," She announced decisively.

She wore the black, oily cloth of Cantonese coolie women, and yet the Afghan had said that she had a chauffeur; a contradiction that introduced speculation. They passed a couple of hotels, several shops, turned a corner, and approached an open-air market. Hardly the place he would have chosen. They sat at a bench with bowls of tea, and for a long while said nothing. Finally, she broke the silence with an astounding statement:

"Bracelet. Need it back now."

When she parted her palms, a cigarette dangled from her fingertips. "Um goy. When fields jade green with young rice, my husband give the bracelet to me. So it is recorded in our Book of Generations. He is dead but his spirit return and say, 'Oh, Tu, where is Manchu bracelet?' And so you see, I must have once more."

Calvados studied her over the rim of his tea bowl. "I believe the shop-keeper sold it."

"Then get it back for me, winter man."

"I can try. How much are you willing to pay?"

She rolled up one sleeve and snapped an elastic band. "See? No money now. Gone to duck farm where I make new home."

"New home?"

"I am not going to this new country with my son and daughter-in-law. I stay here close to where I come from."

Calvados wandered mentally, like a wolf. She would soon be alone. "When are they going?"

"Six days from today."

Six days. Would he dare wait so long? "Surely you understand that you can't claim the bracelet as your own once you have sold it. You will need money, lots of it." He idly watched her, tried to read her thoughts. "Why don't you return to the Afghan's shop and find out who he sold it to?"

"The Afghan is dead."

Her statement sat on the air, malignant against the cries of the vendors. The old dragon had wisdom and strength, and Calvados suspected she knew he possessed the bracelet and had killed the Afghan. The perception came together like a network of nightmares and confirmed all of his earlier fears. "Yet you got paid. A deal is a deal."

She refilled her tea bowl, spat onto the ground, and drank noisily. Her third cigarette burned away in her fingertips. "We can bury in us wordless crimes, winter man."

Damnation! He stared around assessing the crowd, the possibilities for accidents. The bench they were sitting on, it could tip... Suddenly she got up and walked away, through the open-air market, and out onto the street. A block behind, he trailed her all the way to the Star Ferry Terminal. Drifts of mist mingled with tropical scents as she disappeared into the second class entrance.

For several days he went nowhere and hugged the walls of his home—the Emperor of Darkness Temple. He touched a taper to the candles after two days, the light mushrooming out of the dark, and prowled walls hung with fourteenth-century scrolls. At dark time, he opened the windows to insects and birds, allowing them the freedom of the temple hallways.

As he was about to retire, the fax announced that a buyer would be stopping by. At midnight, Emir-al-Omer, Prince of Princes, rang the great bell and was admitted to the temple. Calvados descended to the entranceway and conducted his exalted guest to the House of Harmony, a showroom nestled behind secret panels, where they trod softly past the wonders of the ages.

"The ivory is most elegant." The Emir spoke with an Oxford-English accent. "And yet..." He paused before an ornamental green jade table screen from the Ch'ien Lung period, then passed on, touching the Kuan Yin, Goddess of Mercy, on the forehead. Suddenly, his white robe rippled to a halt as he spotted the Manchu bracelet, the gold filigree dragons shimmering in the half-light. Seeking permission, he lifted it to his arm and clasped it lovingly.

"The price is high," explained Calvados, fighting a sense of reluctance.

"No matter, I must have it, old chap."

To celebrate the deal, Calvados prepared Peking duck cooked five ways, the meal beginning and ending with fine dragon-well tea. A servant came to fetch the Emir at three in the morning, and later, as he was drifting off to sleep, Calvados fancied he heard the roar of the Emir's private plane as it dipped in a salute over the cloud-enshrouded temple.

Six days had now passed, and the old dragon's family would be departing for their new land. His role as predator would be reinstated, her role as victim no longer like an iridescent slick on water. He was relieved that the bracelet was not now in his possession, although he knew he would miss the emeralds, glowing like vigil lights in the semi-darkness. For a time he watched a cloud formation beyond the window, an old woman's head with watching eyes of striated grey. Witches, dragons. Peking duck. It all mingled in one hideous dream.

Determination his predominant emotion, Calvados hunted the streets of Hong Kong with renewed purpose. The following afternoon he spotted a thought-provoking limousine while driving through Causeway Bay into the Wanchai District. Because the sun was playing on the car windows he missed fine details, but discerned a European woman driving with an elderly Chinese beside her, a man with a chauffeur's cap in the rear. Twice around the block and he was rewarded with a parking spot in front of the Golden Kat Bar with Muzak. As the limo cruised by, he got an excellent view of the occupants: the old dragon up front beside the driver, who was a severe-looking white woman. Riding in the back was an elderly Chinese man, his chauffeur's cap askew.

The Golden Kat's muzak was out of order, the place stuffed with sailors on leave. Calvados edged into a seat at the rosewood bar and ordered a Guinness. Taking a long pull of his drink, he searched for answers. The old dragon's limo needed a wash, the woman driving hardly the chauffeur type. And staring out of the window, hunched up with dead eyes, the original chauffeur in repose.

Dead eyes. On the cross-harbour run, on buses at festivals, in the Hak Nam. Everywhere. When last he visited his mother in the Walled City, they'd gone to a den and passed the day chasing the dragon. Did the old chauffeur who once drove for the family now belong to the world of yen?

Calvados took the Carpenter Road approach into the Hak Nam, City of Darkness. His presence was immediately noted by the roof watchers, who signalled that he could pass on. Wearing rubber boots against the foulness of the narrow laneways and avoiding apertures, he nodded to old hags and clots of children, and safely reached a doorway leading down watery steps to an opium den. Cots, stacked one above the other, were all occupied. The attendant was perhaps forty, wearing a grey smock and sunglasses. He had tiny, pointed, catlike ears.

"An ex-chauffeur come here?" Calvados asked, handing the man an American five.

"Hai. Used to come Saturday, now every night. Employers leave for Canada and pension him off. Is named Jim-Jan."

"He get to keep the family limo?"

"Hai, but try to sell because can't buy gas."

"He here now?"

The smocked cat's hand made itself visible; Calvados parted with another five. Through the cloying half-light, he was led to the inert form of the ex-chauffeur, a screw of toilet paper, tinfoil and cardboard funnel lay beside him. Not even a decent pipe, thought Calvados absently.

"Somebody come for him? An elderly Chinese woman and a European woman, maybe?"

The den keeper consulted his Rolex watch. "Will be here in three hour."

"A long time to wait. Tung Tau Chuen side?"

The attendant shrugged. A heavy sweetness lay in pockets. To one not participating, the atmosphere was mortifying. For a while Calvados wandered amongst the peaceful forms, deriving a curious satisfaction. His own flirtation with the world of yen was one of choice, not of habit. Yet life was complex and harsh, and there were blank periods when he suspected the he, too, had succumbed. There were two women, side by side, obviously users of low-grade opium, and he thrust the image of his mother aside, back into that subterranean cavern of iniquity.

He made his way out and stood in a narrow, filthy walkway that led through the labyrinth of horrors known as the Walled City. What appeared to be the plane from Saigon was on approach overhead, about to land at Kai Tak. Calvados searched the skyline for the rooftop gang, the 14K boys who controlled the many illegal drug operations within the City of Darkness.

"You want missee white? Red chicken? Smokee?"

"Not today. Is Hank around? Got business with him."

A hand claimed an American five, and before Calvados reached the crumbling vendor stands of Carpenter Road, a Chinese youth jumped from a tin hut and blocked his path.

"You want me?"

Colour, odour, and sound ran together in the heat of the sun. The Walled City was a melting pot. "Yes. Follow me and we'll talk."

"Talk? Want none with you, man." The kid, maybe about twenty, was dressed in designer jeans, gold chains, and a silk shirt that reeked of the odour of the dark city. He had a thin, concave face and a reflexive smile that didn't reach the eyes. "Don't shit me, man."

"Got a job for you. It'll pay well."

"You owe me for last time."

"So? I'll add that on." Damn but the kid had a memory like a hooker after her dough. The devil had been the kid's tutor and mentor, and while Calvados could identify with such logic, seeing it in others repelled him.

"Okay. I take one more chance on you."

Calvados waited in the shadows for the old dragon, a sort of farewell to a woman who had lived with passion, who fought for her independence. Too bad she'd seen him in the Afghan's shop.

She came at last with her servant in tow, a middle-aged, sour-faced European woman in a cape. They parked the muddy limo and edged into the darkness bordering the craggy silhouette of the Hak Nam, the old woman stumbling a bit on tired feet.

And without thinking, without any reasoning at all, Calvados sprang from his car and ran after her. "Wait! I want to talk! Wait!"

Turning, she held a hand above her eyes and stared. "It's you, winter man."

"Yes. I—you don't want to go in there today. Not today."

She studied his physiognomy, stark against the light and shadow. "So. The winter man has been plotting. Go and conduct your affairs while Tu expands her destiny."

Calvados watched them enter the City of Darkness, the servant a nodular cape swaying on two skinny poles. It would be something thrown from a rooftop, most likely.

Damp with exhaustion, tasting the bitterness of regret, he drove away and parked near the sea. Far out, patched sails beat against the skyline. It was the first hour. He felt totally reduced. She had entered his sphere of awareness by her knowing, by her nobility, and in a curious reversal of character, she had become the champion.

The Duke

by Eric Wright

Since he was born in England, it's not surprising that Eric Wright's "The Duke" shares the claustrophobic, brooding qualities of Gothic English novels of the nineteenth century. Its evil lurks in an isolated landscape, finding fertile ground in the souls of men and women who spend too much time with too little company. It's inspired by Eric's own experiences as a fishing guide in northern Manitoba following his emigration to Canada. It also reveals a dark side that doesn't always surface in his longer works.

Creator of the acclaimed Charlie Salter novels and a four-time winner of the Crime Writers of Canada's Arthur Ellis Award (for which this story was nominated in 1992), Eric is also the author of the best-selling memoir *Always Give a Penny to a Blind Man*.

After half a lifetime of not being very much at home in the world, Duke Luscombe had finally found exactly the right job. He was a cook, trained in Montréal by a catering company to run the kitchen of a construction camp. The training could not have been very extensive: the Duke could cook about twenty different menus, though the same vegetables appeared on most of them, but because some of the items, like steaks and chops, were offered at least once a week, and because there was a roast or a boiled ham every Sunday, some of the menus, like pork tenderloin, appeared only once a month, giving the Duke's repertoire an appearance of being much bigger than it really was. But his skills matched the needs of the men. They wanted soup, and then meat, in some form, every night, and while they were prepared to eat canned fruit for dessert occasionally, most nights they wanted pie, with ice cream. The soups were shipped in from Montréal, in drums, and the pies were made from dough prepared in Montréal and from huge cans of pie filling. The Duke had printed instructions for the preparation of every meat dish, so the best test of his skill came at breakfast, where his bacon was crisp and his eggs done to order.

By the time I came to the camp the Duke was well established. He had command of a dining room serving the foremen, of whom there were about twenty, including the timekeepers, the men who recorded the labour and materials used on each contract. Even a kitchen this small called for two cooks, but the Duke did it all with some help from a couple of Ojibwa girls who came in from the Indian camp down by the railway tracks. There had once been another cook before I arrived, but he had only stayed a month. The Duke had complained in head-shaking fashion from the day he arrived about the "goddam useless bum" that Montréal had sent him, and at the end of the month the new man was gone. When the foremen appeared for breakfast one morning, the Duke told them he had put his assistant on the train and told him not to stop until he got to Montréal. "He was just under my feet all the time," the Duke said. "Help like that I don't need. And if the Montréal office don't like it, they can find someone else to replace me."

The new man had tried to get the foremen to hear his side of the story when it became obvious that the Duke intended to get rid of him, but the prime concern of the men in the dining room was that the Duke not be upset. All of them had worked on jobs where one day the cook had been too drunk to make breakfast, or had gone berserk with a knife, and they could tolerate the knowledge of the Duke's unfairness for the sake of their food. No one was surprised when the assistant left. And presumably the Montréal office was happy with the saving in wages.

The Duke got up at 5:00 to pick up the Indian girls. Breakfast had to be ready by 7:00 for a work crew who started at 7:30. Lunch was soup, cold cuts with some kind of vegetables, and pie. Around 3:00, the Duke began on the supper, which had to be ready at 5:30. He closed the dining room at 7:30 and ate his own supper—usually a steak—and the girls helped themselves to what was left over from the night's menu. He waited, then, until they had cleaned up the kitchen, and drove them back to town. The Duke took responsibility for more than their transportation. While they worked in his kitchen they might as well have been in a convent. There were very few women around that far north and inevitably, since all the foremen had pickup trucks, someone would have offered them a ride home, but the Duke watched closely for any suggestion of that and cut it off immediately. One of the men said that he got the impression that the chief sin that the short-lived assistant had committed was nothing to do with the work, but that he had cast his eye on one of the girls, and perhaps even made a suggestive remark to the Duke.

When he returned from driving the girls to their camp, the Duke went to the beer parlour, drank two beers, and went to bed by ten. On Sundays, he cooked a big meal at noon, usually a roast, or—a speciality of the catering company—a New England Boiled Dinner, the only place I have ever seen it on a menu, then at five, laid out a cold supper of platters of boiled eggs, cold meats, pickles, and canned salmon, which the girls served while he looked on, dressed in his best clothes, thus proclaiming that he was not there to work, although there was no question of absenting himself while anyone was in the dining room. He worked six fourteen-hour days, and on Sundays he worked for six hours and watched for three. On Sunday afternoons, before the supper buffet was set out, he joined in the poker game that had been going since Friday night, dropping out when he had won or lost ten dollars, about a day's pay at that time. He usually lost and seemed in this way to be paying his dues. Apart from the weekly poker game, he relaxed by sitting at the foremen's table in the beer parlour, listening to the talk and contributing only confirmatory remarks; he went to the army cinema two days a week; and spent a lot of time looking after his clothes. He was not a dandy, but he prided himself on his ironing, even doing a shirt for one of us for a special reason, to have a clean one when we went to Winnipeg, for example. The Duke never went to town: we understood he preferred to save up his leave and take it in one lump when the contract was finished, but I believe that more important was his distaste for having anyone in his kitchen.

He had no friends. He referred occasionally to a sister in Montréal to whom he sent money to spend on her children, but he never seemed to hear from her. He avoided intimacy, seeming to require only as much companionship as he found at the foremen's table. At first I thought him simply intellectually disadvantaged, as they say now. His obsessive behaviour was something I had come across before when a simple person has been given a responsibility that exactly suits his capabilities—running a dishwasher, say—and blossoms in pride and then becomes fiercely protective of the area he has learned to control. Then I realized that this was an arid understanding of him, and I decided then that he was by nature a monk, a monk who had found his work and his monastery. He burned with a low flame in all other areas; as far as we knew, he was uninterested in sexual matters except to understand that his girls had to be protected. In his spare time he read—westerns, hundreds of them, again and again, as if the West was the paradise it seems to a ten year old, and yet, I think, he had already found his Eden in the place where the rest of us saved up to escape. He was a happy man.

Until Paddy Vernon came along.

Vernon was a plumbing foreman who took over in the middle of the job from a man who refused to come back off leave. He was a gregarious fellow who made it clear immediately that he was used to being regarded as the life of the party. Always joking, he was, mostly practical. I didn't know so clearly then that teasing is a form of cruelty. Vernon was a born tease, and anyone could see right away that the Duke was a natural butt for someone like Paddy Vernon.

The Duke was very vulnerable, of course. He took pride, not in being a chef, but in being able to do his job exactly as he had been taught. If anyone complained, he would taste a morsel of whatever they found fault with, nod, and say, "That's the way it's supposed to taste. Take your complaint to Montréal." Very occasionally, he would acknowledge a problem for which he was responsible. Then he would shake his head. "That's not the way it's supposed to taste," he would say, not apologetically, but in a puzzled way, and offer to cook something else to make up. For the rest of the meal he would try to think his way back over the course of the preparation until he found the point, where, say, too much salt had been added, questioning the Indian girls, solving the puzzle then and reporting back to the diner, who had by now lost interest, "I'd put the salt in, but there was a power failure this morning, remember, when the digger cut the cable, so when the light came back on I saw the salt still out—I always put it away right after I use it—and I must have thought I hadn't put it in yet. That was what it was."

Such an error was rare and always caused by an outside factor. By never allowing anyone into his kitchen space, the Duke kept such factors to a minimum. After the departure of the sole assistant cook, no one was ever allowed into the kitchen area except the two Indian girls to stand behind the steam table and serve. When the place was cleaned up after a meal, the Duke snapped the locks—he kept locks on all the cupboards, including the walk-in freezer. It was obsessive behaviour, of course: he guarded his territory with the passion of a man who had never owned a territory before.

In the way of such things, we affected a pride in him, gave him an "interesting" status. "Old Duke doesn't allow anyone behind that counter," we would tell the surprised newcomer who had found his way barred wordlessly by the Duke. We did the same thing with the secret that everyone felt must lie at the centre of his life. The Duke gave us no context in which to understand him, no past, no family history, no existence outside the camp, and the men used to wonder what he was concealing. On the whole, the reasons men went that far north to work were easy to find. For most in those days, it was money, because the skilled tradesmen could earn three times what they earned in town and keep most of it. Alcoholism was another big reason; the North was the last stop for men who had used up their welcome in town. There were several men on the run from alimony payments, there were a handful of romantics in love with the idea of the North, and there was at least one with a broken heart. The Duke fit none of these categories: he wasn't saving to go back home or on the run. He was home, but not seeing this we assumed he had an interesting secret. "People don't come up to a place like this to cook without some good reason," Tiny Williams, the general superintendent said, and we nodded solemnly until the Duke began to acquire a touch of Conradian mystery which satisfied our need to mythicize him by failing to answer our questions. Personally, even at the time I was skeptical of this enlargement of the Duke's mysteriousness, seeing it as springing more from his customers' desire to make him interesting than from anything in him, but I knew better than to say so.

Paddy Vernon didn't. He was looking for a target as soon as he arrived. He began with a young timekeeper from Newfoundland, telling him tall stories to test his credulity in front of the other foremen. He also constructed an elaborate running joke at the boy's expense, pretending the boy was meeting civilization for the first time, though there can be nothing in Newfoundland as barren as that construction camp. "Pass me the marmalade, Hector," he would say. "That's the orange stuff in the jar there." It was mild and feeble stuff, and Hector accepted it mildly as the proper due of the youngest man in the room, and it only lasted until Vernon saw that his real target had to be the Duke.

He started with a string of jokes about camp cooks—the manure-in-the-pumpkin pie joke was typical. The Duke listened carefully, not to the words, it seemed to me, but to the cadences of Vernon's sentences. I think he had no sense of humour whatever, but he had watched and listened to men making jokes, and laughing at them, and learned to chime in with a smile to avoid being noticed. If the joke was genuinely funny, enough to catch the other listeners by surprise, then the Duke would come in late with his response, as if he had just seen it. Usually, though, he could time his laugh to respond to the climax he could feel in the rhythm of the speaker's words. "Ha!" he would bark, once, loudly, then, "You want beans?" or more eggs, or toast.

Vernon made me nervous when he started to tease the Duke, because none of us was sure then what lay behind the cook's facade, what sensitive area might not explode into violence, a not uncommon occurrence in that place. Fights happened for trivial reasons. But Vernon found the Duke irresistible, and pretty soon he had progressed from jokes about cooks to more active horseplay. Very early the two men had a small confrontation over territory. Vernon wandered behind the steam table for the first time to help himself to some corn, but as he dipped his spoon into the well, the Duke pushed the lid across to close off the reservoir, trapping Vernon's spoon against the edge. Vernon looked up, genuinely surprised, as the Duke pointed to the notice prohibiting non-authorized personnel (everyone except the Duke and his girls) behind the counter. He lifted the lid of the well so that Vernon could retrieve the spoon, and Paddy looked around at us to see if we found it as ridiculous as he was beginning to, but so sacred was the Duke's area by now that I think we were shocked to find Vernon in it, and waited for him to come away. Vernon saw that it was something he didn't understand and decided to try it for laughs. He read the notice again, jumped back in alarm, and made a business of running out of the Duke's area before he could be caught, one hand behind him to protect him from being spanked. Some of the men smiled politely, but Vernon was left looking foolish by the lack of a real supporting laugh. I could see he didn't like that.

So he tried to find a space on the edge of the Duke's territory where he could mock the very idea of a territory sacred to the cook. He would keep his eye on the Duke, and when the cook disappeared for a few minutes, as he did occasionally to fetch supplies, Vernon would race round the counter and help himself to something he didn't want, then run back before or as the Duke reappeared. The point, of course, was to get almost caught by the Duke.

The Duke appeared to understand what Vernon was up to and rather neatly, I thought, turned the joke against Vernon. Now and again he would return immediately, before the door had swung closed, making Vernon hurl himself across the end of the counter to get back without being "caught." "Ha!" the Duke said, thus turning Vernon's tease into a kind of "What's the time, Mr. Wolf" game for grown-ups, and Vernon had to try something else. Once he took our breath away by locking the Duke in his own freezer, a large walk-in locker by the exit where the cook kept all the meat and fresh (frozen) milk and bread. It was hardly necessary for eight months of the year; for part of that time it was probably warmer in the freezer than it was outside, but its main function was security. It was one of the Duke's two lockable storage areas; the other held all the canned goods. They were locked, not simply because the Duke was responsible for the inventory but because they were his. We had a little hot plate in the bunkhouse, a fry pan, a kettle, and a coffee pot, and we could make ourselves a fried-egg sandwich late at night, during the poker game. The Duke supplied us with everything we needed; we only had to ask. But we did have to ask because he would hand over the key to the stores to no one.

The Duke fetched what we wanted.

One day at suppertime, Paddy Vernon asked if for once he could have a little fresh milk in his coffee. Normally the fresh (frozen) milk was kept for special purposes because it was expensive to ship and bulky to store, and we regularly drank Carnation in our coffee. But this time the Duke looked at the ceiling for advice, nodded, unlocked the freezer, and disappeared inside. Vernon was over the counter in one jump and had the door slammed in a second. The idea, I guess, was to wait until the cook was good and chilly, then let him out, but the Duke was out before Vernon got back to his chair. There's a safety lock on those doors; you can't get locked in accidentally, and once more, the joke was on Vernon as the Duke shouted "Ha!" and went back to work.

After that Vernon seemed more or less to give up on the Duke, concentrating on leaving two-dollar bills in the urinals to see who would pick them up, that kind of thing. I say "seemed" because, in fact, he was working on a major joke.

All the elements are now in place; you can write the rest of the story yourself. You must know what comes next. Inevitably Paddy Vernon will have to construct a practical joke involving the Duke's territory, and the heart of that territory, the freezer. Inevitably, too, given the safety mechanism of the freezer door, Paddy Vernon will have the bright idea of getting inside the freezer to surprise the hell out of the Duke when he opens the door. How Vernon does it is irrelevant. Say he goes to town and gets hold of some duplicate freezer keys from a pal in Winnipeg. Anything will do. Now you have to think of a way to give Vernon an audience when he leaps out on the Duke. Make it Sunday at suppertime, when the Duke will not have had to use the freezer for an hour or two. Then set up one of the men to suggest to the Duke that he check his freezer because there was a power failure that afternoon. Will that do?

The important thing is to get all the men assembled in the dining room, waiting for the Duke to arrive and open the door.

Make the Duke disappear after lunch, forgoing the poker game. At this point, you will have to put in the information that one of the timekeepers who prefers the Duke to Vernon has tipped off the cook. Probably the boy from Newfoundland. At any rate, at suppertime, after they have waited long enough, the timekeeper tells them that the Duke knows about the joke and is probably not coming. But why hasn't Vernon already let himself out? Because, someone points out, there is a three-inch nail threaded through the flange of the handle making it impossible to turn. Is Vernon dead, if not of cold, then, of suffocation? Is this going to be the Duke's revenge? I don't think it will do. He's only been inside a couple of hours at most and there's plenty of air for that long.

Someone pulls out the nail, but the door is still locked, so they smash the lock and the door swings slowly open and a frozen, much chastened Vernon stumbles out. Or better, he faints. Yes, because then he has to be taken to the camp hospital, giving time to discover that the Duke left on the afternoon train. This seems excessive behaviour. Was the violation of his territory that important?

Such seems to be the case until Vernon recovers and leads them back to the freezer where he spent two hours in the company of that other cook who had been there for three months.

Leave the rest to the reader.

And Then He Sings

by Stan Rogal

How dark can noir get? Here's an urban-Gothic thriller from one of Canada's prominent literary figures that makes vampires superfluous. Stan Rogal was born in Vancouver but has lived in Toronto for thirteen years. A prolific author, his stories have appeared in such magazines as *The Fiddlehead, Grain, Blood & Aphorisms, The New Quartely* and *Prairie Fire*. He has published six books of poetry, two collections of short stories, and two novels: *The Long Drive Home* and *Bafflegab*, both published by Insomniac Press. In addition to his own writing, Stan spent ten years actively promoting the work of other writers as organizer of the popular Idler Pub Reading Series in Toronto.

Late night or early morning, depending on your view. The sky is overcast and the rain continues to fall in waves. It's been this way for hours, pounding down without the accompanying thunder and fork-flashed lightning. Unusual for the city, rain normally lasting twenty minutes or so, then blowing through. The lake making a difference; the patterns of wind coming and going from the States. One of those mid-September soaking rains that twists and swirls in the breeze, playing havoc with hats, hemlines, and umbrellas. Not that Mitchell cares at the moment. Maybe he doesn't even notice. At any rate, he sits slumped at the base of an ornamental street lamp, his body pulsing, ragged in the rain-sheeted glow, a whiskey bottle pressed between his thighs, his fingers curled around the neck, the cap long since gone, its function grown useless alongside Mitchell's present resolution—to drink himself numb.

He appears comfortable enough—if not content—wallowing in his misery. There had been tears earlier, now erased by the driving rain, and sobs have made way for deep breaths that occasionally catch in his throat, producing guttural sounds that might appear non-human if not for the fact of his bodily presence jerking in sync with the auditory punctuations.

Except for the bottle and the man's obvious distress, a passerby might conclude: *Not smart enough to get in out of the rain*. Or if he was a wino, a bum, might offer: *Nowhere else to go*. Mitchell's physical appearance and personal hygiene seem to counter such remarks. He is early-to-mid thirties, curly-haired, clean-cut and shaved, wearing a dark-green windbreaker, khaki Dockers, and shod in an expensive pair of brown Florsheim brogues. He hoists the bottle to his lips and drinks. Creeping up beside him, a voice catches him rubbing water from his eyes with the heel of a hand. He doesn't startle. He's too far into his cups to startle.

"Hey, Mr. Lonely. Why so blue?"

Mitchell twists his head to see a young woman leaning a forearm against the lamppost. She has a thin body, made thinner with the weight of rain pasting her light print shift to her skin. Mitchell can make out the panty lines and the flow of elasticized cotton cupping the woman's breasts and circling her ribs to the back. Even through the tearful whiskey haze, he can discern the jut of nipples perked by the cool, evening air. She has short-cropped blonde hair and a slash of red that is her mouth. She wears a pair of blue pumps; a small, matching blue purse hangs from a strap at her wrist.

Pretty, he thinks, at the same time recognizing that he may be in no condition to judge.

"Can I join you, or is this a party for one?" She reaches for the bottle and Mitchell hands it over, watching as she trickles the whiskey through a tight circle in her lips, clenching her eyes and tonguing the few drops that settle in the corners of her mouth. "Mmm, warm. Just the thing." She collapses beside him, tucking her feet beneath her haunches.

Mitchell just stares, unsure of what to say or if he should say anything. Nothing coming to mind, he shifts his gaze toward the pavement in front of him. His shoes are in the gutter, and he can see the rainwater swell over and around them, first one shoe then the other.

"Nice shoes," she says. "Are they waterproof?" She grins and takes another hit of whiskey.

Mitchell remains fixed. He wonders how old the woman is. Could be as old as eighteen or nineteen, as young as fifteen or sixteen. Hard to tell. Her confident manner, her ease, the way she carries herself, all lean toward a maturity. And her body—she has what must be described as a "figure." The thin ones though, hard to tell age-wise for sure.

"So, you wanna talk or you don't wanna talk?" The woman cocks her head one side to the other, as if the space around divided equally yes or no. She swipes a raindrop from her nose with a finger and sniffs.

"No." The word situates in his throat, hardly daring to exit his mouth. He must notice and begins again. "I mean, no, they're not waterproof."

"Maybe you shouldn't stick 'em in the gutter, then."

Mitchell hesitates, then succeeds in shuffling both feet forward. The woman laughs.

"That's great! Now, they'll only get run over by a car."

Mitchell checks the street. It has to be one or two o'clock in the morning, by his reckoning, and traffic is scarce, the rare vehicle keeping close to the centre lines. He takes the bottle, tips his head, and swallows.

"You lose your best friend or what?"

"Something like that."

"Girlfriend?"

"Something like that."

"*Something like that,*" she mimics, though not harshly. She appears determined not to be sucked into Mitchell's funk, and he grins slightly, as if appreciating her effort, her attitude.

"She's married. But I loved her. Turns out, she didn't love me."

"Drag. What happened?" She guides his hand with the bottle to her face and sips. He feels her chin nudge a finger. *An accident?* he wonders, *or...*

"I met her a couple of weeks ago at a conference. We both work in computer software. We talked, later we had drinks together, grabbed dinner at an Italian place. She ended up at my apartment. We went to bed, you know, whatever. Afterwards, asked me to call her a cab."

"And you said, *'Okay—you're a cab!'*" The woman shoves her face out, revealing tiny white teeth through her smile. Mitchell goes on like he hasn't heard.

"I told her I wanted to see her again and she said it might be best if we didn't. Said it wouldn't work out in the long run, her being married and kids and older than me. Said it was fun and nice, but that's all. I asked if I could phone, and she said it's not a good idea." Mitchell gives his head a shake.

"'Course, I knew her name and I knew where she worked. Wasn't far from me, actually. I called her everyday for a week; left her messages on e-mail. I kept telling her how much I missed her; how special that night had been for me; how I had to see her again. She finally agreed and came over. When she left, she said that was the last time; she couldn't handle an affair. I told her I wanted more than an affair. I told her I loved her; I wanted to be with her. She just turned and left.

"I found her home phone number and address in the directory. I called her, but she wouldn't talk to me. I kept calling her. If her husband answered, I'd say, 'sorry,' and hang up. I'd go over to her house and watch her through the windows, from across the street. I'd drop in where she worked, over lunch. She told me to leave her alone or she'd report me to the police. But what could I do? She gave me no choice."

"Sounds like you had it pretty bad."

"Mmm. Then yesterday I called, and she asked me to come over tonight."

"To her place?"

"Yeah. Her husband was out of town. The kids were away. She said it would be good if we talked. Told me she'd make dinner. Be there at nine."

"So, you went."

"I got there at nine on the dot. I didn't want to put her off by showing up too early or too late, though I can tell you, it was killing me having to wait for the hours to pass."

"I bet." The woman huddles her knees with her arms, giving her total attention to Mitchell's story.

"We were in the kitchen. She poured two drinks. I could see she was nervous. Why wouldn't she be, her own house and all, me there and her husband and kids not around? I figure she must've started drinking early on. She was a bit drunk. She slurred her words and kept dropping things: spoons, dish towels, food, whatever. She handed me my drink. I noticed a sprinkle of white powder on the lip of the glass. I asked, what's this? Nothing, she said, then went on to tell me again why we couldn't see each other anymore; why tonight was it. She was going to make me understand; she was going to feed me dinner, and then I'd have to leave. *Kaput, fini.*"

"Let me get this straight. She invites you over to her house, right? I mean, what's that all about? She must've figured you'd want more than just dinner, eh? She must've wanted more, too, you know what I mean?" The woman gives a laugh that can only be described as sexually charged in a *nudge-nudge, wink-wink* kind of way. "Huh?"

"I guess. Meanwhile, she's going on and on, and I'm fingering this white powder, and I stop her and ask again, what is it? And she starts to get into a real panic and shouts at me that I'm harassing her and stalking her, and she's going to call the police, and if her husband knew he'd kill me, and so on, and I ask her again in a very direct way—what is this white powder on my glass? I move toward her, real slow-like, backing her up against the sink. I grab her arm, and she looks at me like I'm the devil himself come to punish her for her sins, and I think she's about ready to scream, so I put my glass to her mouth, not like a threat so much, just as to let her know—"

"Something could happen."

"Yeah. And I ask her one more time—what is this stuff? Well, her voice gets all kind of soft and squeaky, and she has trouble getting the words out. Spice, she says, for the sauce. I look over her shoulder on the counter and there's this little cotton bag with no name on it, and it hits me that she planned to poison me."

"Wow! That's wild."

"Sure. Anyway, I smash the glass on the floor and ask her, 'why did you want to do that?' And she freaks out, I guess, 'cause she grabs a knife and tries to stab me with it."

"What did you do?"

"I didn't have to do much. She was too drunk and scared. I just took it off her, and she dropped to her knees, crying and sputtering words—I don't know what, I'm a little crazy myself at this point. I remember I stroked her hair and said, I love you, I love you. She pulled away from me, though, and crawled across the floor, mumbling something about me being obsessed or obsessive."

"Love is obsessive."

Mitchell faced the young woman. "You see, you understand. It's exactly what I told her: love is obsessive. Otherwise, what's the point?"

"Then what?"

"Nothing. I pulled this bottle of whiskey from the shelf, and I left. I just walked. For hours, I guess. I didn't know what else to do."

"Did you hit her?"

"I don't know. I may have. I don't remember. Everything happened so fast. It was all so strange: the house, her being drunk, her trying to poison me, the knife."

"She'd have deserved it, really," the woman drinks, "if you had hit her. She led you on. Toyed with your affections."

"Mmm."

"You loved her, yeah?"

"Yeah."

"And she led you on."

"She did lead me on, didn't she?" Mitchell drains the bottle. He stands and deposits it in a recycling bin.

"What now?" The woman looks up at the sky. The rain has stopped, and stars blink on and off as clouds race between them and the street.

"I don't know. Go home, I guess."

"Shall I walk with you?"

"Okay."

"Is it far?"

"Not very."

"Do you have anything to drink there?"

Mitchell studies the woman. He thinks he should ask something. He doesn't know what. He isn't thinking clearly. Or he had an idea for a question and now can't remember. Doesn't matter. He nods his head, yes, and the two slip up the street.

"Nice place."

"It's deceptive. From the outside, I mean, it looks smaller, dingier. At least that's what people tell me." Mitchell keeps walking toward what must be the kitchen.

The woman surveys the living room. The furnishings are modern: shelves and tables that are black and white mostly, with patches of oak. Tasteful, austere, very male, with little in the way of accessories or highlights. Vertical blinds fit the windows, no drapes, no rugs on the hardwood, the walls limited to cream colours and featuring framed monochrome prints—Ansel Adams and the like. Stereo and TV filling one wall, couch, chairs, coffee table—the basics—as if he stepped into an IKEA and ordered straight from the showroom floor. Sticking out incongruously from the rest of the decor is an old fireplace, obviously sealed over, the hearth tiled in and featuring a fake burning log display that lights up with the flick of a switch. The woman bends to turn it on, then raises her head to mantle level, where she is met by three human skulls. She runs a fingertip across each forehead and rubs the crown of the final skull delicately with her palm. Mitchell enters carrying two glasses of wine.

"I hope you like red."

"Anything, thanks." She takes a large swig and rolls her tongue. "Mmm. You're supposed to sip wine, I know, but it always seems so much tastier by the mouthful. It's like eating grapes. I can never eat them one at a time, I have to eat them by the handful." She pokes at a skull.

"What are these?" She makes a dismissive growl in her throat. "I mean, I know what they are, but why do you have them? Are they real?"

"They're real. I don't know, really. I bought the first one at an outdoor market, on a whim, I suppose. The guy selling it—he was an old guy, right? Ancient. At least he had that look about him: history and truth and authenticity—as if he'd lived through centuries and was now the God-appointed teller-of-stories. Anyway, he told me that this skull belonged to one of the daughters of the aristocracy during the French Revolution. She was decapitated along with the rest of them. Fourteen years old and reputed to be very beautiful. A soldier had fallen in love with her, one of the guards, and reportedly, he somehow managed to steal the head, replacing it with the head of a beggar girl."

"He cut off someone else's head?"

"Mmm. Apparently."

"Weird."

"I don't know. He was in love. He wanted to keep something of her—a memento."

"But her head? Wouldn't a lock of hair have done? Or a pair of underwear?" She laughs at this last remark. The woman has one of those low laughs that emanates from the chest and ends with a sort of snort that suggests a carnal quality, no matter what the subject.

"I suppose, though, it's not quite the same thing is it?" Mitchell moves on. "I bought this from another old guy. It's supposed to be of a young, East Indian prostitute who killed a client because he lifted her veil." Mitchell strokes the skull, tracing the crooked teeth with a fingernail. "This third one belonged to a girl who died in England of the Black Plague."

The woman rubs her mouth with her glass. Her lips are almost free of lipstick. "And you believe these guys that sold you the skulls were telling the truth?"

"Doesn't really matter, does it? The skulls belonged to someone. Besides, better to have an interesting lie than a boring truth."

"I guess."

"I hate to sound like a cliché, but we're both soaked to the skin. I'm going to throw on some dry clothes. I'll bring you a towel and a housecoat. Okay?" Mitchell sets his wine glass on the mantle.

She nods and takes another swallow. "The wine's warming me. And the fire." She wiggles her ass slightly at the fake logs and grins. Mitchell smiles and leaves the room.

The man returns wearing a gray pants and sweatshirt combination. He can see the woman's panties hanging from the mantle, weighted by one of the skulls. She stands near the coffee table, and he ventures toward her, the robe and towel supported in his outstretched hands. The woman sets her glass on the table, folds at the waist, and in one sure, swift motion lifts the shift and bra over her head and drops the clothing onto the floor.

Mitchell freezes. Naked, there is little difference from before, when her shift was all but invisible, soaked as it was into her flesh. True, the hips are perhaps slightly bonier, her legs are now separated into two distinct limbs: smooth, slim, and a bit bowed at the knees. There is a rich tuft of blonde hair apparent, curling from her groin, and her breasts, while not ample, portray a definite shape and form, the nipples erect amid the pink aureole.

"Would you dry me? It's okay. I'm not embarrassed."

Mitchell tosses the robe onto the couch. He unfolds the towel, spreads it across the woman's back, and pats it against her skin. He proceeds in this manner, gently massaging the towel into her flesh with his hands and fingers, down the back side of her, kneeling to dry her feet, then slowly unbending up the front, feeling her body's every rise and fall through the pale green terry cloth, ending with a deep rub of her cropped hair. He allows the towel to drop, picks up the robe and wraps her in it, the article fitting her like a blanket. Mitchell retrieves his glass, and the two sit on the couch and drink.

"Why do you collect them?" she asks. "The skulls."

"I told you. A whim."

"No way. The first one was a whim, you said so. The second one I can maybe understand—a match for the first. Okay. But to get a third one, that's collecting."

Mitchell takes a deep breath, then releases. "I...guess you're right. I don't know. Maybe..." His head drops and he crosses his hands in his lap.

"Don't be afraid. You can tell me. I mean, you've seen me naked, right?"

She hit the nail on the head, thinks Mitchell. It's like being naked—speaking of things, using the words. How can she know? How can she be so perceptive, so understanding, so comfortable, whereas with him...?

"I've never had much luck with women. In a relationship. Long term, you know? Short term, okay. A date, a few dates, but...it's like it changes after we make love. I don't know what happens, but it changes."

"You change or the women change?"

"No. The situation. The situation changes. And then the women...the woman...I don't know. For me, sex is a commitment. I thought that women felt the same. Instead...well, I'm sorry, it's just the way I've been raised. Commitment."

"So you feel that they used you?"

"No. Not that. More that they have no idea what it means to be committed. Totally committed."

"Maybe they just have a different idea than you?"

"Maybe." He blows through his lips. "Anyway, that's why I bought the skulls. I thought they might tell me something, give me a clue."

"Tell you something?"

"Not *tell* me, exactly. I just thought that who knows, maybe if I was able to hold them, study them, look at them, I might come to understand how a woman thinks." He shakes his head. "Crazy, eh?"

"Maybe. Maybe not."

Mitchell reaches out and plays with a strand of the woman's hair. "What's your name? What with my night and the rain and the booze, I forgot to ask."

The woman chuckles and crimps her nose. "Guess."

Mitchell sags. He has never been good at guessing games, whether ages or names or occupations or personalities. He was always wrong so rarely made the attempt anymore. He recalls people telling him: *Mitchell, you're a bad judge of character. That's why you get yourself into trouble so often.* He tries to conjure a recent (or perhaps not so recent, his mind shuffling madly) newspaper article he had glanced at that listed the year's top ten children's names in Canada. Or was it in North America? Then again, this woman is from another era altogether. What movies were playing twenty years ago? What was on TV? Who were the female figureheads? He draws a blank.

Jennifer? Jessica? Diana? For boys you could pretty much rely on the saints, year in and year out, but for women?

"I'll give you a hint. It starts with A."

"An A? I don't know. I...Ann?" As soon as he says it he feels ridiculous. All the names in the world beginning with A, and the only one he can come up with is the most common.

"Close," the woman beams. It is as if she understands to reward him rather than prolong his agony. *Wise beyond her years*, someone might say. "It's Anji."

"As in Anjelica? Or Angelique?" Mitchell relaxes.

"As in Anji. A-n-j-i."

"It's a pretty name." He wants to say, 'It suits you,' but refrains because he is afraid she might ask why, and he wouldn't know what to answer. He is aware that it's a phrase he is familiar with only because he has heard others use it. He would simply be parroting them, and this is a woman who allows nothing to slip by without an explanation.

Anji swings an arm over the side of the couch and feels her hand hit something. She leans and grabs hold of a guitar. She picks it up and cradles it across her chest.

"Do you play?" she asks.

"No. Someone left it here. I'm just...keeping it. Do you play?"

"A little." She strums the chords and twists one of the screws slightly. "It's pretty well tuned." Satisfied, she jumps into a song.

Mitchell listens intently. The woman has a lovely voice with a pleasant range. The song is in French, and Mitchell can understand only a word or two here and there. Something about horses, he thinks. Or hair. *Cheveux. Chevaux.* He has difficulty making out the words or the context. Likely horses, as why would anyone write such a beautiful melody about hair?

"That was terrific."

"Thanks." She returns the guitar to the floor.

"What did it mean? My French—"

"Yeah, mine too. I don't know. A friend taught it to me. She was French. That's the way I learned it."

"You didn't ask her?"

"Ha. Her English was about as good as my French. Or as rotten. Anyway, I didn't know her too long."

"What happened?"

"Don't know. She disappeared—poof!" Anji finishes her wine. "You have more?"

"Yeah, sure." He starts to rise. "Are you...are you going to stay the night?"

Anji smiles and purses her lips. She puts a hand on Mitchell's neck and cocks her head.

"You're a funny guy," she says, and levels her eyes with his.

Mitchell is in a fine mood, without a trace of hangover. Fresh from a soapy scrub in the shower, he stands at the mirror, stroking lather from his face with a new blade. There is much to be done, he thinks. To make room. Clean his closet of items he never or rarely wears, empty out a drawer or two in the dresser—this was the easy part. How much space would finally be required? How much could Anji own at her age? He'll phone a leasing company and order a panel van. But would it be large enough? He wonders where she lives. With her parents? On her own? With roommates? Is she a student, or does she work? Speaking of which, he'll have to take a few days off, for the preparations, the move, the settling-in period. He's owed holidays. What the hell—he'll take them. A week, two weeks, whatever is necessary. After all, this is a big moment. There's the marriage license. And a ceremony. Religious or Justice of the Peace? It doesn't matter to him; let her decide. Whatever she wants. Food, decorations, cake— shoot the wad. Or something small, simple, private? Mitchell thinks: there's so much he has to discover about her; her likes and dislikes. There's so much that goes on to make up a person. A lifetime, no matter how long or how short, comprised of learnings, habits, and predilections. But all this in good time (for they will have plenty of time later). Now, there was the task at hand, the basics: preparing the marriage nest. He smiles at the notion: *marriage nest*. He uses a towel to wipe the excess lather from his face, smacks and rubs his cheeks with aftershave, and gives his eyebrows a smooth. *Sharp*, he thinks, and pops his lips.

Mitchell enters the living room to find Anji dressed.

"I left you in bed," he says. "I thought you might want to sleep."

"I gotta go."

"Go? You don't have to go."

"I gotta."

"But, I've planned everything. I've worked it all out."

"Well, I've got plans, too. Did you ever think of that?"

"You're coming back though?"

Anji twisted her mouth and snorted. "No, I don't think so."

"But..." The two stand across from each other, silent for a second, as if waiting for a cue.

"Listen, I gotta go." Again, they stand silent: Anji as though expecting some word from Mitchell; Mitchell for lack of anything to say. "I was told to ask two hundred."

"Two hundred? Two hundred what?"

"Dollars."

"Who told you?"

"Bea."

"Who's Bea?"

"She's sort of my den mother. She takes care of us girls."

"She told you to ask me for two hundred dollars? For last night?"

Anji nods, like *Are you getting all this?* and *What's your problem?* and *What did you expect?* and *C'mon, chop-chop!* "She also said if you try to give me a hard time I should tell you that I'm fifteen. You understand what that means, eh?"

"Fifteen?"

"Jeezus! Yeah—you understand? I got a birth certificate and everything." She holds up her purse.

Mitchell studies the woman. He tries to imagine her without her dress: the lean, awkward legs, the bony hips, the delicate pubic hair, the firm breasts. Fifteen. Then the other image transposing, erasing: the eager mouth, the practised hands, the manner in which she initiated and controlled the act. *The act.*

"Bea said you were probably the type who carries a wallet full of cash or has a jar full of twenties put away for your retirement or a rainy day."

"Or a rainy night." It is the first time that Mitchell has made a joke or shown any sign of keeping up with events, and it amuses Anji. But the joke is actually lost on Mitchell as he is thinking *Then she was there last night, on the street.* Bea. From the beginning. Watching, assessing, plotting. And here as well, drinking wine, removing her shift, playing guitar, kissing him, stroking him, opening her legs to him. Through all of it, this faceless woman, not merely pulling strings, but maintaining an actual presence in his bed, on his skin. As now, positioned beside the couch, her feet planted solidly, and the words issuing from her lips, plain, hard, and businesslike.

"Well?" Anji shifts her hips and crosses her arms.

"Yes. I'm sorry. Excuse me. I'll just...I have to..." Mitchell turns, wanders into the bedroom and shuffles back with ten twenty-dollar bills. He hands them to Anji.

"Bea was right."

"Yeah. Bea was right." The words have nothing behind them, neither meaning nor emotion. Mitchell's mind is still elsewhere, tracing the slow dissolve of wedding cake, a tux, a white gown, furniture in a rented van, a woman's clothing hanging in his closet, a woman's scent lingering on his skin.

"I'm going," she says, raising her eyebrows when he doesn't reply, spinning on her heels, and sauntering to the door, where she stops and peeks over her shoulder. "You're lucky," she says. "I mean it. I could have robbed you, y'know? It could've been worse." She walks out, leaving Mitchell with a piece of broken film flipping over and over in his brain.

Mitchell hangs his coat on a hook, crosses the room, and flops onto the couch. He grips a plastic bag in each hand. From one bag he draws chopsticks, condiment portions, two trays of Chinese food, and a Coke. He undrapes a cardboard box from the second bag and removes the lid from the box. He fishes out an object and proceeds to unwrap its newsprint covering. From out of the layers emerges a compact, white skull. Mitchell brings the skull near his face, turning it in his hands, pondering its shape, its heft. He rubs his chin and cheek along the smooth bone; he takes two fingers and slips them deeply into each hole, taking time to circle the rims as he withdraws. He kisses the lipless mouth. Finally, he places the skull on the table and tears the cardboard covers from the food containers. He leans back, still focusing his vision on the skull. He reaches over the couch arm, retrieves the guitar and tips his head through the strap, supporting the instrument in his lap.

"Alas," he whispers. "Poor Yorick."

He plays a few chords, his fingers plucking the strings surely, with apparent ease and confidence; the tune light, melodious, and ancient sounding. A lilt, perhaps; perhaps a madrigal. It goes on like this: four bars, eight bars, sixteen bars; his body gently rocking, his eyes half-shut; biding his time, awaiting the final beat with a tilt of his head, a breath.

And then he sings.

After Due Reflection

by Mary Jane Maffini

Mary Jane Maffini knows that sometimes noir can be about sympathetic characters doing ill to the richly deserving. You can take that to the bank. A 1999 double-nominee for the Crime Writers of Canada Arthur Ellis Awards, *Speak Ill of the Dead* was also shortlisted for the Best First Novel and "Kicking the Habit" for the Best Short Story. In 1995 Mary Jane won the Best Short Story Arthur for "Cotton Armour." Her short fiction has appeared in *Chatelaine*, *Storyteller*, *On-Spec*, *Ellery Queen Mystery Magazine*, *Over My Dead Body*, and in many Canadian mystery anthologies. Her second novel, *The Icing on the Corpse*, was published this fall.

It hasn't always been this way. There was a time when I, too, would catch the attention of handsome young men, just like the women who swish past me on the way to the bank. A fleet blooming season, when I walked with my nose in the air, my hips swinging in that will-she, won't-she way. When I was confidently possessed of a slender neck and firm knees.

I recollect young men staring through the ficus branches in restaurants, turning to face me on escalators, revealing smiles of courage and hope. In windows and mirrors I would spot my bright and glorious reflection and glance away coyly. I would observe myself in shiny marble buildings, and for an instant, wonder who I could be. But that was then.

Probably it would have been better if I'd never been beautiful at all.

These days the young men are the worst. Their glances slide from my face as if I were covered with stale grease, leaving behind a streak of disappointment. I can feel them thinking, *Another old one, waste of air.*

The young women are nearly as bad. They look straight through me. I am not a competitor and not worth their time.

The older women next. Swathed in artifice themselves, they check hair, hemline, the quality of double stitching, the shape of heels. Then they look away, smothering small smiles, patting their fresh tints, straightening their cashmere jackets. Trailing L'Air du Temps.

The old men hang in longer than anyone gives them credit for. At least the ones in bad suits and walking shoes do. Always hoping for a glimpse of life. A flirtation as a small reward. Perhaps they're fighting their own invisibility. Who knows? Who cares.

Now I thank God for small children, or no creature would see me at all. You can count on the children. They never know when someone is going to be a good source of tasty chocolate-chip cookies.

But I no longer even see myself.

I cannot go out. Only in my own home am I tangible, a fleeting sweep in the mirror in the hallway, a shade on the enamel finish of the refrigerator. I reflect, therefore I must be.

My hands shimmer on the surface of the copper canisters, in the small, silver salt salvers, in the polished faucets in the bath. My home, a place where I exist and shine.

But what will happen to me?

It is the day of reckoning. I have in my hand the letter from the bank. I understand now the meaning of the word "demand" in demand loan. All I need is time, and I must match their demand with a plea. The money is on its way. Surely receivables must count for something.

The letter is signed by Mr. Sangster. I remember him. He showed not a ray of good will when I arranged the loan. He would not have been surprised by my default. I do not look forward to meeting him again.

In mental preparation I have two pots of Earl Grey. I stare at myself in the sheen of the rose teapot, inhaling the scent of bergamot, fixing on my image—blurry, pinkish, insubstantial. Lustreware is not the ideal medium for demonstrating one's carnate essence.

I do my best to materialize. Clothing should help. I discover that I own nothing that is not a variant of the colour of dust. Why have I bought these garments? They will not advance my visibility one bit. Why am I fussing about my wardrobe? Well, anything to take my mind off the letter.

Of course, it is too late.

Crimson, tomato, plum, nectarine, cherry, carmine, rose, maroon, vermillion, cerise, ruby, scarlet, flame. The dress with a thousand dancing shades of red flickers at me from the window of the boutique, a shop so expensive I have never let myself even peek at it before. But I am sheltering under the wide green awning, shielding myself from the blasting rain that has turned my dusty, all-purpose suit to mud. Shivering. How appropriate this weather. Perfect for one's last trip to the bank.

Whose heart is beating loudly in that miraculous dress? Is it a mistake to stop and buy it? Surely. Surely. All I need is a raincoat, something safe in barely-there beige. Yet I find myself in the changing room, wearing the fiery dress, find myself writing the cheque that will push me well into my delicate overdraft, find myself purchasing not a neutral raincoat but a capacious umbrella, designed to keep the dress from harm.

My mud-suit now resides in the trash at the boutique.

I am late. The dress blooms so beautifully but the fabric traps my anxious sweat against my body. The scent of my panic grows.

The reception area is curved, smooth, flat, deep aubergine, devoid of light. The receptionist has been carefully chosen to complement it. There is nothing to indicate her name. I think it must be Miss Princess. She is as cold as the marble counter. Her fingernails are royal purple. Her eyes emit not a single prick of light, although I fill in this detail because she does not look at me. It would take more than a red dress to get her attention.

Although the purple nails tap the counter irritably, she does not even raise her head from...is that a crossword puzzle? Silly me, no, it is a magazine. She is reading an article on thighs of steel in only ten days.

I give Miss Princess my name. I am sorry to be late. I tell her I have an appointment with Mr. Sangster. I do not mention that it is in connection with a demand loan for which I am in arrears. I do not tell the tediously sad story of my severance package after thirty years with the insurance company. Claims administration, always where they cut the overhead after a merger. When the going gets tough, they say. If life hands you lemons. Opportunity knocks. I do not bore her with the details of my post-retirement business and its outcome.

She might sneer, *Flowers by Fayellen? Do you not know that to succeed you must be visible, and more than that, you must leave the house? Someone has to pay for all those blooms. And how foolish of you to use your home as collateral.*

No. I do not refer to the white rectangle of shame within my purse.

"Take a seat," Miss Princess says. "Mr. Sangster will be with you shortly."

I sit shakily. I examine the words, "Mr. Sangster will be with you shortly," in all their dark, flat danger. With you *shortly*.

Everyone in the waiting area is concentrating on something: a newspaper, a brochure, a file. No one is staring at a letter like mine, but that is natural. If they have letters, they are hidden. I listen to my umbrella drip on the tray in the corner.

A young mother and her daughter arrive and sit two places from me. The mother is sleek, with black hair, and long legs in hose the colour of nightshade; the child is plain and scrawny, a triumph of recessive genes. The mother reaches for *Toronto Life*.

I smile at the child. Apparently, she alone can see the red dress.

Her eyes widen. "Are you a stranger?"

I have never been asked this. It makes me think.

"I suppose I am."

"You mean, yes?"

"Yes."

She is intrigued, but she scurries to the far side of her mother and snuggles in. Her mother does not lose her place in the magazine.

I do not want to be a stranger. A stranger tending towards invisibility, the very worst kind.

From time to time people rise as their names are called and walk with hope or despair to the offices in the back. My name is not called.

"I have to go to the bathroom, Mummy."

I turn away and stare at the prints on the wall, the gloomy greens and browns unrelieved by the matte finish of the glass. You would never find yourself in them.

"Mummeee."

The mother slaps down *Toronto Life*. She walks quickly to reception, with the child running to catch her. Miss Princess gestures toward the corridor. She follows the child's mother with her eyes and touches her own silky hair with those royal nails.

The child gallops to catch up.

Perhaps it is the small surge of adrenaline that comes from anger that sends me back to Miss Princess at the reception desk.

"How long?" I croak.

"Pardon me?"

It takes an effort to keep my vocal passages open.

"How long will it be until I meet with Mr. Sangster?"

"You have to sign in. Your name?"

"I have already given it to you." I point to my name on the list. "Quite far ahead of other people who have already been called."

She shrugs without looking up. She is still reading the magazine. Well, she's not exactly reading. Really she is looking at women in Lycra holding weights. They are all smiling. Perhaps she will learn to smile by reading such magazines. But I wouldn't bet on it.

"How long will it be?" I am tired and need badly to get home to catch my soul in the bevelled glass of the French doors.

She looks up and blinks at me. "What?"

"How long will it take until Mr. Sangster is free? I can't wait forever."

She frowns. It has not occurred to her that I can't wait forever.

"I don't believe he's back from lunch yet."

I am defeated by her vacant gaze.

I sit again and watch the others, one by one, pass through the doors and out again into the light. Not one of them is in tears or looks like they've had a shock. The men swagger, the woman walk with new pride.

The child and her mother return, smelling of soap.

The two pots of Earl Grey begin to take their revenge. I would like to have had my lunch, as Mr. Sangster has been able to. And to go to the ladies' room. Not a bad idea. Public facilities, for all their evil promise of Hepatitis B and worse, are not without chrome fittings.

But I don't want to lose my turn. On the other hand, Mr. Sangster, if Miss Princess is to be believed, is still at lunch.

A cocky young man with square shoulders and gelled hair strides through the front door and fingers the middle button on his suit jacket. It looks like an ordinary suit but it is carrying the hidden colours of ultramarine and cobalt. And it is dry. Of course. He drapes his raincoat on the rack as if it was there just for him. A simple action but every eye watches him. This is how a raincoat should be hung. Casually. Without stress.

Even Miss Princess sees him. *It won't be long.* Ah.

He sits and lets his gaze linger on her. He is not expecting a "no." He does not have a demand note in his ultramarine pocket. He wouldn't know what to do with one. He tosses an appreciative grin at the child's mother. She stretches her long nightshade legs slightly while pretending not to lose her place in *Toronto Life*. The child stares at him. I want to scream, *Now, that is a stranger, a real stranger.*

Of course, he is unaware of me.

I find myself shifting on the seat, squirming, the message that it's time to go is starting to interfere with my thoughts. I have read all the magazines. In desperation, I reread the letters in *Time*.

Miss Princess calls the young man's name. She flicks her hair over her shoulder as he struts by into the secret office areas. Am I the only one waiting for redemption?

I look around the room. Every single person has come after me. The woman and child have been waiting quite a while. I think the young man did not wait long enough. Of course he didn't. He is everything that takes from the invisible people like me. I feel my fingernails digging into my palms.

The room has changed again, the third time. At least.

The woman and the child, my last companions in oblivion, are waved through the door.

The pressure in my bladder has become a roaring in my ears. I stand and move painfully towards the facilities. I expect to make sloshing noises. If you can't be seen, can you still be heard?

Going to the ladies' room turns out to be an excellent idea. I cannot bring myself to look in the mirror, but I catch a glimpse of hair in the chrome paper dispenser. There is a fiery flash of my image in the forced-air hand dryer, distorted, oddly strong, and muscled. I laugh out loud. As if I could have strength! Even the high-gloss white paint on the walls picks up a firmish shadow of me, and that's a first. I appear, therefore I am. Good news all around.

I give my hands one last flick for good luck and move back into the corridor. The rear offices of the bank are filled with soft, dull surfaces, showing no one. The baffles marking off each cubicle are deep eggplant, the offical colour of corruption, suitable for the mottled skin of a corpse. Appropriate for this land of dead dreams.

But where am I? I stop for a second, confused about the direction. Left? Right? Straight ahead?

It is not like me to go straight ahead.

Right turns out to be wrong as it sends me down a corridor with glass-fronted offices. My heart is pumping. I must get out of there before I anger Miss Princess and am forced to wait until tomorrow when it will be too late altogether.

Will I ever get the smell of sweat out of my red dress?

I am dizzy with panic, breathing raggedly, wheeling right, jerking left. What if left is wrong too?

The young man with the gelled hair and square shoulders whips out of an office and struts past me. I do not imprint on his retina, I am sure of that. He heads into the men's room. He is frowning. I cannot imagine why. Still, his image will show in the mirror all right.

Wait. The office he has left says "T. Sangster." A plaque on the wall next to the window.

How can that be? Mr. Sangster is there. Behind a desk. Not eating lunch. Just there. Immersed in paperwork. Proud and smirking as he fills out the papers for the winners and losers. A man born to say no.

I find myself moving straight ahead until I am framed by his door.

He doesn't even see me.

Hear me then. "Mr. Sangster."

"What is it?"

I don't even rate a polite inquiry. I am of no significance, the nonentity that received a summons from the great Mr. Sangster to anticipate my own financial funeral, while he dawdled with the young man and left me to sit in a puddle of pee.

He has turned back to his work. The pinch around his mouth, the raised eyebrow indicate annoyance. Perhaps I am intended to apologize and vanish all at the same time.

"I was sent in," I say, inclining my head back toward Miss Princess, who has it coming. Not that he's looking.

But I am looking, though. Really looking. The man has such power, and yet he really is quite ugly, especially with that blotchy neck. He needs everything around him—metal in-baskets, leather-handled letter opener and matching stapler—all to maintain his aura. He is soft and pink and covered with freckles, like pale punctuation. No. Period. No. Period. No. Period. But does he have this power? Naked, he would be quite pathetic.

Laughable.

I laugh.

Perhaps that is a mistake.

"It is my turn." I have nothing to lose.

I step into the room. What made me do that? Was it seeing myself square and muscled in the chrome of the hand dryer? Perhaps.

On top of the desk is the file with my name on it. "This is me," I say. The yellow Post-it Note says "NO." Not even maybe.

"You'll have to wait your turn."

If only he'd looked up when he said it. But I am not worth looking up at. I do not reflect on anything in that room. Except for the tiniest flash, a pinpoint of light on the stainless blade of the decorative letter opener.

I do not know how I came to hold it. Memory fails me there. But it is in my hand, and as I raise it, he glances up. I see myself in his dilated pupils. Crisp. Hard-edged. Red.

His hands shoot out, knocking files from the desk. Paper swirl. The blue of maybe, the gray of rejection. I cannot be distracted now. It is much too late. He turns from me—falling, falling. The crimson jet shoots from his neck, upwards, outwards, so much, so much, brilliant, and quite beautiful. The arc of a crimson rainbow. I stand transfixed.

My file is still on the desk, as are several others. There is no blood on it. The blood is on the opposite wall, on the carpet, on the ceiling, almost everywhere except the desk. I take the Post-it Note and crumple it. I lift the "YES" from the next file with the tip of a pencil and reapply it to mine.

But that is just the surface.

Someone else's sad story is on the computer screen but that is not my problem.

Thirty years of claims administration may not prepare you to sell flowers, but it does lead you through three generations of computers and office systems. It does teach you the logic of file organization, the standard codes, the behaviour of software.

I am amazed that I have not forgotten any of it. My file is easy to retrieve. Easy to change. For once, I have no trouble finding myself.

Someone in my body floats back into the waiting room.

The child and her mother are gone. There is only Miss Princess. I would have to scream or take my clothes off to get a reaction from her.

Of course, I would never take my clothes off, not just because some of the spray of Mr. Sangster's beautiful blood has soaked through my dress and on to my skin.

So I am still invisible. That is one good thing.

I want to shout, *I can walk through walls, I can probably fly; the sky's the limit for my type—be jealous, be afraid!*

Whose legs are those propelling me across the room towards reception? I lean against the marble counter. Miss Princess is sniffing a sample fragrance packet from the magazine. But all I can smell is blood.

"I have been here for more than one hour waiting for Mr. Sangster."

One plucked eyebrow arches. "I know you're there."

"But I have been waiting. My time is worth something too, you know."

"There is nothing I can do about it. You'll have to be patient," she says, managing a small but strategic yawn. I can read her thoughts. *Pushy old bag you can just stay out here and cool your jets until I'm damn good and ready.*

The letter opener burns in my pocket like a briquette. I must get rid of it before it singes my thigh. Should I drop it into the trash?

The young man's raincoat is still hanging on the coat rack. Has he forgotten it? It seems to me as though years have passed, but it must be only minutes. No one is here except Miss Princess.

Oh, here he comes. He strides back into the reception area and gives Miss Princess the eye. He leans against the reception counter and engages her in conversation. Oh, she is lost all right.

With care I wipe clean the white-hot letter opener on the dress of many reds. But whose hand slips it into the ultramarine depths of that raincoat pocket?

Lilting laughter drifts from the reception desk. Miss Princess will remember this young man forever. Everything about him. Who he was. Where he went and when. Perhaps she will sit in an open-air café and tell her friends about the closest of calls she had. Perhaps.

I sit back to wait patiently, as instructed.

If the police can see me, I am prepared to answer questions. Of course, I don't know much, except how long the young man was inside the mysterious back offices.

To my surprise I am able to see my shadow on the plum carpet. There it is, firm and resolute. I am fascinated. I believe I could gaze at it for hours.

But I do not have long to wait before the screaming starts.

Foil for the Fire

by Vern Smith

Deception. Manipulation. Corruption. Those are three prime ingredients of noir. Maybe it's his work as a reporter for Toronto's *eye* magazine—covering politics, cops, fugitives from the law, and the justice system—that has taught Vern Smith how to mix them together for maximum impact. He also understands that innocence is relative, not absolute. There are levels. And action taken with good intent can lead to bad consequences.

Vern's understanding of how the underbelly works is demonstrated in hard-edged stories he has published in anthologies, small press magazines, and in his collection *Glue for Breakfast*, where "Foil for the Fire" first appeared.

I felt like I was watching my own face grimace, like I could see my eyes darting in every direction. I was conscious of my lungs expanding and contracting, of my heavy arms and legs pumping through a decaying industrial park.

Running past years of neglect through southwest Detroit, Nick kept stride with me, focusing straight ahead. For the first time, I started feeling as though something had gone wrong. We'd just sprinted about 150 yards east on some train tracks between Swain and Vinewood, near West Jefferson. Our gusto was fading, and his dad's bakery shop was going to explode in about ten minutes.

"We're a little off schedule...but we'll be...we'll be okay," Nick huffed while I watched his wild, bobbing eyes.

We turned left, chugging up Vinewood Avenue towards the ride coming for us at the corner on Fort Street. It was as if the whole scene stuttered into slow motion, or maybe that's the only way I can remember it. Anyway, with 300 yards to the corner, I could actually see myself stop. Through a maze of parked trailers, barbed wire, and wooden pallets, I was sure I spotted a square of light. Nick took a few more steps, realized that my army boots had stopped hitting the ground in unison with his sneakers, and then stopped, whirling around to the fear marking my face. I was nineteen, so was Nick, and there we were, standing outside General Mill Supply, glaring at each other in the middle of the street while I stammered, "I think a light...a goddamn light's on. Somebody's...someone is in the building."

Nick gasped impatiently, not bothering to look back, dropped his eyes to the concrete and pinched the bridge of his nose.

"It's supposed to be empty...free and clear until four this morning," I went on in a screaming whisper. "You said this was a sure thing. You said this wouldn't fucking happen."

"Look, Jonzun, whatever you think you saw, forget it. Stay cool and let's get back to Canada. Not now, but right now."

He seemed a bit too calm for a guy who could be causing somebody's spontaneous combustion, so I ignored him, breaking into a run back towards his dad's bakery. Before I took four strides, he dove at my legs, bringing our bodies crashing onto the cold, cracked concrete.

"Get the fuck off me," I said, struggling underneath him. "Get—"

The smacking sound was the back of his right hand pimp-slapping me across the face, his knuckles biting my cheeks. In the next moment, his same hand enveloped my mouth. With his knees on my shoulders, he began speaking, choosing his words with chilly precision. "Relax, Jonzun. That light's probably just a reflection from the *Detroit News* or one of the other warehouses. Look, we know the routine too well, and nobody's in there baking pitas. Now, I'm calmly getting across the border now, and you're coming, right?"

"Yes," I said, white breath hovering in the cold February night. In the distance, the horn of a tugboat toiling on the Detroit River acted as a pin-drop, breaking our silence.

"Now run like hell and don't look back," Nick said, picking himself up and helping me to my feet. "Remember, straight up to Fort Street, and then right. Latino Family Services is the first doorway. Zoe will be cruising by every two minutes."

So we ran.

We ran past burnt-out homes, dodging a broken couch, discarded clothes, and broken trash bags strewn across Vinewood Street.

It wasn't supposed to happen this way. In fact, the original plan called for the bomb to go off *after* we crossed the border. Nick said it would be "a walk in the park." We figured on watching the explosion from the tiny one-bedroom apartment my girlfriend, Andrea, and I had rented on the Windsor waterfront. She was off visiting her parents in Toronto, so Nick, Zoe, and I had the place to ourselves.

Yet there we were—running hard and running late because Nick forgot the electronic security code to his dad's shop. We ended up losing about twenty minutes, doubling back to St. Andrew's Hall to get it out of my dad's K-car.

Nick had hand-picked the corner of Vinewood and Fort because it was close to the Ambassador Bridge to Windsor. Also, the neighbourhood was so violent that police had unofficially slowed down on answering calls there. So unless we were shot-up, the Detroit Police wouldn't want to be around to catch us running to our checkpoint. But then when I hit the doorway of Latino Family Services, steps ahead of Nick, Zoe was nowhere.

"Maybe she got scared," I said, panicking, looking to and fro.

"My little sister's got balls bigger than you and me together," Nick scoffed. "She'll be here, but not a word of that light you think you saw. She has to do the talking at the border, and she just doesn't need to know right now. Just stay cold, and I guarantee you we'll never end up traded for a pack of menthols at Jackson State."

"Prison?" I said, nodding my head. "That's great psychology. We're standing in North America's most violent neighbourhood after planting a bomb in your dad's bakery. Something's wrong, terribly fucking wrong— our getaway car isn't here, and you're cracking jokes about me in prison before we cross the border. It's not like you can tell we're in the Midwest or anything."

"Look, I'm just fucking around," Nick laughed. "We're doing fine, just keep your head, and—here she is."

It's been more than ten years now, but I don't have to go through the news clippings to remember we timed that bomb for 1:45 a.m. on February 11, 1986.

I'd met Nick doing volunteer DJ duty at the University of Windsor's radio station the previous fall. His slot was right before mine, and we spent every Monday night drinking and arguing over who came up with the trashier play list. He was the one who introduced me to Andrea. Aside from her, he was my only real friend on campus.

I was studying English, and Nick was a Business major. Neither of us really managed to mingle with our faculties, so we spent most of that year smuggling cheap liquor back to Windsor and wondering what we were going to do with our lives. I went to U of W just because it was my hometown school. Nick crossed the Detroit River for his education after his dad refused to put him up in an apartment near Wayne State University in downtown Detroit. It was a good school in a pretty violent area back then. Still is.

Whatever. I think Nick's wild eyes made me do it. The same wild eyes I watched while we ran from his dad's bakery. The same eyes that glared with the disturbing passion of audacity when he hatched his plot at some dive called Steve's Place in Greektown. Every time the waitress brought more drinks, our voices drifted to silence. When she left, Nick's brown eyes ballooned into this wet well of pride. Littering his plot with rants about bankers, he gave me the history of Pappa's Bakery, explaining that it had been in the Pappadopoulos family since the turn of the century.

It was located on West Jefferson Avenue, but even though I grew up in nearby Windsor, Nick had to explain that it was a rough area. Still, the bakery had survived just about everything, including race riots, the infernos of Devil's Night, and a savage World Series celebration when the Tigers won in 1984.

The way Nick said it, Pappa's Bakery was never what you'd call a real cash cow, but he said the family had done all right selling spanakopitas, baklava, and other Greek baked goods to restaurants and grocers. At least it was doing fine until Nick's dad, Georgios Pappadopoulos, opened a chain of Pappa's coffee shops. One was in Dearborn, one in Greektown, and another in Livonia. Nick said they were all failing badly.

Since Georgios had mortgaged the original bakery to open the storefront operations, Nick said the whole family business was broke and soon going to fold. With a quick cash infusion, he told me, the family business just might make it. I never met Georgios. Taking from Prudential Insurance to stop the Bank of Detroit from foreclosing seemed like the right thing to do, especially when Nick started talking about a time bomb. It was being assembled by a childhood pal of Nick's who ran with Young Boys Inc., a street gang that ruled the Cass Corridor in the late seventies and early eighties. The bomb would consist of two-dozen dynamite sticks wired to a blasting cap, an alarm clock, and two plastic Faygo bottles filled with gasoline. Georgios, of course, wasn't in on the plan. Nick said he was too honest for his own good.

Zoe pulled up in my dad's blue K-car, and Nick quickly jumped into the front passenger seat.

Just as I dove into the back, I heard what sounded like a round of gunfire in the distance. I rolled down the window to listen. Zoe had the radio locked onto WRIF and Mitch Ryder's "When You Were Mine," which stopped me from hearing what was later described on the news as "a series of outbursts ringing out near the riverfront."

"Everything ready to go boom?" Zoe asked, flushed with adrenaline.

"We're on," Nick said, awkwardly pulling off his leather jacket. "Now it's your turn. You got the route down?"

"Yeah, straight on Fort, left on 25th, and then a right on Lafayette West," Zoe said quickly. "We pass the Duty Free Store and flip onto Fisher Service Drive for a few seconds, until we hit the bridge cutoff."

"Good. There's a token in the ashtray," Nick said, reaching forward and opening the tray to ensure the coin was there.

"You've got a lot to say for a guy who forgot the security code," Zoe giggled.

"Just do your thing, Sis, and save your commentary," Nick said, unbuttoning his denim shirt before whirling around to check on me staring into the darkness. "It's not over yet, pal," he said with a forced smile, tossing a black concert T-shirt into the back seat. "Get into the shirt. Know your script. Be the character Jonzun Riley."

I squirmed out of my navy peacoat. My black, collared shirt went next, exposing my torso to the cold. In one motion, I reached for the black Ramones T-shirt with white, yellow and red inscriptions, pulling it over my head. Zoe had bought the T-shirts hours earlier at the concert. She also had three torn ticket stubs and a hasty concert review ready for Nick and me. With my shirt open to expose the Ramones' emblem, I struggled back into the peacoat.

With Zoe guiding Dad's K-car toward the bridge, I looked to the riverfront. Stardust smoke against the night sky was unmistakable, even through rows of industrial buildings.

"Okay, here's the scoop," Zoe rehearsed, passing the torn ticket stubs to Nick. "The Ramones did all their biggies, except for 'Teenage Lobotomy.' While you men were supposedly slamming near the stage, I stood in the back. The concert wrapped up after midnight. We're getting close to two now. We stayed for a few drinks, then left."

"What if they pull some Colombo horse shit?" Nick smiled, testing Zoe. "Why are we taking the bridge when St. Andrew's is so close to the tunnel?"

"We stopped at Mexican Village for takeout," Zoe said. "There's nachos, refried beans, and tacos in the back. We got them for you, Jonzun, honey."

"Perfect," Nick said. "Fucking perfect."

As we approached the tolls, Zoe reached into the ashtray, pulling out the token along with some of my dad's leftover cigarette ashes. She threw it into the white change tub for tokens and exact change. The striped arm lifted, allowing us onto the Ambassador Bridge and past buildings blocking the riverfront. A shower of blurred flames, rising ashes, and flat-black smoke blasted all around Pappa's Bakery hundreds of feet below.

None of us needed to strain to see the destruction to the west. Street lights clearly exposed the thick clouds of smoke. Flames shot into the air over the *Detroit News* warehouse. Glowing debris climbed before falling to the ground as fire trucks rushed to our blaze on West Jefferson near Swain.

"What a beautiful orange boom," Zoe beamed. "Very thorough job, especially for a first, Mr. Riley and Mr. Pappadopoulos."

I studied Zoe's eyes through the rear-view mirror, watching her head shoot quickly to our destruction, then to the car in front, and back again. *Her eyes are gleaming*, I thought, *almost glowing.*

From the middle of the bridge, I looked back down again, watching the tiny fire engines. It was about then that I started to think about how my dad warned me against taking his K-car to Detroit.

Through the back window now, I watched climbing flames tearing into the sky. We're fucked, I decided. Then another small explosion barrelled into the flat-black plume. Tiny orange balls careened off one another, skidding awkwardly into the cover of night and smoke.

My eyes strained through the haze of colours until I heard Nick's voice again. "Okay, stay in this line...we've got a guy," he told Zoe, looking to the male customs officer in the booth ahead.

Zoe sneered as the customs officer whisked the three cars ahead of us through in less than two minutes. The light at the booth turned from red to green. Zoe whispered, "Showtime," gently tapping the gas and pulling up to the window.

The customs officer looked into Zoe's eyes, remaining silent for a few seconds before blurting out his one-word question. "Citizenship?"

"We're American, my brother and I. He's a student at the university, and I'm just visiting. He's Canadian," Zoe said, pointing to me in the back seat.

Without a dead-air lapse, the officer looked to me. "How long was your trip?"

"About six hours," I said, remembering Dad's border-crossing tip about keeping my answers short.

"Where are you coming from?"

"Concert at St. Andrew's Hall," I answered.

He looked back to Zoe. "Why are you driving his Daddy's car with Ontario plates?"

"It's my turn to be the designated driver," she said, smiling.

The officer's glare stung Zoe's eyes, making her want to look away and blink. I watched her in the rear-view again. Her eyes begged to water, but she continued the brief stare-down until the officer finally peered into the back at my shadow and said, "Your daddy know you had his car in Detroit?"

"Yes, sir," I said.

"Go ahead then."

We drove to my place on Sandwich Street, where we alternated between news reports and blurred views of the fire from my balcony on the Detroit River. Nick was channel surfing when a *News Four* reporter broke into a late-night Joan Collins movie. Detroit Police had several blocks cordoned off with flashing squad cars. Behind the night reporter, Detroit cops smoked cigarettes and drank coffee from disposable cups. I don't know why I expected the phone to ring just then. No one knew Nick and Zoe were at my place.

Fingering her earpiece, the reporter said she had an unconfirmed report that the blast had left at least one man dead. Zoe carefully rose from my couch and turned off the television before we heard any more. She reached into my open package of cigarettes and lit one. Her hands trembled, but just a bit.

The Detroit detectives talked to me for about three minutes when I drove Nick and Zoe home in the morning. As agreed, I said we had just heard the news on WJR, and they rattled off a few routine questions. I don't know how far their investigation went because Nick and I drifted apart after Georgios' funeral, as intended.

Andrea didn't quite get it, but she was busy finishing her degree, then moving onto grad school at the University Toronto, and I went with her. Dad gave us the K-car as a moving gift, even though he thought we were rushing into things.

I didn't find out that Nick had dropped out until the following February. Andrea and I were living on Brunswick Avenue, and my mom had sent me an article from the *Detroit News*. It was a feature on Georgios, marking the first anniversary of his death. There was a picture of Zoe and Nick looking sombre with their arms around each other.

It turned out that Nick greatly exaggerated the demise of the Pappa's chain. Contradicting his tale of financial woe, the *News* said Pappa's storefront coffee shops in Dearborn, Greektown, and Livonia had thrived since Georgios opened them. On top of that, Zoe and Nick had opened a new Pappa's Bakery in Eastern Market, and two more store-front shops in Dearborn and Royal Oak. Old customers were quoted, each talking glowingly of Georgios and the courage of his kids.

The clincher came at the end of the newspaper story. That's when I finally let myself believe what Nick said all along: he knew Georgios' routine too well for this to have been a mistake. In a few breaths, he gave it all away, but only to me. "Pappa Georgios didn't just own the bakery," Nick told the paper. "Like his father, and his father's father, he was the first one there at precisely 1:30 every morning. He took pride in the fact that he sold the freshest Greek baked goods in town, and we're carrying on in that great family tradition."

So the Pappa's chain had been profitable all along. Given the new openings, Georgios obviously had a whack of money Nick forgot to tell me about, too. Top that off with some building and life insurance, and it must have made for a tempting package. There was no other reason for the Pappadopoulos kids to torch their dad's bakery. Still, they needed an alibi. At some point, they decided the only way to get one was to make someone part of it, to make me part of it. That's when Nick started in on me, carefully picking my limits before working up to a crisis he'd created. The best part was that he never had to check up on me again. As far as alibis go, I was as solid as they came. I was foil for the fire.

Can You Take Me There, Now?

by Matthew Firth

Bad relationships. Bad companions. Bad choices. Bad timing. Mix them together and let them simmer over high heat. That's a sure recipe for blackened fiction. It's what Matt Firth does in this story, which appears in his second collection of short stories, also entitled *Can You Take Me There, Now?*

Born under the slag heaps of Hamilton, Matthew now lives in Ottawa. His fiction has appeared all over the world—well, Canada, the U.S., the U.K., and Australia. He is co-editor of the fiction and review magazine *Front & Centre*, and was editor of the now-defunct literary magazine *Black Cat 115*. An earlier collection of his stories entitled *Fresh Meat* appeared in 1997.

I spent most of last night dodging cops and queers, so obviously I'm not at my very best. The cops harassed me down by the harbour, glaring at me from their cruiser behind cheesy moustaches. One of the fat thugs clambered out of his car and stood over me.

"What's your business here?"

He took out his nightstick: a big inverted crucifix.

I didn't answer. I was just trying to pass the night, leaning back against a Baskin-Robbins, using the lights from inside the ice-cream parlour to read *Notes of a Dirty Old Man*, but the fucking cops just wouldn't let me alone. If I'd had a brick, and not a book, in my hand, I could have seen their point. I wasn't looking for trouble. If asked, I couldn't have said what I was looking for. I pushed on.

Up past Citadel Hill the queers became a problem. I settled on a park bench for a breather, hoping to sleep. Wasn't it more than five minutes before some fucker with dyed-black hair offered me twenty-five bucks to suck my cock. I was skint but not that desperate. Told the queer to make it an even fifty and he was on. He got all huffy. Sulked off somewhere to find a more willing prick. Next, some asshole was flashing his high beams at me from the curb, blinding me, keeping me from catching a few zeds. What the hell he wanted I wasn't interested in waiting around to find out. I gave up on the park bench and shuffled away, back down to the town centre to find a doughnut shop or burger joint, anything all hours. Spent the rest of the night guzzling coffee at a Hortons, reading Bukowski, trying to mind my own business.

Eight or nine o'clock finally rolls around, and I get up to take my tenth piss in the last four hours. I douse my face with lukewarm water. Blow hot air into my face. Scratch stubble and stumble back out to my cold coffee. Sit back down, and ten seconds later, this black guy's in my face like a shot.

"You hitchhiking?"

I look at him and recognize street-crazy instantly. He's wearing the uniform: soiled greatcoat, fingerless gloves, the modern equivalent of hobnail boots. He's got on a frayed, red and green toque that barely covers his head; clumps and tufts of hair jut out. I can see bits of lint in his 'fro, Christmassy, sort of. He's a month early for that.

I pause for a second longer, then answer his question.

"No, not hitchhiking. Not right now. Later, if I have to."

He sits down across from me, his scent wafting over me.

"You mind?"

"A little late to be asking," I bark, my head buzzing from all the caffeine. Then I give him a congenial nod. I can use the company.

"Name's Winston," he tells me. "Winston Whitehorse."

"Like the town up in the Yukon?"

He rolls his eyes.

"You think you're the first wiseass to use that line on me? Yeah, like the town way the fuck up in the Yukon. Cold as fuck, as far as I know. Never been there."

He's drumming his fingers on the table madly, looking left and right, left and right.

I look at the lint in his hair.

"Sorry, I wasn't trying to be a smartass. I've never been up there either."

"Where you never been either?"

"The Yukon. Whitehorse."

Winston leans back and starts in again. "Right, Whitehorse. What kind of a fucking name is that for a black man? Should be *Black* horse. Got a Indian's name, for fuck sakes. Look at me. Do I look like a Indian to you? A very black-assed Indian, maybe."

I sip coffee and gaze around the doughnut shop. I can't tell if Winston is yelling, whispering, or speaking at a normal volume. The other customers ignore us completely. We're the only ones sitting at a table. All the others are queued up.

I look back at Winston. "Whitehorse, Blackhorse, I never thought of it that way."

"Course you haven't. We just met. Why the fuck would you thought about my name before?"

He waggles a grubby digit in my face.

"It's like that Barry White fucker. Guy should change his name to Barry Black. That's a name for a black man."

I lean back. Rub my eyes. "Hmmn, yeah."

Winston moves in closer, giving me a stronger whiff of him. "What'd ya mean, 'Hmmn, yeah'? Makes perfect sense if you think about it. White man, white name. Black man, black name."

I do think about it for a few seconds. Then come up with, "I guess you're right. But there's always Frank Black."

Winston glares at me, skeptical, puzzled. "Frank Black? Who the fuck is Frank Black? Some dumb-ass white man?"

"Frank Black. Used to be in that band, the Pixies."

"Don't talk to me about no fucking pixies. Fuck up my head with that shit."

I wave my hands in air. "No, no. The Pixies. Rock 'n' roll band. He's another musician, that's all. I thought it was relevant. You know, Barry White's a musician. So's Frank Black."

Winston looks at me deeply. He's mulling it over. "Maybe so," he goes.

"But no one gives a rat's ass about Frank Black."

I can't argue with him there.

I look at the lineup of bored office workers, civil servants.

Me and Winston fall silent for a minute.

Then Winston's on his feet, gesturing out to the street. "Let's get us something to drink before you hit the road. Get your duffel bag and I'll give you a reading somewheres."

For the first time I notice that Winston's toting a Bible in one hand. He sat down in such a flurry that I didn't notice the Good Book.

"Come on. On your feet."

I look at Winston and shrug. My mind numb from coffee, I do as instructed.

At the first stoplight he wheels around and steps back towards me. "What'd you say your name is, by the way?"

I tell him and he shifts the Bible to his left hand. I drop my duffel bag and shake his fingerless-gloved hand. The light turns green. I follow Winston across the pavement.

A few blocks along my shoulder starts to ache.

"I gotta dump this bag at the train station."

Winston looks me over, sneering a little, assessing my character, something. "I thought you said you was hitchhiking."

"Yeah, I *was* hitchhiking. That's how I got out here. But I'm taking a train to Montréal. Maybe thumb it back through Ontario after that. See how cold it is first."

I drop my bag on the sidewalk and rub my sore shoulder.

"Montréal? Fuck sakes. What'd ya wanna go there for? Full of snobby Québec whores. They *will* suck your dick, though, no doubt about it."

I look at the Bible in Winston's hand.

"You read that thing or just carry it round?"

Winston's eyes alight. He holds the Bible over his head. "Don't get fucking smart with me, white boy! 'Course I read this fucking book. All the time. Been through it dozens 'a times. Only book anybody oughta read."

I lug my bag back up onto my shoulder. "Just that you don't sound too religious when you go on about cocksuckers from Québec."

Winston snorts. He follows a pace or two behind me for a moment, then races up in front and spins around. Walking backward, he wags a condemning finger in my face. "The point is, white man, I just want you to be sure that I ain't no queer, see. *That's* all. That's not what this is about, in case you had any funny ideas. That's why I mentioned Québec whores."

He stabs a finger at the cover of the Bible. "Don't question my reasons. My religion. I'm a fucking priest, buddy. Don't you forget it."

He turns around again and starts walking away from me. Over his shoulder he points down a side street. "Train station's down there. Come on."

This is my eighth day in Halifax. I stayed a week at the YMCA, renting a tiny room for seventy bucks. Most of my money ran out, so I spent last night on the street, knowing I had a train ticket booked for today.

I've not done a hell of a lot since I've been here. Skulked around this maritime city. Drunk coffee. Eaten cheap dinners at some Hare Krishna vegetarian place. Hung out with other bums in the public library. Ogled university women near Dalhousie. Made a couple of pilgrimages to the oceanside to stare out to sea. Thought about the wide expanse of water.

About what lies on the other side. Past Newfoundland, anyway. Europe. Thought about how I have no interest in seeing the shores on the other side. That's where she went, after all. Lucy. The one I'm hung up on. She of the tedious, clichéd, post-university jaunt to Europe types. Train passes. Backpacks. Fucking Canadians, Americans, and Australians everywhere you look, I'd guess. All of them searching for some link to the past, full of stupid, romantic ideas. Stupid, romantic students. I couldn't afford it anyway.

Lucy ended our three-year romance without batting an eye and bought a flight to Amsterdam. Probably fucked the first pot-smoking Dutchman she bumped into. Him rubbing hands greasy with mayonnaise all over her body. She sent me a couple postcards. *Such* sympathy. *Such* bullshit, we're-still-friends-aren't-we sentimentality. London. Paris. Rome. Castles. Museums. Cathedrals. Each time the cards arrived all I imagined were the cocks of different grubby Europeans fucking her. I could picture it: Lucy'd be drunk on cheap Hungarian wine. Sunbathing nude somewhere. Chatting up any prick that came her way.

I pitched the postcards, quit my job, and thumbed to Ottawa. Spent a month there doing nothing but getting pissed, drowning my sorrows.

Moved on to Montréal next. Slept on an old friend's couch. We'd fucked a couple times way back when. No fucking this time. So I took a Metro to Longueuil and thumbed through the rest of La Belle Province to New Brunswick, finally to where the highway stopped—Halifax—to contemplate my misery, to exorcise some demons, to eventually turn around and piss off back to Ontario's fertile belly and all the sour memories that it holds.

In the train station Winston scurries off to the nearest toilet. I think about dumping my bag and nipping out a side door somewhere, ridding myself of the guy. But by the time I've deposited my duffel bag in a locker, he's back.

"Watch this and learn," he says, thumping the Bible in his right hand with his left fist.

I watch Winston work a few weary travellers. He barks quotes at them, Old Testament stuff, hard-assed passages from Leviticus, shit about who should lie with who. It doesn't get him many converts to begin with, the hard-line approach. He should back off a bit, ease into it with some Psalms and then try the fire-and-brimstone stuff. A couple of suits eventually relent, tossing loonies at him. Winston drops to his knees and scampers across the station's dirty floor, chasing a couple of measly bucks.

Up off his knees, he's back in my face. "Easy money. What'd I tell you?"

I look at the two, one-dollar coins in his hand and shrug, unimpressed.

A minute later he approaches a couple of blue-rinse grannies. For them he reads from the Gospels, walking backward as he praises Christ. It works like a charm. Maybe he does know what he's doing. Both grannies pry crisp five-dollar bills from their purses. Winston smiles and bows, tipping an imaginary cap at them. Twelve bucks in ten minutes. Not bad work if you can get it.

Now he's back over beside me. "You dump your bag, buddy?"

"Yeah, in a locker. Train doesn't leave till three."

"Well, then we got plenty of time. Clock on the wall says ten to eleven."

I look over Winston's left shoulder. He's right about the hour. But I'm growing a bit weary, a bit leery of him. I search my head for excuses to cop out, to lose him, but draw a blank.

"I got money burning a hole in my pocket. First one's on me."

Again Winston leads, and again I follow.

Outside, Halifax is its perpetual November grey. Winston points across the street.

"The Harbourview. Cheap beer and plenty of sluts. I'll meet you there in ten minutes. Got an errand to run first."

He hands me one of the fins.

"Buy us a couple of beers, my man."

I look at the bill.

"With a five?"

"Fuck yeah. I told you, beer's cheap at the Harbourview. And I'm a preferred customer. Mention my name and just watch the service you get."

Again he wags a finger in my face.

"Off you go. Like I said, the first one's on me."

I stand on the curb, the blue bill fluttering between my fingers in the sea breeze. Winston shuffles up the sidewalk. I think he's muttering to himself, but I can't be sure. I could use a drink. One or two beers and then that's it. Then back to the train station to catch my ride out of this damp city. Back to Montréal for a few days, then Hamilton.

Inside the Harbourview, Winston arrives almost exactly when he said he would. I'm sitting at a table in the virtually empty bar, nursing a bottle of Moosehead. Winston pulls out a chair opposite me and sits.

"What the fuck you buying that piss water for?"

He points at the green bottles.

"I thought this's what you drink down here."

Winston bolts forward in his chair, starts preaching again. "The fuck it is. We sell that shit to Americans and assholes like you down in Ontario. Nobody drinks Moosehead in Halifax. I hope you didn't mention my name to the bartender."

He's really worked up, genuinely upset. I ease back in my seat, keeping his breath at bay.

"No, Winston, I didn't mention your name. No harm done."

He scoffs at me and picks up the bottle. Takes a hard hit of it, emptying half the contents.

"Better get this drunk. Then *you* buy the next round!"

He waves the bottle in my face.

"But not this shit. Oland fucking Export, my friend. That's what we drunk here."

I don't say a word. I slouch back in my chair and drink my beer. I gaze around the dimly-lit bar. The usual east coast crap on display on the wood-panelled walls: ship's wheels, a couple of stuffed fish, a lobster that's probably plastic, neon beer signs (Schooner, Oland Export, Keith's; no Moosehead, I now notice).

At the front of the bar is a squat stage and a dodgy disco ball dangling from a cable. A stripper's pole stands dead centre at the front of the small stage.

I look over at Winston. He's finished his beer.

"Girls dance here?"

"What the fuck do you think that fat chick at the bar's doing here at 11:30 in the morning on a Tuesday?"

At the bar, a large woman in a black leather mini, a ratty white sweater under a black leather vest, and black fuck-me boots sucks on a butt, flipping through an *Auto Trader*.

"When you're at the bar ordering us a couple Olands, ask her what time her shift starts."

Winston swings his empty beer bottle in his hand like a pendulum, letting me know it's empty. I trot over to the bar, riffling through my wallet. I've got three tens left, plus maybe forty bucks in a chequing account that I can access from a bank machine in an emergency. But there should be no need for that till I get to Montréal tomorrow. One more beer with Winston and then I'm heading back to the train station. I got no sleep last night and could use a snooze before my train leaves.

"Two Olands," I say to the bartender.

I turn and look at the stripper beside me. She takes a long, hard drag on her cigarette and ignores me. Blows a cloud of smoke out over the bar. Her lips are painted deep maroon. Her cheeks smeared in gaudy rouge. Black shit circles her eyes. I think for a minute about leaning left and feeding her my tongue, sucking on her smoky mouth, and running my hands all across her lumpy, leather-clad body. I want to pull her foreign form in close to me. Meld with her. Stick my dick in her right there at the bar while Winston watches and applauds, offering advice like a ring-side trainer.

"Four-forty," the bartender says.

I hand him a ten, my reverie interrupted. The stripper doesn't flinch, doesn't acknowledge my presence at all, even though I'm an arm's length from her, spitting distance. I want to say something now. Get her to at least look at me. I could ask her about her act, what time she's going on. Chat her up a little. But where the fuck would that get me? Nowhere. Nowhere fast. She stubs her cigarette, squeaks off her stool, and waddles away from me. I catch a whiff of leather as she leaves.

Lucy never wore leather. Apart from leather shoes, anyway. There was no way I'd ever have gotten her into a leather miniskirt, never mind out of one. She was a conventional dresser. Proper. Sweaters, blazers, expensive jeans, the occasional long, colourful skirt. Under that, boring, bland, matching bras and panties; always pristine white. I tried once on Valentine's Day with something red and sparse. She was genuinely appalled by the panties. Called me a pervert, refused to wear them. Forty bucks pissed away that night.

The sex we had was also boring and predictable. She was boring in bed. No imagination. No sense of adventure. It got mundane pretty fast. The whole relationship got mundane pretty fast. But for some fucking reason that escapes me now, I didn't realize it, didn't see that tedium was soon leading to a complete demise. I guess, despite my beefs now, I was happy with the mundane, with the mediocrity.

She wanted something else, something grand. Her head was full of university crap. Not a practical bone in her body. Deluded. She talked about finishing her degree and moving to New York. What the fuck for? What was she going to do in New York City with a lousy degree in some shitty arts program? Didn't know a soul there. Had ideas that living in the States was her future. Then, just when all the talk about that ended, she switched to talking shit about a trip to Europe. Never once asked me if I wanted to go. What would I have said? "Yeah honey, me and you up the Eiffel Tower, fuckin' brilliant! Just let me quit my job first." Nope. She had no plans of including me in her future. I was a footnote. A mistake. A memory.

After three beers—the last two paid for by yours truly—Winston decides he wants something to eat.

"They got these great open-face sandwiches. Roast beef and a stack of mashed potatoes, peas, and carrots. The works. We should get us some food if we're gonna drink all afternoon."

I look him over. I'm on the brink of exhaustion and I think he knows it, knows he can take advantage.

"I am kinda hungry."

"Let me take care of the next drink."

He reaches over and scoops up my empty, drawing it under the table.

"Told you I had an errand to run."

He flashes a mickey of rye, snickering.

"CC. Only the best for you, my friend."

Under the table Winston splashes about three fingers of rye into my empty bottle of Olands. He smiles, devious, mischievous. Then fills his bottle about halfway, probably five fingers worth.

"Now you get us some food and they won't be none the wiser."

I rub my chin and look around the bar. We're still the only ones here. The bartender is watching TV, oblivious to us. I don't know where the stripper went.

"They serve food in this place?"

"The best. And cheap, too. Come on, spring for it. It's $3.95 for a big plate of hot food."

I take a sip of the rye, diluted with the dregs of my beer. I lean back and rub my stomach. Then reach for my wallet. I take one of the tens out and head to the bar. I have to call to the bartender to get him to stop watching TV for a minute. He looks at me and reaches into the fridge for two more Olands.

"No. No more beer. We wanna get some food. You got open-faced roast beef sandwiches?"

The bartender grunts and steps over to the till. He rings in $7.90 and I hand him the ten, collecting all of the change. He scoffs at me and traipses behind the bar. I look up at the TV. Phil Donahue pushes his glasses up the bridge of his nose and thrusts a microphone into someone's face. Someone somewhere offers their opinion on something. It doesn't interest me. I don't care about their problems, wherever they are in the States. I've got my own problems up here.

Halfway through our meal, the stripper reappears. She's changed out of the leathers and is now decked out in a slutty red number. Frilly. Folds of fat droop out from her tight panties and bra. A little drunk, I start to applaud as soon as she steps onto the stage, trying to whoop, but my mouth's full of mashed potatoes.

"Take it easy," Winston says. "You're acting like you've never seen a dancer before. Fuck sakes."

The stripper nods at the bartender, and he slaps in some music: The Cars, from their first album. I recognize the guitar: "Let the Good Times Roll." It reminds me of high school. She's probably about the same age as me. Probably loved this album when it came out. She gets up on the small stage and starts strutting around, trying to dance, trying to look marginal- ly interested in what she's doing. She jiggles everywhere. But I'm loving every minute of it. I want to move closer, get right down in pervert's row and concentrate long and hard on what she's doing. But I don't. Instead, I push the remains of my lunch aside and sit back and watch her flaunt her stuff from a comfortable distance.

During the second song—a slower tune I don't know—Winston turns to me.

"You like white girls, then?"

"I'm not that fussy one way or the other."

He's looking a little restless now, distracted.

"You wanna go meet a black girl? I know one that'll fuck you this after- noon."

I look at the stripper. She's down to her panties. Rubbing her big tits. Jamming them against herself. Making the shape of an egg with her mouth.

"I got a train to catch, Winston."

He looks me over, unbelieving. "I'm talking about getting you laid!"

He flashes the mickey of rye and offers me a drink. The bottle's almost empty. I look back at the stripper. She turns to show us the thong running up the crack of her ass. She bends over. Pulls on the thin strip of fabric. It bisects her flesh perfectly, symmetrically. She looks back over her shoulder, pouting, a classic pose. It does something for me, to me.

"Where we gotta go for this?"

"Not far. We got time."

I look back at the stripper. She smiles at me, I'm certain of it, even at this distance.

"What's the catch? You her pimp or something?"

Winston leans forward, towards me, his back to the stripper. His plate is empty. His beer bottle is empty. His Bible sits on the table to his left.

"No, nothing like that at all. She's a good girl. Just needs it a lot. And she likes white boys, that's all. No catch. Nothing."

I'm drunk now, no question. I look back up at the stripper. The music has gone off. She's still in just her panties, bending over, collecting her belongings, her tits hanging from her like bags of wet cement. She stands up straight and gives me a smug look. I applaud again. Then raise my beer bottle to my lips and face Winston.

"Can you take me there, now?"

I stumble along the sidewalk, my eyes adjusting slowly to the natural light outside the Harbourview. Winston's half a step ahead of me, leading as usual. A light drizzle falls from the sky.

"How far we gotta walk?"

Winston looks back over his shoulder and sort of laughs.

"Not far. Not far at all."

He leads me on to Robie Street. After one block, I stop in an alleyway to take a piss. I lean one hand against the red brick of a building. I tilt my head back. Drizzle sprays my face. Winston talks to me from the street.

"You got any cash left?"

I look heavenward, his voice drifting over me.

"We should get us something to drink. Something to take to Wanda. That's her name: Wanda. A bottle. A token of our appreciation, *your* appreciation."

I finish pissing and walk back out to the street.

"You said no catch."

"This is no catch. I'm talking about simple manners here. Remember, she'll fuck you as sure as the day is long."

I've got ten dollars and some change left.

"There's a liquor store along here."

He points down the street. I stuff my hands into my pockets and start walking.

"Now, how's about that reading?"

I look over at Winston. I erupt in laughter. I am drunk in the early afternoon. I got absolutely no sleep last night. I have spent several hours with this stranger, getting drunk, listening to his bullshit, and now I am letting him take me to see some woman who, he assures me, will fuck me this afternoon before my train leaves. It's all a bit much, too much. I toss my head back as far as it will go, opening my mouth wide, and roar with laughter.

Winston is unbothered by my outburst. He ignores my laughter and reads his Bible aloud. He reads from Samuel about David's reign: "Once again the Israelites felt the Lord's anger."

I want to tell him about my anger but I'm too busy laughing. The thought makes me laugh even more. *My* anger. That's a joke. A damned good one.

Lucy was religious. She had faith. But not in me. Who can blame her? I seem to lack free will, direction, vision, certainty.

We stop at the liquor store and I spend most of my remaining money on a bottle of red wine. Winston takes it from me on the street.

"I thought it was for Wanda?"

He looks me up and down. He pulls a Swiss Army knife from his pocket and pries open the bottle. Drinks. Offers it to me.

"Wanda don't drink."

I laugh and jingle a few coins in my pocket. It's all the money I've got left in the world until I get my hands on the forty bucks in my chequing account.

Wanda isn't black. Winston introduces us, straight-faced, as if nothing is wrong.

"This's Wanda. Who I was telling you about."

I shake her dewy hand. We're inside a religious bookstore. Wanda is a clerk. She is tall and blonde, gaunt and withdrawn. She's wearing proper clothes. Like Lucy. Some kind of dull brown skirt-cardigan combo. Beige blouse. Under it all—I'd wager—pristine white panties and bra.

"He's here for the group?"

Winston nods.

I'm confused now. Winston holds the empty wine bottle out for Wanda.

"We had the communion wine already."

She tut-tuts and walks to the front of the store, locking us in. Winston steps over to a curtain at the back of the store and opens it, revealing a small chapel: Christ's image in neon on the wall. I want to laugh some more but I'm too tired, completely exhausted, defenceless. He gestures with his head, and I step behind the curtain. Wanda follows a minute later. She lights candles that form a circle around a crucifix six inches tall, sitting dead centre on a small altar. Winston sits on a fold-out chair. I inspect the small room, chock full of Christian bric-a-brac.

Wanda leads us in prayer. I find myself down on my knees, hands folded in supplication in front of my chest, listening to her speak. Her voice rises and falls, lilts occasionally. It is beautiful. It is soothing, soporific.

Winston sits on his chair behind us, snoring. I reach out and take Wanda's hand in mine, lean forward, and pull her towards me. She smiles. I kiss her. She holds her pursed lips against mine, resisting me and my advances, not giving me what I want. I'm imagining that she's Lucy with all my might.

She rises up off her knees.

"Lucy?"

"That's not what we're here for. We're here for Jesus."

Her face is flushed red. Some colour, finally.

"Lucy?"

"Winston? Winston, who is this friend of yours?"

She's on her feet now, straightening the pleats in her skirt, brushing away something invisible.

"Lucy?"

"He come on to you? This fucker come on to you in the house of the Lord?"

I look over at Winston. I can't tell if he's serious or not. He rises out of his chair and blunders out through the curtain, drunk.

"Cast him out, then. Cast him out. CAST THE MOTHERFUCKER OUT!"

In the other room, I can hear him fucking with the cash register, pounding on the keys. She steps through the curtain to check out the commotion. I look around. Christ's eyes blaze right through me. I snuff a couple candles, grab the crucifix in my left fist. For some reason, I attempt the sign of the cross, messing up the order, then kick through the curtain, back into the store.

Winston is laughing, holding a palmful of blue and purple bills in the air, like he's keeping candy from a kid. She is close to tears, disconsolate. I'm not sure; I think she might still be praying. She seems to be muttering something. I step towards her armed with Christ's likeness on a cross. From the back, she looks just like Lucy. Upright. Proper. Pristine. Pure. Everything I can't stand.

I raise the crucifix in the air. To my left, Winston blurts something but I'm not hearing him now. I've listened to too much of his bullshit today. Wanda turns to face me, and I catch her across the top of her right eye with the cross. Her flesh opens, blood all across her forehead and nose. She crumbles to the floor like a detonated building, rolls and settles, staring up at her assailant with glassy eyes. I look at the damage I have done. The welt swells. She's got a mouse above her eye like she's gone twelve rounds with George Chuvalo. Blood on the carpet. Not a peep, not a prayer from her.

"Lucy?"

Winston looks over at me. He's in some kind of shock. He can't speak. There's blood splashed on his greatcoat, more in his hair, shimmering with the lint.

I squat over her, check if she's breathing, check for a pulse.

I bunch up the sleeve of my shirt in my fist and wipe blood from her brow. Then swipe a finger across her nose, smearing blood on my trousers. I look at Winston. He jams the cash in his pocket and sprints out the door. I lean over her and kiss her lily lips. Then stuff the weapon in my pocket and chase after my witness.

Back in the centre of Halifax, a few blocks from the train station, Winston turns to me. "I told you she'd fuck you, didn't I?"

He's in denial about the assault.

"Winston," I start and then stop.

"Let's get us a drink. Celebrate your fucking," he sputters, drooling a little.

"My train."

I point vaguely in the direction of the station.

"You've missed it and you owe me a drink."

I look at a digital clock above a bank: 2:38.

"No, no time. Tell you what. Take the cross. Pawn it. Buy yourself a bottle on me."

I put the bloody crucifix in his hand. He wraps his fingerless gloves around it. Then stares at me. He holds the Bible in his right hand and extends his left arm in my direction, pointing the cross at me.

"Sinner, leave."

I take his advice. I bolt across the wet pavement, ignoring honks. It's all downhill to the station. I get my duffel bag from the locker. Take my seat in coach class. My mind draws a blank; no thoughts now.

I start to nod off as the train jerks into motion. Grey rain spatters the grubby window. Someone nudges my shoulder roughly.

"Ticket."

I lean right, give it to him, then settle again.

Wipe Out

by Matt Hughes

At the heart of noir lie disappointment, loss, and despair. Ultimately, nothing goes right and the gods are always ready to punish those who think they've got the thing pegged. That's the theme at the core of Matt Hughes' series of stories about Mikey, the Vancouver-based burglar blessed with brilliant ideas and lousy luck. The stories are lean and hard-boiled, and one of them, "One More Kill," took the Crime Writers of Canada's Arthur Ellis Award for Best Short Story in 2000.

Matt lives in Comox, B.C., teaches creative writing, and writes speeches for political leaders and corporate CEOs, as well as other crime fiction. His novels include the 1997 semi-comic political suspense thriller *Downshift*, as well as two fantasies, *Fools Errant* and its forthcoming sequel *Fool Me Twice*.

Mikey waits by the elevators until the receptionist comes out and heads for the washroom, then he walks into the law firm's offices. He tilts back the baseball cap with the Purolator logo and says, "Here for a pickup?"

Several women are in a corral of desks behind the receptionist's empty seat. One of them looks up briefly from her computer screen and says, "Should be right there, somewhere."

Mikey makes a show of looking on the chest-high counter that separates the receptionist from whatever drifts in the door. "Nothing here," he says.

"Kay-Lynne'll be right back," says the woman. Her fingers don't stop rattling the keyboard in front of her.

"Sure," says Mikey. His eyes haven't stopped moving since he came in. He's making a list: good quality motion detectors, positioned right where they need to be; a hemisphere of dark glass on the ceiling by the back wall almost certainly houses a video camera; a wire running under the carpet beneath his feet—*pressure plate*, he thinks, and better than even money, they got laser tripwires and maybe even thermal sensors in the walls.

The receptionist comes back in. "Pickup for Purolator?" Mikey says.

That makes the girl look puzzled, so Mikey gives her a show of him checking his clipboard, then puts on his I'm-so-dumb face and says, "Sorry. Wrong floor."

Two minutes later he's in the underground parking garage. He dumps the Purolator hat and clipboard on the passenger seat of the Toyota pickup and heads up the exit ramp.

"No way to go in and out of that place, nobody sees it," he tells the steering wheel. The thought of giving Angie T. the bad news sends an involuntary shiver through his back muscles.

The mid-afternoon traffic around Georgia and Granville is just as crazy as you'd expect in a major city with neither a downtown freeway nor a decent transit system; where the city council has decided to dig up major streets to lay an earthquake-proof water system. Mikey finally makes enough right turns to add up to a left and gets onto the Viaduct heading for East Vancouver.

He decides he's not going to tell the client the job can't be done. "I gotta think about this," he says to the windshield.

Mike finds Angie Tedesco sipping murderous black coffee in the bare back room of a trattoria on Commercial Drive near East First Avenue, a neighbourhood they used to call Little Italy before everything got multi-cultural, though it's still at least as easy to find pasta as Thai noodles.

Angie T. is a short, balding loan shark and money mover with a little black moustache and a lank comb-over. The hands that cradle the diminutive espresso cup are big enough to conceal a bocce ball. Mikey has heard that those hands have done things nobody's hands should do.

Sitting next to Angie is Carmine Zuccaro, who would need only a ten percent increase in body hair to qualify as Bigfoot. Angie keeps Carmine around for when he has to rearrange somebody's agenda.

"Youshouldn't deal with this guy," Carmine says when Mikey sits down across from his boss. "He's a mook."

"Did I ask you your opinion?" Angie says, and looks at Carmine until the big man looks away. Then he asks Mikey, "Well?"

"I guess I got good news and bad news," Mikey says.

Angie turns and gives Carmine a different look. Carmine reaches over and puts a hand on Mikey's shoulder, then somehow manages to insert a thumb between muscle and bone in a way that makes the arm feel like it's coming off.

"Jesus, Carmine!" Mikey says, squirming.

The giant's expression never changes. He keeps up the pressure a few more seconds until Angie wriggles his thick eyebrows. Mikey rubs the spot where the thumb was, trying to get the blood moving again.

"I'm waiting here, you're gonna come tell me jokes?" Angie says.

"I was just trying to put it in perspective for you, Angie," Mikey says.

"For perspective, I don't hire a burglar. I hire a..." Angie can't think of anybody he would hire for that purpose. "Just tell me, how does it look?"

Mikey takes a breath. "Okay. How it looks is there's no way I go into that place and nobody knows it. They got the whole catalogue, all top of the line. You just walk by thinking about going in, they probably got something reads your mind and speed-dials the cops."

Angie says a short word, then slams down the little coffee cup and says it again. He looks at Mikey, and his face works its way into an expression the burglar has never seen on the man before—kind of *help me, I'm sinking,* Mikey thinks—as Angie says, "Suppose somebody, maybe a security guard, was to cut the power?"

Mikey shakes his head. "I'm figuring battery backup, hundred percent sure."

His client lets his hands lie flat on the chipped formica tabletop. He looks down at them as if they could give him the answer to his problem, and Mikey is thinking those hands have probably solved most of the problems Angie T. has bumped into over the years.

"What did we say, two Cs?" Angie says, without looking up.

"Yeah, but—"

"I don't wanna hear no buts, Mikey, " the loan shark says. Still looking at his hands, he tells Carmine, "Pay him."

Mikey takes the two bills and puts them in his shirt pocket. "I said there was good news."

Angie T. looks up. This is where it all happens, Mikey knows. A mouse pulls a thorn out of a lion's paw, it can do the mouse some serious good. But if the mouse messes up, maybe drives the point in deeper, the last thing the mouse is going to know is how it feels to be ripped apart. Mikey swallows.

"You were saying," Angie says.

"You asked me to look over this lawyer's set-up," Mikey says.

"I know what I asked you."

Mikey keeps on. "You wanted to know, could I go in, get a package out of the safe, nobody knows it's gone. And you said the package was, like, so big." Mikey holds his hands as if they were moulded around a pound of butter.

Angie's jaw moves sideways, like a lizard chewing a beetle. A joint under one ear creaks. "I'm not hearing any good news," he says.

Now Mikey goes for broke. "Well, that size," he says, "I'm thinking computer diskettes."

There is a silence in the little room, a stillness so profound that Mikey can almost hear individual dust motes rubbing together in the shaft of light that slides in from the curtained window.

Angie T.'s brown eyes stay on Mikey. They don't blink or shift their focus by a hairbreadth. Mikey finds it hard to breathe.

"You don't got to tell me what's on the disks," the burglar says, the words tumbling into each other like falling dominoes in a commercial. "But if that's what's in the package, I can solve the problem."

Angie blinks. His eyes flick toward Carmine. He says, "Carmine, whyncha go put a dollar in the meter?"

The giant's face shifts its placid expression toward a question, an uncomfortable transition, like a man trying on a coat that's too tight in the shoulders.

"Just go and do it," Angie says. Carmine's features reset to blank. He rises from the little square table like a big old moon rocket inching up off the launch pad.

When he's gone, Angie turns back to Mikey. "I know you, what, six, seven years, right?"

Mikey nods.

"I see you're always trying to get out of this nickel-dime B&E crap."

"I got a brain, Angie," Mikey says. "I see angles, opportunities."

Angie's short laugh has no humour in it. "The thing is this," the loan shark says, "the stuff you do, you screw up, you get six months, maybe a year. The stuff I'm into, a guy screws up and *pffft!* he's dead."

Mikey nods again.

"Don't sit there nodding at me," Angie says. "I'm telling you something you don't know. This business, it's got floors and it's got ceilings. To you, me, and Carmine, we're the ceiling. But there's guys look at us, we're just the floor."

"I get it," Mikey says.

The loan shark looks at the table, looks up at the burglar again. "You better get it. I'm gonna offer you something now. You take it, you take it all the way. What I'm gonna tell you, it can get *me* whacked, somebody hears about it. You, they step on like a bug."

Mikey's mind shows him a picture of a dark forest, bad things shifting and lurking behind black trees. Somewhere down the trail, made faint and misty by distance, is the golden light he's always wanted to get to. *Whatever it is*, he tells himself, *I can do it.*

"I get it."

Angie T. looks over his shoulder, although he knows the room is empty. He lowers his voice. "It's this asshole, Terry Alizotto, married my Angelina. For her sake, I give him some things to do, but every time, he makes a godawful mess. I mean, forget about it—there's guys passed out in alleys, you wake 'em up, they gonna do better work.

"So I tell him, 'Terry, this life ain't for you,' and I get him a straight job hauling stuff off building sites. Two grand a week, all he's gotta do is show up, sign in now and then."

"He didn't go for that?" says Mikey.

Angie T. rolls his eyes. "He gets my own daughter bitching at me. Then they come for dinner, and while he's in my house, he goes into my den, copies some stuff off my computer, gives it to this lawyer to hold. Then he says, 'Put me back on the count, or I start showing your business around.'"

"Sheesh," says Mikey.

"Sheesh, my ass," says Angie T. "It's not just *my* business on those disks. There's things I'm doing for other people, you know what I'm saying?"

Mikey knows, and now he has an inkling just how bad the beasts in the dark forest might be. But what Angie T. is telling him brings the warm golden light a lot clearer and closer.

"I can fix this," he says. "If it's just disks, I can fix it."

"You fix this, I'll give you the opportunities I gave Alizotto. But it's gotta be quick—I got till the weekend to fix him up with what he likes, or he's back at the lawyer's Monday to collect the disks." Angie looks out into the trattoria's main room, where Carmine is coming back in from the street. "The meantime, any of this gets to the wrong people, all bets are off, you know what I'm saying?"

Mikey checks his watch. "It's noon. I can put something together this afternoon, then forty-eight hours and you're clear. You want me to tell you what I'm gonna do?"

Angie looks to see if Carmine is coming back. "No," he says. "Just do it."

"I'm going to need a couple of grand for supplies."

The loan shark reaches for his roll. He peels off twenty hundreds and passes them across the table. Mikey puts them with the other two. "I gotta hurry," he says, and starts to rise.

Angie reaches over and puts a big hand on Mikey's arm. "Stay in touch," he says.

Carmine is outside on the sidewalk. "What's that all about?" he wants to know.

"I can't tell you."

Carmine's face never shows much, but then it never has to. People study it closely because it can be directly relevant to them to know what Carmine's about to do.

Mikey doesn't like what he sees in the big man's face. "He told me I can't tell nobody," he says.

One of Carmine's hands reaches for the burglar. Mikey says, "You got me scared, Carmine. But he's got me more scared."

Carmine puts his hand down.

"I'm just looking to move up," Mikey says.

"Everybody's looking to move up," Carmine says. But now there is an identifiable expression on his face. Somewhere inside Carmine's head, ponderous wheels are turning. He watches Mikey walk away, then goes back into the trattoria.

Mikey goes four blocks down Commercial to an electrical supply place he almost hit once, when he had a potential buyer for big spools of copper wire, but the guy changed his mind. Now he goes in and buys the materials he needs for under fifty dollars. The rest of Angie's two grand he spends at a coin shop buying silver, in dollars and ten-ounce ingots, along with a couple of commemorative sets from the Montréal Olympics.

He takes it all back to his one-room apartment in a crumbling high-rise overlooking English Bay, and spends an hour at his kitchen table winding thin copper wire around a flat piece of iron, then connecting it through a timer switch to a compact, heavy-duty battery. He sets the timer for ten seconds and watches to see if the switch will open. There is a faint hum, and then a pair of needle-nose pliers slides across the table and sticks to the homemade electromagnet.

Now he puts a formatted blank disk into his computer's floppy drive and copies onto it a few files chosen at random. He pops the disk out of the drive and lays it on top of the magnet, waits a minute, then puts it back in the drive. *Disk error. Disk not formatted*, appears on the monitor. Mikey repeats the experiment with another disk, this time letting it sit for ten minutes, a foot away from the electromagnet. When he puts the plastic square into the floppy drive, the computer tells him that it, too, is unreadable.

Mikey kills the current to the electromagnet and resets the timer switch to reactivate it at nine o'clock that night. He figures the battery is juiced enough to keep it running for an hour. Then he packs it into the bottom of a wooden box that once held a bottle of Okanagan wine, covers it with a page torn from the newspaper, and fills the box with the silver.

Kay-Lynne doesn't recognize him in a suit and without the Purolator hat. When Mikey tells her his name is Ron Fenshaw and he wants to see a lawyer, she takes him to an office that has the name William Takashita on the door.

Mikey explains that he is holding a box full of silver as security in a business deal and wants somewhere safe to keep it overnight. He opens the lid of the box and shows the lawyer the heaped coins and ingots.

"Cost you fifty," says Takashita. Mikey pays cash and accepts a receipt. The lawyer has him sign "Ron Fenshaw" on a gummed label, which he then pastes over the box's side and lid so it can't be opened without breaking the seal. Mikey asks to see the box put in the safe. The lawyer shields the combination lock while he spins the tumblers, but when the thick door opens, Mikey sees the package Angie T. described. The lawyer slides the box in next to it.

He tells the lawyer he'll be back in the morning, then goes downstairs to the shopping mall to phone Angie T. "It's in place," he says. "Ten o'clock tomorrow, I'll go in again, see if it worked."

"Let me know, soon as," Angie says. For the first time, Mikey hears in the loan shark's voice the kind of shake that Angie T. must have heard a thousand times. He wonders if his client is as good at bearing pressure as he is at applying it.

Mikey is at the lawyer's a little before ten. There's a small crowd in the reception area: a silver-haired guy in a hand-made suit that might as well have "senior partner" stitched across the back, and a couple of other guys who don't need to have "cop" stencilled on their off-the-racks. The big lawyer scans a blue piece of court paper, then kneels to open the safe.

William Takashita is off to the side, with Kay-Lynne and the women who do the word processing. Mikey puts himself beside the lawyer. "I come for my package," he says.

Takashita keeps his eyes on the cops and talks out of the side of his mouth, like he's auditioning for an old-time gangster movie. "It'll be a minute."

"What's up?"

"Search warrant," the lawyer says. "Evidence in a homicide, they're saying."

The kneeling lawyer straightens up and hands one of the cops Terry Alizotto's package of disks. The cop tucks it under his arm like he's a running back with a touchdown in his future, then he and his partner are out the door.

Takashita stoops and gets Mikey's box before the senior man closes the safe and hands it to him. "Homicide, eh?" Mikey says. "They say who it was?" The lawyer has spent his career doing wills and real estate, Mikey figures, or he wouldn't be so excited about what he has been seeing. "It was on the warrant. A client of Mr. Plimley's, guy named Alizotto."

As he boots the Toyota back to Commercial Drive, Mikey is struggling to see the golden glow somewhere up ahead. Black shapes are moving around the edges, shading the light, trying to compress it to a pinpoint and smother it. The closest parking spot to the trattoria is almost a block away, and he leaves the pickup and legs it fast down the sidewalk. But halfway there, Carmine Zuccaro is standing in a doorway. The giant steps out and puts a hand like a grizzly's paw on Mikey's shoulder. Mikey stops.

"It worked, Carmine. It's totally cool. Just let me go tell the man."

Carmine says, "Forget about it." He is between Mikey and the restaurant, standing sideways to watch the trattoria's front door.

"That thing he was worried about. Man, I fixed it."

Carmine shakes his head, still looking the other way. "We've moved on."

The restaurant door opens. A knot of men in suits comes out, swarming around Angie T. like Secret Service agents around the President, hustling him to a car at the curb. For a second Mikey sees the loan shark's eyes, wide and flicking around like a cow's when it's being pushed into the slaughterhouse, then somebody puts a meaty, pinky-ringed hand on Angie's head and pushes him down and into the back seat. The car pulls away.

"But he's clear," Mikey tells Carmine. "The disks, they're wiped."

"Don't know about no disks," the big man says. He looks at Mikey. "You're smart, you don't know nothing neither."

"We had a deal, Angie and me," Mikey says.

"Angie don't make deals now," Carmine says. "I do. And I got no business with you." He sniffs and moves his neck like he needs to rearrange its position inside his shirt collar, then heads down to the trattoria. There's a difference in the way he walks. One of the guys out front opens the door for him.

Mikey watches the car carrying Angie T. dwindle in size as it goes down Commercial Drive. A gleam of sunlight reflects from the chrome trim above the rear window. Mikey watches the glimmering spark grow smaller and smaller, until the car turns the corner on East First Avenue and the light is gone for good.

The Package

by Brad Smith

In the worlds of James M. Cain, Jim Thompson, and John D. MacDonald, the good guys are bad, and the bad guys are worse. That also describes the existentialist purgatory of the characters Brad Smith writes about so powerfully. Brad is also proof that noir grows just as abundantly in the country as it does in any metropolis. Born in the hamlet of Canfield, Ontario, and currently living in Dunnville, Brad dropped out of school early to travel and work his way across Canada, the southern U.S., and Africa. His list of jobs is the kind that's perfect for a book jacket. Farmhand, bartender, truck driver, pipe insulator, railroad signalman, and others too numerous to list or too vague to remember. His recent novel *One-Eyed Jacks* is a hard-boiled gem set in 1950s Toronto; and it was shortlisted for both the Hammett Award from the International Association of Crime Writers, and the Crime Writers of Canada's Arthur Ellis Award.

The rhythmic clicking of the train fills the room. Royce sits at the controls, an O-gauge Lionel, his great belly straining against the fine silk of his belted robe. There are open doors leading to a terrace facing west, and the room is bathed in soft afternoon sunlight. The train set is mounted on an immense oak table, and the room itself is a shrine to the golden days of railroading. Coal-oil lanterns on shelves, a stationmaster's swivel chair, signals, telegraphs, caps, coats, watches. Royce hunches over the line, adjusting the speed as the train chugs dutifully along—over the trestle, through the tunnel, past the little lake coloured with blue dye.

Lewis stands, Buddha-like, along the wall, beside the brass-trimmed doors, his eyes blank as he watches the circuitous route of the train, his hands hanging at his sides—indeed, Royce had never seen Lewis put his hands in his pockets, or behind his back, or anywhere.

With a deft touch, Royce glides the train into the station, brings it to a perfect stop.

"Safely in, Lewis," he says. "Safely in."

He heaves himself to his feet, crosses through French doors into the living room. He pours himself a shot of bourbon from a decanter on a sideboard and turns to look into the open doorway of the bedroom. There is a naked woman on the bed. Her eyes are cold as a snake's, staring back at him. Her left hand is visible, handcuffed to the brass railing of the bed. Royce looks at her benignly for a moment, then turns away. The woman watches him as she raises her right hand and takes a pull from a cigarette. Sighing audibly, she produces a key and releases herself from the cuffs.

Carrying his drink, Royce returns to the game room, where Lewis stands, watching the train even yet.

"Lewis, my boy," he says. "Why do you watch when there's nothing to see? The train is at the station, the adventure is complete. It is the journey itself which fascinates—the perils of circumstance and choice. The arrival is anticlimactic. It means nothing."

Lewis' eyes are diverted momentarily as the woman, wearing a short black dress, walks out of the bedroom. Her expression still vacant, she glances about the room, spots an envelope on a glass end table. She picks it up, peers inside, and slips it into her purse.

"I'm goin' then," she announces.

When Royce smiles, the woman turns and leaves without another word.

"I find her rather truculent, Lewis. Don't you think?" Royce asks. "I don't believe we'll have her back. I feel the need for companionship of a more stimulating nature. A positive attitude would be a start."

Royce has a package in his hand and he wraps it neatly with binding as he speaks. He hands it to Lewis.

"There you are, my boy," he says. "Remember, it is the journey which excites us. Circumstance and choice, the outcome unknown. Circumstance and choice."

He sits down and puts the train into motion again. He watches critically as the little engine moves away from the station, takes the switch to a spur line, which leads up a slope to the papier mâché mountains.

"They say that Mussolini made the trains run on time," Royce says thoughtfully. "Other than that, he was a despicable man. Lewis, are you still here? Go, my boy. Go!"

Slider talks himself into a three-on-three game on the court at the old collegiate. Slider, with his baggy pants and his ghetto talk and bad tattoos—everybody wants what they can't have, and all he wants is to be a brother. But he can play a little ball. He hits a three pointer, falling away, and when he turns, Lewis is standing there, watching. Slider waves the ball carrier by, walks over.

"Hey," he says. "Word up."

Lewis pulls the package from his jacket and hands it over. Then he gives Slider a slip of paper and a fifty-dollar bill. Slider checks out the address, then looks up at Lewis' impassive face.

"How 'bout another ten?" he asks. "My girlfriend's birthday."

Lewis' eyes go dark at the suggestion.

"All right, bro," Slider says at once, throwing his hands up. "Don't be freakin' on me."

The office is deserted, as is the rest of the building, an eight-storey red brick waiting for the wrecking ball. The door was unlocked, just as they'd been told. They walk in cautiously, find the light, and turn it on. A single overhead bulb, maybe forty watts.

"There's nobody here," Dave says.

"I can see that," Sam says. "You think I can't see that?"

Sam walks over to a grimy window, looks down at the street below.

"Lookit this place," Dave says. He walks to the desk, examines an old rotary pencil sharpener mounted there. In the process he somehow gets his pinky finger caught in the works. He yelps in pain and removes the bloody digit from the sharpener.

"The fuck you doin'?" Sam demands, turning.

"Nothin."

"Just relax," Sam says, and lights a Players.

"I'm fucking relaxed," Dave tells him, and to demonstrate his relaxed state, he sits down behind the desk and puts his feet up. He is wearing brand new sneakers, with Velcro fasteners instead of laces.

"So, where is this guy?" he asks.

"He'll be here."

"What's his name—Lewis?"

"Lewis," Sam says.

"I hear he's a bad motherfuck."

"That's what they say."

"I hear he killed a guy once over a pool game. Beat him to death with a fucking cue, man."

"That's the story."

"I heard it was all over a dollar," Dave says. "What kind of an animal kills a guy for a buck?"

"I don't think it was the money," Sam says. "I think he was trying to make a point."

"Some point."

They wait in silence. After a time, Sam finishes his smoke, crosses over to butt it in the ashtray on the desk.

"What's with the shoes?"

"They're my new runners," Dave says. "Bought 'em today. Walmart."

"They got straps."

"Yeah.Velcro."

"What are you—a fucking retard?"

"What?"

"They make those shoes for fuckin' retards," Sam tells him. "People who can't tie their own shoes. You look like a fuckin' retard."

"I ain't a fuckin' retard," Dave says angrily. "I can tie my shoes. You've seen me tie my shoes, Sam. I ain't no retard."

"Well, you look like one."

"Fuck you."

"You look like a fucking retard in those shoes, man."

"Yeah, you know what you look like?"

"What?"

"Aw, fuck you."

"Good one."

The door opens and they both jump. Slider walks in. He's got his Walkman on, some Snoop, and he's got his shoulders working to the rhyme.

"Hey," Sam says.

"Hey." Slider pulls the 'phones off.

"We been waiting," Sam says, and then he realizes how it sounds. "Not long! I didn't mean we were...you know."

Slider shrugs.

"So what's the deal here?" Sam asks. "We supposed to give you anything?"

Slider begins to speak and then he stops, his wheels turning.

"Yeah, you gotta give me ten, dog."

Sam's eyes pop and he turns toward Dave.

"Ten fuckin' grand!" Dave says. Trying to whisper, panic in his voice.

Sam exhales heavily and turns back to Slider, trying to act cool.

"Hey, now. The man never told us nothing 'bout no ten grand. I mean, we don't have..."

Slider shrugs again, reaches under his shirt. The boys misinterpret the move.

"Hold on, man!" Dave yells.

"Hey, hey, we can work it out," Sam says. "Nobody told us..."

"Nobody said nothin'."

"We can give you something though," Sam says. "Good faith, you know what I mean?"

Slider is easily confused on a good day, but this is too much. He decides to go with the flow, though. Sam and Dave have their backs turned, their wallets out.

"We got, like, a hundred and twelve bucks," Sam says, turning. "That's just for now, understand."

"We woulda had more but I bought new runners today," Dave explains.

"Shut the fuck up," Sam says. "Mr. Lewis doesn't want to hear about your fuckin' retard shoes."

When he hears the name, Slider smiles, nods at the goof. He pulls the package from under his shirt, tosses it on the desk.

"I know it ain't no ten grand," Sam says.

"I'll take the hundred," Slider says.

"And twelve," Dave reminds him.

"Keep the twelve," Slider says. "Get some juice, dogs."

The taxi pulls up outside the bar, sits by the curb idling for maybe a minute. Then the door opens and the Blonde gets out. She's a little over-dressed for the hour and way overdressed for the neighbourhood. She stands looking at the rundown tavern—the broken plastic sign above the door, the graffiti-stained brick, the smell of urine and beer and decadence. She glances down at the scrap of paper in her hand—the familiar hand-writing—and checks the address. She squares her shoulders like a lad marching off to war, and walks inside.

Sam and Dave sit at the end of the bar watching as the Blonde walks in, has a short look around, and then sits at the opposite end.

"Oh, man," Dave says when he sees her.

"Oh, man is right."

The bartender approaches her. He wears a greasy mustache and a shirt that must have been white at one time. He fancies himself a ladies' man.

"Hey there. What'll you have?"

"I don't know," the Blonde says, looking at the drink specials on the board. "What's good?"

"What's good? The bartender."

"How 'bout that—I'm in a comedy club," the Blonde says. "Vodka martini. Rocks."

The bartender moves off to make the drink. Dave watches the Blonde like a dog watches the grill at a family barbecue.

"Probably one of those supermodels," he says. "Like on Letterman."

"What's a fuckin' supermodel doin' in here?" Sam asks. "Checking out your new shoes?"

The bartender delivers the martini, raises his hand when she attempts to pay.

"I got it."

"I don't think so."

"Why not?"

"Let's just say I'm a liberated woman," the Blonde says. "I light my own cigarettes, I buy my own drinks." She smiles. "And I don't fuck sleazy bartenders who look like they haven't had a bath since the Leafs last won the cup. Okay?"

Down the bar, Sam finishes his beer. "Let's go," he says. "We got a delivery to make."

Dave involuntarily touches the package on the bar. "Let's stick around. Let's buy her a drink."

"With what? We only had twelve bucks, remember? I gotta take a leak. Drink up."

Sam walks into the back. Dave lifts his glass to his mouth. Taking a peek over the rim, he is surprised to find the Blonde looking back at him. Smiling.

In the gents' Sam pisses and washes his hands. The towel dispenser is empty. He looks about in vain, finally wipes his hands on his pants. Then he looks in the mirror, checks his profile, left and right. He isn't surprised that there are no paper towels.

He is surprised, walking back into the bar, to find that Dave is gone.

The Blonde, too.

Jessica sits before the easel, legs spread, glasses perched on her nose, paint smeared along the line of her chin. On the canvas is a landscape, a river winding through pastoral farmland.

Daniel enters the apartment, wearing jeans, boots and his leather jacket. He comes up behind her and kisses her on the neck as he looks at the painting.

"I like it," he says, and he slips his hands under her shirt.

"Recognize anything?"

"Yeah, your tits."

"The painting, moron."

He has a long look. "The farm," he decides. "Along the Grand River."

"Very good."

"You do that from memory?"

"You betcha."

"You're a talented woman."

"I keep telling you that," she says and looks at her watch. "You better hustle, you're gonna be late."

His face changes then, and he walks away, goes into the bathroom. A teapot whistles on the countertop. She walks over and makes a cup of tea.

"I almost forgot," she calls. "Jimmy phoned. His truck is fried. He wants you to pick him up."

Daniel comes out of the bathroom, wiping his hands on a towel. "Yeah, well, I'm not going in."

"Aw, I know you hate afternoons, but it's your last shift."

He turns and carelessly tosses the towel back into the bathroom. "Got things to do."

Not looking at her.

"You fucking asshole," she says. "You're doing a delivery for Royce, aren't you?"

"Don't," he warns her. "I don't want to get into it."

"Well, we're into it," she says. "Is that what you're doing? Daniel, look at me."

He peels his shirt off, tosses it aside, and walks into the bedroom. Seconds later, he comes out, pulling a clean sweatshirt over his head. She stares him down.

"Hey," he says defiantly. "I can go to work for eight hours and make a hundred-and-fifty bucks, or I can run a parcel across town and make a grand. Is that a tough choice, babe?"

"No, it's the smart move, Daniel. And when your son's born, you can teach him to run drugs, too. Think about it—it'll be a Hallmark moment."

"It's not drugs. I've told you that."

"Then what is it? Why's he pay you all this money. The dude never heard of FedEx?"

"I *told* you—he's a collector. Artifacts—old coins, maps, shit like that. Some of it might have gotten here through illegal channels, you know? It's *not* drugs."

He reaches above the fridge, produces a .38 revolver, checks the load.

"Then why do you carry that?"

"You know the old saying," he says smiling. "Better to have it and not need it than need it and not have it."

"I got an old saying for you," she says. "Fuck you."

He regards her darkly for a moment, then puts the gun back. He walks over and indicates the easel with the point of his chin.

"You're the one who wants the place in the country," he says. "Well, I'm gonna buy you that place. But I can't swing it working at the plant. Every time I do this, it all goes into savings."

He starts for the door.

"That fucking Royce," she says. "He's not straight. I don't know what he's into, but he's not straight."

"Nobody around here is, babe. That's why we have to get out."

Eleven in the morning and Sam's sitting on the stoop in front of a decayed walk-up in the East End. He's smoking a Players and waiting, watching the traffic, both powered and pedestrian. Dave finally shows, looking like a hound caught creeping out of the chicken pen.

"Well, if it ain't Romeo."

"Hey."

"She's got it?"

"Yup."

"You're a fucking idiot."

"Don't call me that," Dave says softly. "I'm sorry."

Sam flicks his cigarette into the gutter and watches Dave for a long moment. Dave turns and looks out over the street.

"Well, we better go find her," Sam says. "We're dead fucking meat if we don't get it back, you know that?"

"Yup. I know it."

Sam gets to his feet. "Well—did you at least fuck her?"

"Of course I fucked her."

"You're lying. You never fucked her."

"I guess I fucked her in my head," Dave says then. "In my head I fucked her."

"In her head she fucked you. Let's go."

Royce sits down to an enormous breakfast on the terrace. There are eggs and sausages, pancakes and toast, fried potatoes and ham. Royce, wearing a mauve robe, eats like a man who grew up without utensils. Lewis stands nearby, silent, watchful.

"She picked the dumb one, did she?" Royce asks, his mouth full. "Good for her. You know, Lewis, I always had respect for her intelligence. In spite of everything else that happened, I always admired her brain. I admired her ass, too, but that's another story."

Lewis is gazing intently at the train set.

"So, now young Daniel enters the lion's den," Royce continues. "He'll need all the resolve of his biblical forefather this day. Wouldn't you say, Lewis? Of course not. I forget sometimes that you don't actually say anything, do you?"

A soft yet distinct sobbing is heard from the other room. Stuffing a link sausage into his mouth, Royce rises and walks over to pull the bedroom door shut. Then he returns to his repast.

"Poor Alicia, she really is too emotional for her vocation. I fear this might be her last visit here. It is getting so difficult to find interesting people in the city. I do look forward to Amsterdam next month."

Lewis stares at the train, as if trying to will it into motion.

The living room is high-ceilinged, spacious, beautifully appointed. The carpets are Persian, the trim walnut. The Blonde wears silk pajamas, in spite of the hour, and carries a cocktail in her hand. Daniel follows her into the room.

"Do you drink, Daniel? It is Daniel, isn't it?"

"I'll take a beer. How do you know my name?"

"I have domestic and I have Heineken."

"I'll take the home brew. You didn't answer my question."

There is obviously some sort of refrigeration unit in the panelled wall. She pours beer into a pilsner glass and brings it over.

"Royce," she says.

"Royce didn't tell me your name."

"Names are not important, Daniel," the Blonde says. "Especially to people like Royce. People don't matter to him—how could a name? Sit down."

They sit on a plush leather couch, the smell of the leather so fresh that Daniel assumes it is new. The Blonde crosses her legs, displaying a fetching ankle. She sips from her glass and then fishes an olive from the drink and places it delicately between her lips.

"Do you like martinis, Daniel?"

"I never developed a taste for them."

"They can be dangerous. I think it was Dorothy Parker who said it best, 'I like to drink a martini, two at the very most.'"

"I know all I need to know about Dorothy and that bunch at the Algonquin," Daniel says. "You have a package for me?"

She stands at once, crosses the room for a cigarette. She appears offended.

"You're very touchy, Daniel."

"I'm not big on games, that's all."

"Neither am I," the Blonde assures him. "So what're we doing associating with a freak like Royce?"

"I'm just doing a pickup and delivery," Daniel says. "What your involvement is, I don't know and I don't need to know."

She shrugs in resignation, drops the pose. She walks to a cabinet and produces the package. Returning, she hands it over.

"You have the pictures?"

"What pictures?" Daniel asks.

"The package for the pictures, that's the deal."

"Listen," Daniel says. "I don't know shit about any pictures. I was told you had a package for me."

"Christ, I can't believe this," the Blonde says and she sits down heavily. She looks like she's about to cry. "You really don't know, do you?"

"I really don't *care*."

"You know anything about the guy?"

"He pays well."

She regards him a long moment, as if making up her mind. "Royce is a psycho, man. His whole life is a game. He's a fucking puppeteer, you want to know the truth."

"I don't need to know it."

She gives him the look of indecision again, then gets up and walks over to refill her drink. She speaks without turning; a theatrical touch.

"I met him at a gallery opening," she says. "What can I say? I mistook him for a human being. We had dinner. One thing led to another."

"So these pictures—they're of you and him having dinner?"

"I'm glad you find this amusing," she says, turning to him. "They're pictures of me sucking his limp dick. And worse. Scotch and cocaine, bad for a girl's judgment, you know what I mean?"

"Probably not."

"Oh, man, I just want the fucking prints. I don't need this in my life. You think I want that shit floating around town? I'm a respectable woman."

"Take it up with him. I'm just a bystander."

"You're a fucking infant. You have no idea. Do you know what's in the package? Do you?" She waits for a reply that doesn't come. "You're a puppet, Daniel. We're both puppets. And Royce holds the strings."

Daniel drinks off his beer and gets to his feet. He has the package in his hand, a look of apology on his face.

"Well, I gotta hold up my end," he says. "Thanks for the beer."

"Wait," she says and she stands as well, walking coolly up to him. "You want another beer? We could party a little..."

"No," Daniel says. He looks her in the eye a moment. "I'm married."

"So what's that make you—an honourable man?"

He shrugs and starts for the door.

"An honourable man," she says again. "You're gonna be lonesome where you're going."

There is a city park across the street from the Blonde's house. Swing sets, slides, a backstop for baseball. Sam and Dave wait in the darkness by the screen. Sam smokes down his Players and watches the house. Dave has a baseball bat, and he is tossing stones into the air and launching them toward the outfield.

"Pow! Another homer," he announces. "That's six he's hit. What an awesome display of power."

"You're an awesome display of something," Sam says. "Why don't you try and keep the fucking noise down? We're kinda—what do you call it—conspicuous here."

Dave tosses another stone in the air, takes a mighty swing and misses. "How do you know she's even coming out? Maybe she's keeping it."

"Not according to the man. She doesn't want it to keep. She wants it to move. Whatever the fuck it is, it's got to move."

Dave belts a grounder up the middle. "Sometimes I got no idea what you're talkin' about, man."

"There's a lot of things you don't—" Sam starts, but he spots something across the street. "Whoa, what've we got here?"

Daniel walks out of the house, is seen plainly beneath the porch light.

"Oh, man, look at this!" Sam says. "He's got the fucking thing in his hand. Can you believe this?" He looks at Dave. "Come on, put that slugger under your coat."

They keep to the shadows, catch up to Daniel as he's unlocking his truck, which is parked on the side street. Sam sidles up along the rear fender.

"Hey!"

Daniel turns and takes a quick inventory. He is not impressed.

"Hey, what?"

"Give it over," Sam advises.

"Fuck you."

"You wanna get hurt, man?" Dave asks.

Daniel looks him over, turns to Sam. "Where'd you get the imbecile?"

"Don't call me that," Dave says.

"Make it easy on yourself," Sam says. "Give us the fucking package. Don't be a tough guy."

"Tough guy," Dave says.

Daniel opens the truck door, looks at Sam. "Why don't you take your retarded friend for a long walk off a short pier?"

Dave leaps forward, pulling the bat from his coat. "Don't call me that!"

Daniel ducks beneath the blow. The bat hits the open door and splinters in half. Daniel shoves Dave away, then turns and slugs Sam twice in the face, dropping him to the pavement. He turns back as Dave is lunging toward him. The broken end of the bat goes in one side of Daniel's neck and out the other. He falls to the ground, the bat wedged in place, and is dead in seconds.

Sam gets to his feet, holding his jaw like a man with a toothache. "Shit, man."

"I told him not to call me that," Dave says weakly.

There are exterior lights flashing on from the surrounding buildings. People are stepping out onto their porches.

"We better get going," Dave says.

"Where's the fucking package?" Sam demands.

They find it under the truck. Dave stuffs it in his pants. They begin to walk, affecting nonchalance. When they hear the sirens, they break into a run. Dave, panicking, tosses the package over a fence into a yard.

Royce sits on the terrace in the morning sun. Lewis is just inside the door. Royce is looking through a Viewmaster; its steady click is heard as he moves from scene to scene.

"Shocking news, shocking," he says.

Click.

"You know, Lewis, I have never encouraged violent behaviour in these matters. This...this is an unspeakable horror. It destroys the spirit, the gamesmanship."

Click.

"Poor Daniel. I can't say that I really knew him, but still..."

Click.

"Of course, the fact still remains that we've lost our cargo. It must be returned, Lewis. Any other conclusion is unacceptable. Now more than ever, in light of this tragedy."

Click.

"Oh, yes, you'll have to lay in some champagne, Lewis. I have a new lady friend coming over tonight."

Click.

Jessica stands in the park in the darkness, scant yards from the spot where Sam and Dave waited the night before. She stands by the swing set, looking across to the side street. Under the street lamp, the bloodstains on the pavement are still visible. Although there are tears in her eyes, there is a fixated, deliberate air about her.

A girl of perhaps ten approaches her. She has curly brown hair and she carries a stuffed giraffe.

"Why are you crying?"

Jessica shakes her head. "You wouldn't understand."

"Was he your boyfriend?"

"He was my husband."

"My mother said that some bad men killed him."

"Yes, some bad men."

"Do you know what they were fighting over?"

Jessica turns away, shakes her head in dismissal.

"I know," the little girl says then.

"No. You don't."

"Yes, I do. They threw it in my yard."

Royce, wearing a crisp linen suit, sits on the couch, eating large shrimp from a platter and drinking cold Chardonnay. The TV is on, the sound off. A high-quality porn film is on the set. Royce occasionally glances at the screen, although it is obvious that the shrimp are his main focus.

Lewis stands inside the French doors, his big hands hanging down, his eyes as flat as creek water.

"I suppose the thing to do is bail Abbott and Costello out of jail," Royce says. "Perhaps they stashed it somewhere before the arrest and are unwilling to disclose the whereabouts while still incarcerated," he smiles over at Lewis, "lest they be abandoned in that place."

He watches as Lewis steals a look toward the train set.

"Yes, we'll arrange for the lads to make bail. Then we'll send them on a long trip. They needn't suffer the indignity of a trial. After all, they're not football heroes, they *might* be convicted."

Something on the screen catches his interest. He reaches for the remote, runs the film back and watches. He sighs and then smiles, as does a man who is greatly satisfied with life.

"I won't be needing you tonight, Lewis. I'm quite anxious to meet this new girl. I do enjoy meeting new people. I assume she'll be beautiful, I only hope—"

He's interrupted by the doorbell. Royce gets to his feet, gives Lewis a look.

"Well, well. How apropos. And twenty minutes early—a sign of eagerness, Lewis."

Lewis goes to the door and opens it. Jessica steps into the apartment, dressed casually—skirt, blouse, flats. Daniel's leather jacket.

Lewis retreats across the room. Royce gives him a look as he passes.

"I'm not mad about the wardrobe, but..." he says under his breath.

Jessica steps purposefully into the room, moving on resolve and adrenalin.

"Which one's Royce?" She stops to look at the two, sees the obvious. "You're Royce," she says to him.

"My oh my," Royce says, again to Lewis. "This could be interesting. Well, I guess introductions are in order. You are, of course, Maria—"

"I've got your package," Jessica says.

She produces the package from inside the jacket. Then she opens it to reveal the caboose from the train set. Royce is taken aback.

"How did you ever...?"

"This belong to you?"

"Why, yes."

Royce steps forward to reach for it, but she tosses it on the floor. It rolls across the marble and stops against the leg of the coffee table. Then she pulls Daniel's .38 from her pocket and shoots Royce in the chest three times. He falls backward, crashes onto the table and sprawls across the wreckage, stone dead among the shrimp and the crackers and the wine.

Jessica immediately puts the gun on Lewis. He moves toward her, his eyes narrowed, head turned to one side as if in anticipation of the bullet. She prepares to shoot, but then he stops and leans over to pick up the caboose. He turns and walks into the game room, attaches the caboose to the train. Then he takes down an engineer's hat from a brass hook on the wall and puts it on his head. He sits at the table and puts the train in motion. It chugs out of the station on the main line, heading for the little forest made of real pine branches.

Jessica turns and leaves. The rhythmic clicking of the train is all that is heard.

Life Without Drama

by Crad Kilodney

In describing the essence of noir, Anthony Boucher talked about characters whose lives are subverted by "the everyday gone wrong." Their world is turned upside down, and from that perspective, it looks a lot like hell. But what of lives subverted by an everyday that never goes wrong, that never deviates from the mundane? In this evocative and moving story, Crad Kilodney takes every cherished noir convention and gives us a distinctively different view of hell.

Crad Kilodney is a legend in Canadian letters. From 1978 through 1995, he stood on the streets of downtown Toronto selling his books—titles such as *Sex Slaves of the Astro Mutants* and *Lightning Struck My Dick*. Now officially retired, he still writes new short work for the Web site *www.jagular.com*, and lives comfortably off the stock market.

He did not awaken in a strange hotel room, with an empty bottle on the floor and a beautiful woman asleep beside him.

He did not put a gun in his pocket before leaving.

He did not have an appointment in a dimly-lit bar with a powerful person representing a secret organization.

He did not find anything unusual on his desk.

There were no complex decisions or moral problems to wrestle with. He had no power over others. He was not called into an important meeting. He did not receive sly looks from a beautiful co-worker. He overheard nothing of importance in the washroom. He did not have a confrontation with his superior, in which he surprised him with his boldness.

He did not take the afternoon off to keep a rendezvous with a rich and famous woman.

On the way home, he did not fight off an attacker, or rescue children from the second or third floor of a building on fire.

He was not caught in a crossfire between police and armed robbers.

He did not find a briefcase full of money, jewels, or secret documents.

He was not handed coded instructions by a man in black to take the next flight to Tangier, Amsterdam, Paris, or Moscow.

He did not meet a beautiful woman sitting alone in a dimly-lit bar, who smiled at him seductively.

His pager did not sound once.

People did not notice him on the street, and there was no one following him.

He experienced no unusual physical sensations, and no ideas, fears, or recollections came to him in a flash.

When he returned to his apartment, he found that no one had broken in and ransacked it, and nothing was missing.

There was nothing important in the mail, and there were no messages on the answering machine.

Going out later to buy cigarettes, he did not observe any crime or accident, nor did he chance to meet a beautiful woman who needed protection and a place to hide.

His lottery numbers did not come up.

When he looked out the window at the city, he saw only buildings and cars.

He did not hear any strange sounds from the apartment next door.

When he climbed into bed, he had no premonitions of evil, nor was there a crucial deal on the agenda for tomorrow that he had to think about.

He had no dreams that would prove to be prophetic.

Needless to say, he did not awaken in a strange hotel room, with an empty bottle on the floor and a beautiful woman asleep beside him.

"Two Fingers," copyright 2001 by Kevin Smith.

"Her Voice on the Phone Was Magic," copyright 1984 by William Bankier. Originally published in *Ellery Queen Mystery Magazine*.

"The Stand-In," copyright 1999 by Mike Barnes. Originally published in *Aquarium*, Porcupine's Quill.

"Winter Hiatus," copyright 1991 by James Powell. Originally published in *Ellery Queen Mystery Magazine*.

"Head Job," copyright 2001 by Kerry J. Schooley.

"Coup de Grâce," copyright 2001 by Barbara Fradkin.

"Avenging Miriam," copyright 2001 by Peter Sellers. Originally published in *Ellery Queen Mystery Magazine*.

"Winter Man," copyright 1995 by Eliza Moorhouse. Originally published as "Death of a Dragon," in *Cold Blood V*.

"The Duke," copyright 1994 by Eric Wright. Originally published in *2nd Culprit*.

"And Then He Sings," copyright 2001 by Stan Rogal.

"After Due Reflection," copyright 2000 by Mary Jane Maffini. Originally published in *Ellery Queen Mystery Magazine*.

"Foil For the Fire," copyright 1996 by Vern Smith. Originally published in *Glue for Breakfast* and *Rush Hour Revisions*.

"Can You Take Me There, Now?", copyright 2001 by Matthew Firth. Originally published in *Can You Take Me There, Now?*, Boheme Press, 2001.

"Wipe Out," copyright 2000 by Matt Hughes. Originally published in *Blue Murder Magazine*.

"The Package," copyright 2001 by Brad Smith.

"Life Without Drama," copyright 1992 by Crad Kilodney. Originally published in *Suburban Chicken Strangling Stories*.